SOLD TO MISS SEETON

THE HERON CARVIC MISS SEETON MYSTERIES

By Heron Carvic

PICTURE MISS SEETON
MISS SEETON DRAWS THE LINE
WITCH MISS SEETON
MISS SEETON SINGS
ODDS ON MISS SEETON

By Hampton Charles

MISS SEETON, BY APPOINTMENT
ADVANTAGE MISS SEETON
MISS SEETON AT THE HELM

By Hamilton Crane

MISS SEETON CRACKS THE CASE
MISS SEETON PAINTS THE TOWN
HANDS UP, MISS SEETON
MISS SEETON BY MOONLIGHT
MISS SEETON ROCKS THE CRADLE
MISS SEETON GOES TO BAT
MISS SEETON PLANTS SUSPICION
STARRING MISS SEETON
MISS SEETON UNDERCOVER
MISS SEETON RULES
SOLD TO MISS SEETON

"HERON CARVIC'S MISS SEETON"

SOLD TO MISS SEETON

HAMILTON CRANE

BERKLEY PRIME CRIME, NEW YORK

Mystery
Cra

SOLD TO MISS SEETON

A Berkley Prime Crime Book
Published by The Berkley Publishing Group
200 Madison Avenue, New York, New York 10016

Copyright © 1995 by Sarah J. Mason.

Book design by Jill Dinneen

All rights reserved. This book, or parts thereof, may not be reproduced
in any form without permission.

First edition: October 1995

Library of Congress Cataloging-in-Publication Data

Crane, Hamilton.
    Sold to Miss Seeton / Hamilton Crane. — 1st ed.
        p. cm. — (Heron Carvic's Miss Seeton)
    ISBN 0-425-14936-6
    1. Seeton, Miss (Fictitious character)—Fiction. 2. Women
detectives—England—Fiction. 3. England—Fiction. I. Title.
II. Series.
PR6063.A7648S65 1995
813'.54—dc20   95-6298
                                                                   CIP

Printed in the United States of America

10 9 8 7 6 5 4 3 2 1

SOLD TO MISS SEETON

CHAPTER 1

Pentonwood Scrubs is not a high-security prison. True, the main building has clearly been designed to prevent the occupants from escaping: the ground-floor windows are barred, others are too small to permit human egress, and every door directly communicating to the outside world is double in design, with a twin locking system and the keys kept at all times on a chain about the warder's uniformed waist.

Viewed, however, from that outside world to which its inmates—understandably—aspire, Pentonwood might at a quick glance be mistaken for nothing more than some bizarre Ministry of Defence establishment, or a boarding school for disruptive pupils. There are no massive wooden gates, ribbed with oak and studded with iron; visitors enter through an opening blocked only by a striped wooden pole, raised or lowered by a man on duty in the nearby kiosk. The perimeter is bounded not by looming granite walls, but by an eight-foot chain link fence crowned on its inward overhang by a dozen strands of strong barbed wire. Pentonwood prisoners are not regarded as any great risk to the civilian populace; they are men who are nearing the end of

their time in gaol, and who have no wish to risk the loss
of their approaching freedom by any foolhardy schemes.

Or so the theory goes.

But theories, from time to time, may be exploded . . .

Three days running in the week after Christmas, a helicopter of unknown origin had clattered its way across the
airspace directly above the grounds of Pentonwood Scrubs.
Its visits delighted and amused the prisoners beneath, but
caused perplexed annoyance to the governor, who ordered
an identity check to be run on the metallic spy in the sky:
and discovered that the numbers on the fuselage—which
were altered each day—belonged, according to all known
records, to no known registration scheme. The governor
dug out his army-issue binoculars, and on the third day took
a long hard look at the pilot, in case he was an old friend.

He might have been: nobody knew. Like all good mystery men, he was masked. The governor had to admit he
might even have been *she*. Behind the mask, and with the
helmet and earphones very much in place, it was impossible
to tell: impossible, also, to tell what he (or she) wanted.

After the more obvious solutions had, for lack of hard
evidence, been dismissed, it was concluded that the visits
must be caused by an attack of some manic philanthropism.
Boxing the compass, the anonymous chopper arrived on the
first day from the east, on the second from the south, and
on the third from the west. On the occasion of its eastern
approach, the helicopter, circling above the prison playing
field, deposited upon that field a cloud of white envelopes
which the governor—having sent a detachment of warders
to collect them—discovered contained Christmas cards for
each prisoner, addressed by name, with apologies for the
late delivery and best wishes for the remainder of the festive season.

The governor had all the cards bundled up and sent to
the local hospital to be X-rayed. He then (with marked reluctance) authorised their delivery, even later than the helicopter pilot might have expected.

Approaching from the south during the exercise hour, the helicopter next day delivered a further selection of cards, addressed, as before, by name. Unlike before, the tone of the good wishes was decidedly muted, since the addressees were, without exception, members of the prison staff; which proved that the pilot—whoever he (or she) might be, knew rather more about the workings of Pentonwood Scrubs than the governor could possibly like.

There also drifted from the helicopter an assortment of white plastic hexagons with delicate spurs and lace-like patterns, suggestive of giant snowflakes. Once more, the governor ordered the offending items X-rayed: once more, it seemed no harm had been done—except to the prisoners, who had been rushed indoors at the first wind-borne rattle of the rotors, and were feeling not a little disgruntled at so sudden a curtailment of their daily quest for fresh air.

On its third visit, the helicopter appeared for the first time to be uncertain about what seasonal offering it should bring. It circled the grounds twice, waggling its rotors and rocking from side to side as those below studied it with care. Suspicious or sensitive natures might have supposed the pilot to be thumbing his (or her) nose at the authorities, except that the governor could confirm that he (or she) was doing no such thing. His, or her, deportment was decorous in the extreme—as far, that is, as anyone's can be who flies helicopters in plain defiance of all known laws directly over one of Her Majesty's prisons . . .

The pilot was eventually seen to pull a lever; at which a scarlet banner, embossed with green letters, streamed out at magnificent length from beneath the anonymous fuselage to wish the staff and inmates of Pentonwood Prison a Belated Merry Christmas, and a Happy New Year. Another lever was pulled: the outsize streamer drifted free of its fastenings, falling to earth (the playing field again) in a riot of billowing silk. The helicopter hovered for a few moments more, observing with interest the flurry of activity from the warders as they ran from the main building to investigate this latest occurrence; then, with one final waggle of its bulky underbelly, it lumbered to the fence, hovered again as it released another plastic blizzard, and rattled briskly away into the distance.

The governor, watching its antics through his binoculars, was so busy trying to read the flashing Morse message of farewell it signalled that he did not notice the half dozen small, round, white objects, camouflaged among the myriad drifting snowflakes, that tumbled from the undercarriage as the helicopter reached the perimeter fence and bounced as they hit the ground, and, rolling, vanished into the tangles of longer grass beside the wire.

Nobody else noticed them, either.

Nobody, that is, on the prison staff—and almost nobody among the prison inmates.

Almost nobody: but not quite.

Cutler noticed. He had been watching. Closely.

For it was Cutler who had planned the entire three-day operation to the very last detail. There is no problem that is insurmountable, if a mind sufficiently quick and cunning is brought to bear on it, and Cutler's was one of the quickest and most cunning minds ever to have enjoyed the hospitality of Her Majesty. A disgrace to the ancient university that had awarded him first class honours in chemistry, the man was in prison for having used his chemical knowledge to mastermind a forgery scam. He was now nearing the end of his sentence; and he would happily have served out the rest of his term, organizing from inside the various outside activities of his gang by a complex system of coded messages in letters home, had not intelligence reached him of what even the most meiotic of his colleagues—did they but understand the word—must have called a piece of uncommonly bad luck. For once, one of Cutler's schemes had failed. As in Tennyson's celebrated poem, someone had blundered . . . yet Cutler did not feel the need to escape from gaol merely to administer the appropriate punishment. Reprisals, while effective, could generally be left to underlings. But there were times—rare, indeed, but such times there were—when only the physical presence of the master could avert a catastrophe . . .

The interrupted exercise hour was resumed. Cutler, with a few cronies, ambled across to the place where the red silk banner had wrapped itself around the wooden crossbar of the football goal mouth.

"Not there now," said Snipey after a long, thoughtful pause. Snipey was a sharp-faced, wiry little man whose looks had earned him his nickname—looks that belied his true character, for his wits were notoriously dull. Snipey had been convicted of receiving stolen goods, and even his defence counsel could only suggest that it must have been a genuine mistake, since nobody who knew him would ever trust his client to receive anything.

But Cutler trusted him—or, rather, was relying on him. He had been courting Snipey's intimate acquaintance for the past few days: the little man and his friends were essential to his plan. He needed them for camouflage . . .

"Not there now," agreed Cutler calmly.

"Any more snowflakes?" enquired Budge, who had the build of a bulldozer, and slightly less brain.

"Screws'll've picked 'em all up," said Long John with scorn. Long John was at most two inches taller than Snipey, his small cellmate, and his given name was Egbert; but he walked with a decided limp. Prison humorists had promptly hailed his stick as a crutch, and adorned his shoulder with an invisible parrot; over the months, Long John Silver had been shortened to Long John. He was perhaps the most vital member of Cutler's unwitting team. "Running abaht like blue-arsed flies, wasn't they?"

"Might have missed one," said Budge in dogged accents.

"They might, indeed," interposed Cutler smoothly, but with a quick, conciliatory smile for Long John. "Let's take a stroll about the grounds. Finders, as the saying goes, may

be keepers—if you'll excuse that word's unfortunate con-
notations, of course.''

Snipey, Budge, and Long John would have gladly excused him far more than the odd unfortunate word. Cutler's
personal magnetism, when he chose to exercise it, was remarkable; and he had been exercising it much of late.
Moreover, in the opinion of Snipey, Budge, and Long John,
there was always the chance he could do them a bit of good
once they were out of Pentonwood, and free agents again.
Wasn't he well known among the fraternity for being a man
with bright ideas? And didn't ideas men need other men to
help them see them through?

In an amicable silence, the four duly strolled—Long
John limping, swinging his stick in an easy rhythm—about
the grounds, passing between groups of their fellow prisoners who were, on such a chilly morning, more energeti-
cally disposed. Some men ran on the spot or did physical
jerks; some kicked a football, others played leapfrog. Some,
like Cutler and his colleagues, merely walked.

An impartial observer would have been interested to observe just how many of the walkers were drifting, with the
most casual of zigzag movements, in the direction of the
barbed wire fence . . .

But the governor had put his binoculars away, and was
busy studying the silken banner that lay draped in graceful
folds across his desk. He never thought to look out of the
window; and the watchful warders, far colder than the men
they watched, stood brooding on their burgeoning chil-
blains, blew on their mittened hands, cast surreptitious
glances at the clock on the prison tower, and sighed. They
had been instructed to allow their charges an extra quarter
of an hour outside, as compensation for the time lost during
the helicopter's latest visit; the minutes were creeping by
more slowly than a caravan of snails.

''Hello,'' said Cutler as they drew near the perimeter
wire. ''Do my eyes deceive me? Or could it be that we may
expect mushrooms for supper, my friends?''

He pointed to a cluster of small, round, white objects lying among the tangles of long grass. "Perhaps not mushrooms," he said, "on second thought. But certain species of puffball are, I believe, edible. One fries them. With caution," he added, and chuckled.

Long John and Budge echoed the chuckle, but Snipey was even more determined to curry favour. He scuttled across to the cluster of white spheres amid the grass, and bent down.

"Couldn't fry these," he said after no more than ten seconds' scrutiny. "Not that they're poisonous, mind. Not if gutta-percha's safe to eat, they ain't—which I wouldn't rightly care to say it is or it isn't, one way or the other, though I wouldn't've thought as it was."

"Perch?" echoed Budge, frowning. "Gutted perch . . ." He made a face. "Cod, now . . . quite fancy a nice piece of cod for my dinner, I could—but I dunno about *perch*." He sighed, dreaming of happier times. "With chips—a nice piece of cod . . ."

"Passeth all understanding," muttered Cutler against his better judgement. Luckily nobody heard him.

"If them's fish eggs," said Long John, limping across to peer down into the grass, "then that's the richest load of caviar any of us is likely to see in our sweet lives. Just look at the size of 'em!"

Snipey, who'd had longer to look than the others, here uttered a remark that made his friends roar with laughter. With an effort, Cutler contrived to smile: but his less than buoyant response was lost amid the welter of coarse comment that now erupted from Long John and the thoughtful Budge. Cutler crossed mental fingers, and prayed that one of them would lead the conversation where he needed it to go . . .

"Golf balls," said Snipey at last, and sniggered. "More likely to be a bird than a fish, eh? With golf balls flying through the air, and fish—"

"Swimming," said Budge, giving the nearest ball a wary

prod with his foot. "Can't say as I care overmuch for exercise. It ain't healthy. Think of all that . . . that chlorine
muck messing up yer lungs, not to mention hopping abaht
in one place for hours on end filling 'em with freezing cold
air." He directed a scornful look towards his more energetic peers as they jumped and jogged and flung their arms
in vigorous display.

"Right," chimed in Long John as Budge continued to
gaze with contempt upon the jumpers and joggers. "Cheap,
though, innit? If yer minded to follow such pursuits, I
mean. But golf, now," he said, patting another ball with
the tip of his stick, "that ain't fer the likes of us. Begging
yer pardon," he added hastily to Cutler, who was widely
known to play—when at liberty—off a handicap of three.
"But it's true. What's the chances of the likes of us ever
getting to play golf? Golf's a rich folks' game, and there's
nobody in here with two pennies to rub together. Present
company always excepted, of course."

"Of course," said Cutler, promising worlds in two mere
syllables: if they would only follow his example, Snipey
and Budge and Long John might one day be as he . . .

Idly he bent down to pick up one of the small, white
spheres. "Not my usual brand," he murmured, scratching
at the embossed trademark, "but, my word, how it reminds
me of the good old days." The murmur was just loud
enough for the others to overhear: in such matters, Cutler
was an artist.

He achieved a deep sigh. "Right now, the good old days
seem a long way off—yet so much the better, when they
come again, for the anticipation, no doubt. Freedom." Another sigh. "The freedom to hit one of these little dears
where and whenever you please . . ."

He tossed the golf ball from one hand to the other and
smiled a whimsical, wistful smile. "Ah, the good old days
at the club—the fairways, the greens, even the bunkers, I
miss them all. The laughter and chat at the nineteenth
hole—not that I miss any of them to the same degree that

I miss the game itself, of course.''

Another smile. Those sensitive to mood might have observed something wolfish, rather than wistful, in the curve of the lips, the flash of the teeth.

Snipey, Budge, and Long John were, fortunately, unobservant. "Not with such good friends in here . . ."

Would the idiots never take the next step? How heavy a hint did he have to drop?

It was the golf ball that he dropped.

It fell to the ground with a doleful plop and rolled no more than a few inches before bumping against a tussock and stopping. Cutler chuckled and clicked his tongue. "Dear, dear, the green-keeper must be disciplined. We'll rescind his Christmas bonus, shall we? Such a poor putting surface—not," he said with yet another sigh as the reality of his situation struck home, "that anyone can hope to sink a decent putt without a decent club. Failing which, memory alone must suffice . . ."

"Here," said Long John, "have a bash with this, if it'll make you happy." He handed his walking stick to Cutler, who received it with a smile and a sigh which, for once, he made an effort to smother. It was not a sigh of longing, or realization: it was a sigh of relief.

But "Thank you" was all he said; though he said it with a fervour even his self-control could not entirely suppress.

Long John grinned. "Pleasure," he said. "Anything to oblige a friend—go on, quick, afore the screws sees yer."

His hands trembling with excitement, Cutler picked up the golf ball and examined the maker's mark once more. His fingers flickered strangely over the dimpled surface; it was as if he searched for something. Then he nodded, took two steps forward, placed the ball on the ground, and stepped back, fiddling with the lace on his shoe as he did so.

"I wonder," he remarked, reversing Long John's stick and taking a few experimental swings, "how far I could send it?"

"Over the wire," said Budge on cue, though in complete innocence. "Hot stuff, you were—eh, Mr. Cutler?"

"Still are," said Snipey at once, looking ahead to freedom and the need for a patron.

"You bet," said Cutler, the most colloquial they had ever heard him. He gave one more practice swipe at the ball, then opened up his shoulders and swung mightily.

The handle of Long John's walking stick met its target with a loud crack. The ball soared away, speeding up and over the fence in a swift parabola, landing with a merry— but surprisingly light—thump on the ground beyond.

"Coo," said Snipey. "Said you could do it, dint I?"

"Have another go," begged the admiring Budge; and would immediately have scurried forth to gather the remaining balls visible against the grass, had he not been halted in his eager tracks by the unexpected sight of strangers emerging from the distant bushes and running towards the fence. Running towards the fallen golf ball . . .

There was a flash of light as the first man to reach the ball bent and made severing motions with a pair of scissors as the second man fumbled with something in midair above his head. Both men straightened and gave the thumbs-up signal.

Cutler merely straightened. While Budge and his friends had been watching the antics of the running men, he, too, had bent, fumbling once more with his shoelace. As the signal was given, he began to pull, repeatedly, hand over hand, at something none of the others could see . . .

Not, that is, at first. But as his hands moved faster, Snipey, Budge, and Long John focused on the space between them and saw a faint, threadlike gleam stretching upwards. They looked down and saw that same gleam, a thread in ever-growing coils, spiralling to earth about his feet as he pulled—and pulled—and pulled.

"Blimey!" said Budge. He spoke for them all.

The gleam grew stronger: the thread had become a line. And still Cutler pulled, faster and faster; and the coils about his feet spread wider and wider. The line became a cord; the cord became a rope.

The rope became a ladder, knotted with handholds . . .

And Cutler was away, climbing, up and over the fence, tumbling on the freedom side into the arms of the men who now, with him between them, ran even faster than before back to the bushes, from which came the sound of a car engine at full speed, and the sudden squeal of tyres, and the slamming of doors, and a triumphant pip-pip-pipping of a horn . . .

And Cutler was gone.

CHAPTER 2

It was not altogether a happy new year.

For some people, of course, it could well have been one of the happiest mornings of their lives. For Major-General Sir George Colveden, KCB, DSO, JP, this was not, however, the case. He lay in bed with his eyes closed, listening to the rain as it lashed against the windows, and wincing; wincing also as he listened to the sadistic clatter of the little man who tapdanced just behind his eyeballs wearing metal-tipped, hobnailed boots.

The baronet essayed a groan. He ventured to open his eyes the merest fraction of a crack. The little man at once stopped dancing to produce from somewhere a miniature longbow and a quiver of red-hot arrows, which he proceeded to loose in distressingly accurate sequence towards the top of Sir George's skull.

Sir George closed his eyes again. He sighed. He dragged a feeble hand from beneath the bedclothes and raised it weakly to his fevered brow. He managed another groan.

He received no response. He took a deep breath, forced his eyes farther open, and turned his head—very gently—in the direction of the neighbouring pillow, on which the soft, waving brown locks of his spouse should have been tumbled in sleep: or rather, in drowsy waking, in readiness to administer such sympathy as he required.

He blinked. Meg wasn't there—must be later than he'd thought. Light showing through the curtains, come to think of it. Time to get up . . .

"Ugh."

Or maybe not. His eyelids drooped again. Hammer and tongs inside his head this morning. His own fault, he supposed, but New Year's Eve only came around once every twelve months, dammit. Had to celebrate in style—proper toasts, and so on. Just seemed to have lost count, somehow . . .

In the distance, he could hear the welcome clatter of a breakfast kitchen. His stomach lurched. Maybe, after all, not so welcome. Not breakfast, just black coffee. Strong. With sugar. Aspirin, too, perhaps. Meg would see him right: a few minutes more, and he'd feel a new man. Ready for anything, raring to go . . .

Go? Where? The breakfast clatter was suddenly drowned out by a further onslaught of rain on glass: heavy, vicious drops, driven by the single-minded wind from the north, icy cold and splintered with hail. Sir George groaned again. Sort of rain they'd had every day for dashed near a whole week. Fields flooded—waterlogged, anyway. Impossible to plough, with the tractor up to its axles in mud as soon as it got through the gate. Could always do a spot of hedging, of course, but hedging was a skilled job: easier ditching, though with the ditches full of water that was no joke. Up to his knees or deeper, half the time. A wonder he wasn't dead with pneumonia instead of . . . well, half dead. With a hangover: call a spade a spade. Or—talk of ditch-clearing—a billhook . . .

Sir George managed a chuckle, and it didn't hurt as much as—for one dreadful moment when it was too late to stop it—he'd been afraid it might. Heartened by the little man's apparent loss of Terpsichorean fervour, he opened his eyes again. He gulped, and breathed deeply, but left them open. He raised his head from the pillow to gaze in the direction of the curtains, through which a grey, wintry light made its shadowy way. Yes . . . time to get up.

"George, you made me jump." Lady Colveden turned from the toaster to stare at her husband, who had eschewed his ordinary shoes for soft-soled, blessedly silent slippers. "Coffee or tea? And I'm making more toast, if you'd like it. Nigel and I have been awake for hours."

"Minutes, she means." Sir George's son and heir popped his head through the serving hatch to grin at his honoured parent. "Happy New Year, Dad. Mother's already told me how you saw the old year out in style at the admiral's party." Sir George tried to frame a suitable reply, and shuddered with the effort. Nigel's grin mingled sympathy and amusement for the folly of his elders. "We enjoyed ourselves at the Young Farmers, too, thanks for asking. Er—shall I pop upstairs for the aspirin? I know just how mean a pink gin the Buzzard can mix."

Sir George closed his eyes. Memories of the bartending skills of his friend, Rear Admiral Bernard "Buzzard" Leighton, were returning in horrid detail as the blood began to flow faster through his arteries and the supply of oxygen to his brain increased. He achieved a monosyllabic reply which Nigel interpreted as a vote of thanks, and shuddered again as he heard his son's feet thunder along the hall and up the stairs to the bathroom overhead, where a series of bangs and rattles indicated that the future baronet was having trouble with a cupboard door.

Ten minutes later, Sir George was in his usual place at the head of the dining table, drinking his second cup of black coffee and venturing to nibble (warily) at a slice of unbuttered toast while he turned the pages (very gently) of *Farmers Weekly*. He had—as the undutiful Nigel pointed out—to get into the right physical and mental state for the rigours of the working day to come . . .

"Though what else we can profitably do until the rain

stops besides clear ditches and lay hedges, I'm not sure. Bang a few nails in the odd loose tile, I suppose, even if going up a ladder on a day like this isn't exactly a bundle of laughs.'' Nigel glanced at his mother as his father, who had endured hammering enough already that morning, winced.

''Of course, if we had a team of heavy horses, we could always clean the tack . . .'' Lady Colveden had more than once expressed a sentimental yearning for the days of jingling harness and plume-footed majesty working their way across freshly turned furrows. Her husband and son had always reminded her that horses were hard work, and they were running the farm for profit, not out of some misplaced sense of nostalgia; her ladyship had countered this argument with one of her own, that there was bound to be a profit in horses, if they only thought about it. In the end.

''*From* the end, you mean.'' Nigel had choked over his coffee, while Sir George chuckled behind his newspaper. ''Were you thinking simply of your herbaceous borders, Mother darling, or did you have some farsighted scheme to bag the stuff up and sell it from door to door?''

''I don't see why not,'' returned his mother, pouring herself another cup without, unusually, offering to help either her son or her spouse. ''Well rotted, of course, and I didn't mean selling it, but using it for—oh, raffle prizes and things. You know how people are forever dropping by the forge with buckets when Dan Eggleden's been shoeing. And it wouldn't just be my borders, of course, but people used to spread it on their fields all the time in the old days—think of the saving on fertiliser. You know,'' she added with a quick glance at the far end of the table, and the upheld broadsheet spread of a breakfast *Times*, ''how your father's always grumbling about bills.''

''Always grumbling, full stop,'' came Nigel's prompt revision. ''Farmer's privilege. Practically the first thing we were taught at Wye . . .'' But the alumnus of the celebrated agricultural college had an unusually thoughtful note in his voice as he spoke, and this thoughtfulness had continued, on and off, for some days afterwards.

"Horses," he said now, "might be able to get over heavy ground rather more easily than a tractor, I suppose. There isn't much chance of this rain letting up, never mind what the barometer says."

"I can't think what's got into the wretched thing." Her ladyship shook her head. "If it was human, I might have said it was suffering from—from the same as your father," she amended hastily, as *Farmers Weekly* rustled with indignation.

"Decidedly under the weather," came Nigel's ambiguous gurgle. "It's been set fair," he went on quickly, "for the last week, at least. Do you suppose someone's dropped an atom bomb somewhere?"

Farmers Weekly came down with an exasperated scrunch. Sir George rolled his eyes and groaned. Her ladyship shuddered.

"Nigel, don't joke about such things." Bombs, atomic or otherwise, were currently a sore point with Lady Colveden. Her nerves, she maintained, were still quivering from the recent shock of having a chance-disturbed World War II hand grenade blow up the oldest oak on the Rytham Hall estate. "It's far more likely to be statistics." Her menfolk blinked in startled unison. She ignored them. "The earliest frost, you know, or the hottest day, or the heaviest rainfall. Half the time you feel nobody would notice if the radio and television didn't make such a fuss."

"They would," said Nigel, "if they had their living to earn out of doors."

"They do," said his father grimly, forgetting to wince. "I do. Set fair, indeed. Blasted thing ought to be in parliament."

More than a quarter century of marriage assisted Lady Colveden to interpret this remark after only a moment's hesitation. "Being, um, economical with the truth, you mean? That's rather unkind. I'm sure it's doing its best."

"Not good enough." Her husband huffed irritably through his moustache. "Tapped it on the way to breakfast. Damned thing didn't even wobble."

Lady Colveden began to gather plates and cups. "Do be fair, George. I shouldn't imagine you could have tapped it very hard. Not before your aspirin, I mean. It's probably just stuck."

"Stuck?" Irritation huffed again. "Be suggesting a drop of oil next, I dare say. Stuck!" And he pushed back his chair with an ear-splitting squeal of solid carpentry on polished board. "*Stuck . . .*"

Nigel, knives and forks in his hand, looked across at his mother as his father stumped out of the room. "I think we may assume he's over the worst." He cocked his head to one side, listening. Sir George's slippered footsteps had soon become inaudible on their way down the hall. "But he's not his usual sunny self just yet, by any means. Should we slip out to watch the fun?"

"It was a wedding present," said Lady Colveden, made suddenly nervous by the gleam in the dancing eyes—Nigel and his father so often thought the same way about things—on the opposite side of the table. "It's never gone wrong before—at least, not that I've noticed anyway . . ."

By unspoken mutual consent, mother and son set down their spoons and crockery on the white cloth and hurried from the dining room. Whatever fate might befall the hapless oak-mounted weather forecaster, it surely behoved the entire family of its owners to bear witness to that fate.

What they witnessed was the family's infuriated head, standing by the front door, glaring at the wall, reaching out to tap, and to tap again, the glass face of the barometer, the whole time muttering under his breath. "Set fair, indeed! Tell the truth for once, you devil—every damned day this week the same!"

Sir George gave one final, definitive tap, stepped back, and fixed the barometer with an eye which—even from the far end of the hall—was baleful in the extreme. "Still set fair, you idiot? Well, be damned to you!''

He darted to the front door, wrenched it open, leaped back to the barometer, and snatched it from the wall.

"George!" cried Lady Colveden: but too late.

"Go and see for yourself, you blasted fool!" thundered the beleaguered baronet; and he hurled the offending barometer as far as it would go, out into the torrential rain.

CHAPTER 3

Sir George Colveden, Justice of the Peace, was not the only arbiter of the law to be feeling more than slightly fragile that New Year's morning. In Ashford police station, headquarters of the local force, Superintendent Brinton sat at his desk with his head in his hands, very much the worse for wear. Mrs. Brinton was ten years her loving spouse's junior, and on close terms with her brother, a hard-drinking young man whose succession of blond lady-friends was a source of constant wonder—and secret envy—to the husband of his sister. The latest in this glamorous succession had been brought round to the Brintons' last night to see out the old year with a bang . . .

"Ugh." The very idea of noise made the superintendent squirm. Someone was letting off fireworks—neon-bright fireworks, with needle-sharp sparks—inside his tortured eyeballs. His ears were ringing with the banshee howl of rockets, and his mouth was filled with cayenne pepper, mixed in equal parts with gunpowder and with sand from a very salty beach.

"Ugh . . ." It was a judgement on him for having allowed his fancy for fair hair to become rather too apparent to the redheaded wife of his bosom. Mrs. Brinton's temper matched her fiery locks. Having blown up at her husband last thing last night, she'd gone through a repeat performance first thing this morning, and thrown him out of the house without breakfast—not that he could've faced breakfast, feeling the way he did. "Ugh . . ."

"Cup of tea, sir? Or would you prefer a peppermint?" Detective Constable Foxon, irrepressibly chirpy and the bane of Brinton's life, bounced up from his corner of the office with nothing but benevolence in his tone. Foxon had joined Nigel Colveden and his colleagues at the Young Farmers' New Year jamboree, and the younger men had proved wiser in the ways of alcohol than their elders. Still, there had been times . . . And Foxon spoke with genuine sympathy, tinged with not even the least hint of schadenfreude.

"A cup of tea, sir," he coaxed his suffering superior. "Two spoons of sugar, and no milk—you'll be a new man before you know it."

Brinton raised despairing eyes to the bright face above his own, and issued a mute appeal for understanding and assistance. Foxon, detective constable, deduced immediately what was required.

"Coffee, not tea—right you are, sir. Be with you in two shakes of a brand-new truncheon."

He was gone; he was back, bearing a tray on which stood two steaming mugs and—Brinton averted his gaze with a groan—one loaded plate. "Didn't have time for a proper breakfast, sir, sorry." And Foxon deposited his chief's caffeine fix on the blotter in front of him before retiring to his own desk to lament the late waking that had deprived him of his porridge, bacon, eggs, and marmaladed toast. Iced buns from the canteen just weren't the same somehow.

He munched warily, with one eye on Brinton and the other on the paperwork he'd made it his new-year resolution to clear out of the way. Part of the way. Well, to the other side of the desk, maybe . . .

"*Must* you make such a noise?" Brinton's voice broke in on Foxon's careful study of an accident report which might or might not hint at darker doings. The young constable looked up, blinked, and swallowed hastily.

"Er—was I munching my bun too loudly for you, sir? Sorry, but—"

"Blast your bun—and you, too, for being as half-baked as that—that chunk of canteen concrete! You know very well I was asking why you had to rattle every damned piece of paper as if it was one of those hellish thunder-sheets you wanted to use the other week . . ." For Foxon had been an enthusiastic cast member of Plummergen's recent Christmas pantomime, waxing eloquent around the office on the subject of props and effects even as he attempted to persuade Brinton to buy tickets.

"Sorry, sir." Foxon's reply was barely above a whisper. With exaggerated care, he slipped the sheet he held into its folder before laying it cautiously to one side.

Brinton glared at him over his coffee and took a deep, defiant swig. His internal fireworks flared up, flickered—and went out, as triple-strength caffeine knocked his hangover for six. He took another swig and sighed.

"I'd never dream of stopping you working, laddie—if only you didn't make so much of a song and dance about it!" He shuddered. "I'd gag you myself, if I had the strength. When you've finished over there, you can come and have a go at my bumf, too. I'll watch you with the greatest pleasure. I fancy a clean desk, for once."

"Don't we all?" Foxon peered at a slip of paper jotted with indecipherable telephone numbers, frowned, and threw it in the wastepaper basket. "Chance'd be a fine thing, sir. I know the villains enjoy a holiday as much as anyone else, but for all things've been reasonably quiet over Christmas—thank heaven—I could work my trousers to the bone—you too, for that matter—and it wouldn't make any real difference, would it? There's a sight too much being carried over from last year for us to have much hope of seeing the bare wood this side of *next* new year, if you ask me.''

''The Quendon killing, for one.'' Brinton drained the last drops of coffee, and risked a gloomy nod. Since his head neither fell off nor exploded, he took a further risk and leaned in the direction of his own paperwork mountain, beginning a hunt for the file he knew wasn't so very far from the top. ''No leads at all—and it happened over a month ago. The poor bloke's dead and buried and forgotten by everyone except us, and we still don't even know why he died, let alone who killed him.''

''A burglary gone wrong,'' said Foxon, whose theory this had been from the start. He was leafing through his own notes on the Quendon case, refreshing a memory that had no real need of refreshment: Professor Eldred Quendon had, in his eccentric way, been a neighbourhood celebrity, whose death did not pass unnoticed in the local newspapers, even warranting a few paragraphs in the national press. *Brettenden Boffin Battered to Death by Burglars* had been one of the most offensive headlines. Since few of the general populace had much idea where Brettenden might be, however, and since the police, when pressed, were forced to admit that they had no clues, the story had soon given way to others more exciting, or more seasonal.

Nobody seemed to know what Professor Quendon's special subject had been. Nobody knew at which university he had studied, or even whether ''Professor'' was an earned honorific as opposed to one merely adopted by himself to impress. The postman reported that it might from time to time be observed on some of his—admittedly rare—letters, but that meant nothing: more than one generation had known Eldred Quendon as the Professor, and the name had certainly stuck. It was, it seemed, perhaps not undeserved. The police, on breaking into his house after the alarm was raised, reported in their turn that there wasn't a room without several shelves of technical and scientific books along at least one wall, and what must have started as the dining room had been turned into a laboratory full of cryptic notes and complicated equipment concerning whose purpose no constabulary expert cared to hazard a guess.

"So what," mused Brinton aloud, as he studied the Quendon file for the umpteenth time, "were the blighters looking for? I *can't* believe any of those bottles and jars and bits of tube and coils of wire were really worth pinching. There's got to have been something more to it than that."

"An awful lot of those tubes were copper, sir, and scrap copper's worth a few bob, I gather. They might have seen the Prof. as an easy target—it's not as if he had any burglar alarms, or anything—and you know how people talk about even the most ordinary people, which you can't say he was, can you? Why, my gran's heard rumours that he was trying to find a way of turning iron into gold, for goodness' sake. Sir," added Foxon quickly, as the wrathful eye of the superintendent withered him where he sat.

Or tried to wither him: but Foxon was not so easily suppressed. "Well, she has, sir. Not that she believes it, of course, but there must be plenty of others who do—who did, I mean, and that's what they were hoping to pinch when they broke in, and he disturbed them, sir, and they hit him a bit harder than they needed just to shut him up. Sir."

Brinton sighed. "I wish *you'd* shut up, laddie, and get on with your tidying. The sooner you finish, the sooner you can start on mine, because I'm not doing a stroke to help you—I want to *think*." He tapped the cardboard folder with a daring finger; the sound did not make him wince. "Poor old Quendon. No clues, no idea what's going on, and nobody but us to care one way or the other. What a miserable end to a bloke's life, when legal types have to put notices in the papers asking for the heirs, and nobody turns up—not even to nag us about why we haven't caught up with the devils who did for the poor bugger." He shook his head, and winced only slightly. "You can't help thinking about it, with Christmas just gone. Makes it that much worse, somehow—no family, and no friends . . ."

He had opened the file as he spoke, and was scanning the most recent additions. "The solicitors've been keeping an eye on the post, in case the long-lost heir, whoever he is, turned up, but he didn't, and neither did she. A couple of duty cards from tradesmen, and that was it. So much for the festive spirit."

"Could be," ventured Foxon, "they'd all heard what happened to him and saved themselves the stamp, sir."

Brinton grunted. "Could be—but I doubt it. If they knew he was dead, I'd have thought anyone with even half a claim would've been camped on the doorstep to stake it— but there hasn't been a sausage. Poor bugger . . . It all seems so pointless. Like his death. If only we knew . . ."

"If only," said Chief Superintendent Delphick, "we knew, for certain, our lives would be a great deal easier—but then, what copper in his right mind ever expected an easy life? Anyone in the least desirous of having things handed to him on a plate should refrain from the slightest contemplation of the very idea of the notion of joining the police in the first place."

From the window of his office on the umpteenth floor of New Scotland Yard, the Oracle gazed out with a thoughtful frown upon the spreading streets of London, which hummed with the busy traffic of the post-holiday return to work. From the reinforced chair at his own desk, the massive Detective Sergeant Ranger—six foot seven in his socks, seventeen stone (and, since Christmas, a few suspect pounds more) on the scales—uttered a quiet sigh of agreement as he turned to the next page in the Pentonwood Escape file.

"Why?" he murmured, half to himself, half in response to the Oracle's remark. "*Why* does a bloke so near the end of his sentence risk the lot by suddenly making a run for it? Like you say, sir, if we knew for certain, instead of guessing, we could do something about it—but we don't. So we can't. And even if we *did* know it was all tied up with the Rickling business, the villains won't be too happy if we start locking 'em up as soon as look at them . . . and they'd never believe it was just out of the kindness of our hearts, to stop the blighters slaughtering each other. If," he added conscientiously, "that's what they really want to do."

"Their suspicions could even be justified. Would our motives, Bob, be entirely altruistic?" Delphick addressed his enormous sidekick with a faint smile in his grey eyes. "*Would* it be such a great kindness for us to prevent our homicidally inclined criminal acquaintances from despatching one another in an outbreak of gang warfare? A cynic might argue that it must surely be to the benefit of all law-abiding citizens, should membership of the opposite fraternity be, by whatever means, reduced . . . while, on the other hand, one must accept that there would, in such circumstances, be a corresponding increase in the work of the street maintenance department, which could prove unpopular in certain quarters.

"Waste disposal," he enlarged, as Bob stared, "costs money. Corpses littered about the capital would give a decidedly untidy appearance. There would undoubtedly be pressure applied on the City and Council cleaners to rectify the situation. And the cost of such rectification is bound to be reflected in a subsequent rate increase, which the honest citizenry might well resent . . ."

At the look on Bob's face, he laughed. "I'm talking nonsense, Sergeant Ranger."

"If you say so, sir."

"I am not alone. You say so, too—by your tone, if not by your words. Yet nonsense can sometimes help to distract the mind sufficiently to allow the subconscious inspiration to begin work . . ."

"And has it, sir? This time, I mean."

Delphick drifted away from the window and sat himself

down on the visitors' chair at Bob's desk. He stretched his long legs and sighed. "No. Inspiration, I fear, has failed. It must be that my mental processes are still suffering from a surfeit of Christmas pudding and New Year scotch." He sighed again. "As, it appears, are those of our friendly neighbourhood snouts. Not a single sighting has been reported—which, of course, does not unduly surprise me: Cutler is an intelligent man. But none of the strangely few hints we have received has merited any close investigation. Which suggests either that the festive spirit has indeed addled our informers' wits, or that Cutler has put the frighteners on . . ." He sat up. "Or . . ."

"If we'd posted a reward," said Bob after a courteous pause that remained unbroken, "they'd have risked the frighteners and come crawling out of the woodwork with the answer fast enough."

The oracular eyebrows arched in a look of astonishment. "Now who's being cynical? Cutler, I would remind you, is a surprisingly popular man, as well as an influential one . . . but he is not, we should also remember, the only criminal with influence around Town. To my two earlier hypotheses, we should add a third: that someone else other than Cutler has put the frighteners on . . ."

"You mean Rickling, sir?"

"He is a distinct possibility, yes."

Bob nodded, turning back to the file. "There *have* been rumours, all right . . . about Rickling trying to muscle in on Cutler's lot while their boss was in jug, and hotting things up before his parole board met . . . According to Artie Chishall, though, Rickling missed out, once they heard it wouldn't be long before Cutler was released. So why," he asked again, "should Cutler go over the fence the way he did, if he knew Wimbish was taking care of everything back home?"

"According to Chishall," Delphick echoed, with emphasis. "Hardly one of our most reliable sources, friend Artie. One would hesitate to entrust him with any task or message of importance: he has an unparalleled capacity for being economical with the truth, when it suits him. Compared to Artie Chishall, a corkscrew is a model of rectitude.''

''He's come up with some useful gen. in his time, sir.''

''But not this time. No hint of Cutler's whereabouts since he vanished: no idea of what reprisals Rickling might have in mind after the apparent failure of his bid for power; no inkling of Cutler's purpose in making his escape, or of the identity of those who helped him. Nothing from Artie Chishall—and nothing from anyone else.'' Delphick's tone was bleak, his eyes dark with anxiety. ''Bob, I'm not given to wild prophesy. But I'll take a gamble and predict that if we don't find Cutler soon, certain areas of London are about to become places where nobody with a healthy wish for self-preservation would care to be, not if he was in his right mind. Not even an innocent bystander . . .''

CHAPTER 4

Of the myriad innocent bystanders to whom Delphick might, or might not, have been referring, none could be considered more innocent than Miss Emily Dorothea Seeton. Formerly of Hampstead, for the past seven years, since her retirement, she has lived in the Kentish village of Plummergen; and the little art teacher is innocence personified . . .

In certain senses of the word, that is.

The dictionaries define ''innocent'' in various ways. *Free from moral wrong, blameless:* well, this is undoubtedly true. Miss Seeton has been described—described by Delphick, no less—as everybody's conscience, humanity's backbone; and Delphick is an excellent judge of character. *Ignorant of evil:* this ignorance should be qualified, since Miss Seeton, unutterably honest herself, cannot in honesty deny that evil exists. The eyes of an artist see only the truth, and in Miss Seeton's case even more of the truth than most. The existence of evil is, all too sadly, true—yet Miss Seeton somehow always contrives to think that it was a mistake, and firmly believes that good is sure, in the end, to prevail. *Not legally guilty of crimes:* this, of course, goes without saying, although Miss Seeton's absence of guilt is not quite as straightforward as at first it might appear. She is not only honest, she might almost be called painfully honest, in that her wish for complete honesty at all times frequently involves her in such convoluted explanations that considerable mental pain may be caused to those hearing the explanations. *Harmless . . .*

Harmless? Miss Seeton stands five foot nothing in her unshod size four feet. She weighs, at most, seven stone. She does not rage about the countryside with a machine gun, an axe, or a set of carving knives; she does not drive under the influence of drink, peddle drugs, or administer still more exotic poisons to helpless and unwitting victims. Miss Seeton has never deliberately done any injury or moral wrong to a fellow human being in her life . . .

Yet there are those who would claim—and rightly—that unintentional damage can be far more devastating than any deliberate attack; and among such claimants must be counted a growing number of criminals now behind bars, together with several members of Her Majesty's Constabulary, whose paths have been crossed by Plummergen's perhaps most celebrated resident in the course of one or other of her frequent, and remarkable, adventures—adventures which, in her innocent (*guileless, simple, naive*) fashion she can never quite appreciate that she has undergone. Miss Seeton's life, in Miss Seeton's opinion, is quiet, calm, uneventful: the life—no more, no less—of an ordinary English gentlewoman. It remains forever peaceful, well regulated, and devoid of any untoward incident . . .

Life was indeed sadly devoid of incident and activity that morning: or seemed likely to prove so, if the rain didn't stop. Miss Seeton, standing before her kitchen sink to rinse the last of her breakfast dishes, was moved to sigh as she stared through the window at the same steady downpour that, for goodness knew how many days past, had prevented her from busying herself in the garden as she had planned. True, she had indulged in an orgy of old films on television, had caught up with her Christmas correspondence, and had read several books during the day which in normal circumstances she would have kept for non-television evenings: but she still regretted the external (as it were) opportunities she had lost. There was soil, for instance, to be firmed about the base of plants loosened by the recent bad weather, though one might, perhaps, do better to wait until the bad weather had completely finished. Except that by then (for one had no idea when that would be, since winter was very far from over in January) they could well have become *too* loose, and uprooted, and dead. Which was hardly, she felt, the intention of the author of that invaluable gardening handbook *Greenfinger Points the Way* when he pointed out that there was little sense in the keen gardener's keenness resulting in either pneumonia (for him or her self) or death (for the plants) . . .

"Moderation," mused Miss Seeton, spreading the tea towel on the rack, "in all things—where moderation is possible, of course. What a pity it is not possible to moderate the weather." She wandered into the sitting room for a better view of her little kingdom. "And the leaves." Greenfinger also instructed that the January gardener must (weather permitting) rake up any last fallen leaves from the lawn and add them to the compost heap, with the inference that in an efficient garden there should be few leaves to rake by this stage of the gardening year. Miss Seeton feared that she was a far from efficient gardener. There had been several recent occasions of frosty mornings and windy nights; the very last leaves had been blown from the branches to the lawn in unusual quantity; Miss Seeton now looked out upon their soggy brown blanket and sighed again.

For Christmas she had treated herself to some rolls of nylon netting, which Greenfinger recommended for tying about small trees and shrubs of particular value, to protect them against heavy snowfalls. There had as yet been no snow, but this did not mean there would be none during the rest of the winter. Miss Seeton quoted to herself the old saw about a stitch in time, and shook her head as she contemplated the grey, cloudy, ill-tempered sky. At least while it still rained there could be no chance of snow: but one had to confess that one was more than a little weary of being cooped up indoors, day after day after day . . .

Not, of course, that one was, in the sense of being a prisoner in one's own home. And it seemed so very ungrateful, when there were many who didn't have the good fortune to possess a home of their own, as she now did after so long in rented accommodation. Like the chickens. Miss Seeton's gaze drifted to the bottom of her garden, and she smiled at the unconscious pun. And prisoners had no choice, whereas she did. Except, of course, that she supposed she should call it a house. To go in or out, when there were always gumboots, and her mackintosh, and of course her umbrella, which she carried even when there wasn't a cloud in the sky. Indeed, she had even heard it called a cabin, although that did sound rather too . . . nautical for birds which were most definitely land-based, even if it was made mainly—she smiled for another pun—of wood. Hen-house, chicken-house, chicken cabin, chicken coop.

"Cooped up," remarked Miss Seeton, still smiling. Twice in as many moments, when really one had never thought of oneself as having any particular sense of humour: it must be the influence of those amusing mottoes and riddles in the Christmas crackers. Which nobody could say of today, with all too many clouds pouring down all too much rain, and no sign that they were ever likely to stop for long enough to let her out in the garden again. Perhaps she could make profitable use of this time in further study of the seed catalogues with their bright colours and appealing descriptions, although when dear Stan heard her proposals she suspected he would—and not for the first time—choose to dispute the printed word, even when printed by professional seedsmen. Which might make things rather awkward, since he had far more idea than she of what would be suitable, though this wasn't saying much, because Stan was an acknowledged expert, and she would never dare to say so of herself. But one did find the catalogues so . . . well, enticing. Which was of course the intention. Even after seven years' close study of Greenfinger's advice, which sometimes agreed with Stan's, and sometimes . . . well, didn't. Which—or so she'd gathered during those seven years—was quite common, among gardeners, who each had his or her favourite way of doing things. And really, unless the way was especially unusual (as Stan so often insisted Greenfinger's was) it had to be admitted that most of the Plummergen gardens—at least those worked by keen gardeners, like dear Lady Colveden, or Miss Treeves—were much of a muchness. Though of course one would never dare say so to Stan . . .

Miss Seeton was musing fondly on Stan Bloomer, the farm worker husband of cockney Martha who cleaned her cottage twice a week, when the telephone's jangling trill broke into her thoughts. She replaced the seed catalogues in her bureau, and hurried out into the hall.

"Miss Seeton? Meg Colveden. I haven't rung too early, have I? Are you still eating breakfast?"

Miss Seeton, with genuine pleasure in her voice, assured her ladyship that she was interrupting nothing more important than one's perhaps rather foolishly self-indulgent contemplation of the weather.

"Yes, awful, isn't it? I know it hasn't been forty days and forty nights, but it certainly feels like it. Nigel's begun threatening to demolish the largest barn and use the wood to build an ark. He says with so much hedge-laying and ditch clearing, he's grown quite skilled with an axe."

Miss Seeton smiled: the humour of the aristocracy. It would be only courteous to reply in similar vein. "I had no idea," she ventured, "that any of the Rytham Hall barns were constructed of gopher wood. And what does dear Sir George think of the idea?"

Lady Colveden giggled. "Actually, that's why I rang. In a roundabout way, I mean," she added as Miss Seeton uttered an involuntary squeak for the thought that perhaps Nigel's desire to imitate Noah wasn't a joke after all. "George has been even worse about the weather than Nigel, so you can imagine what life's been like here for the past week or so with the pair of them brooding all over the place about the work they can't do until it stops. To be fair, I suppose I can see their point, though it's quite as annoying for me, with the garden. And nobody," said Lady Colveden firmly, "has caught me smashing barometers to pieces up and down the house, no matter how heavily it was raining."

A second exclamation from Miss Seeton, shocked. Meg Colveden hastened to explain.

"So you see," she concluded, "because it was a wedding present, now he's had a few days to calm down George feels it ought to be replaced, if it can't be repaired. Well, so do I, of course, but I knew if I said anything before George did I'd end up having to spend the housekeeping. And now he says he'll treat it as a belated Christmas present, only I said I'd make all the arrangements, because if there's the slightest let-up in the rain they'll want to be out in the fields, and by the time they got back from Brettenden it might have started again. So I wondered whether you'd care to come with me. I'm sure you must be quite as tired of stewing indoors watching puddles as I am."

Miss Seeton admitted that indeed she was, and accepted the invitation with thanks. She would be ready, she told Lady Colveden, within a quarter of an hour . . .

One's winter coat, or the mackintosh? When the day was not only cold, but wet, she supposed it depended on how far one might anticipate having to walk in the open air. Lady Colveden had said that a trip to one or other of the Brettenden auction houses could be on the agenda, if the jeweller said that the barometer was beyond repair, as from the description sounded all too probable. Which would mean parking behind the shops, and cutting through one of the many little alleys to the main street, which would be sheltered from the worst of the weather; yet puddles, of course, there would undoubtedly be, no matter how much shelter the walls might give.

"My mackintosh, then, and gumboots," said Miss Seeton to herself, pinning on her hat before the mirror. "Rather than galoshes, today. And, of course, since it is my first real outing since Christmas . . . my new umbrella."

Miss Seeton's lifelong habit of carrying an umbrella, in every conceivable climatic condition, has been the cause of some innocent amusement among her friends: but that same habit has spared these friends much racking of their brains each time a present for the little spinster is in order. Another brolly for Miss Seeton's by now remarkable collection is always welcome. She would never be so extravagant as to purchase technically unnecessary accessories on her own account, but she takes a secret (albeit guilty) delight in her ability to choose, from the many clipped in the rack beside the hall table, the correct umbrella to match whatever outfit she might wear on any particular occasion.

Miss Seeton's very best umbrella she keeps for the very best occasions. She values it highly. It was given to her in appreciation of the invaluable assistance she once rendered to the police during a drugs-and-murder investigation, and was made especially for her with a handle of real gold. Not *solid* gold, she will quickly explain to any who might ask; solid gold would have been far too heavy, as well as— Miss Seeton blushes, for a gentlewoman does not discuss money—far too expensive, and more than she deserved, in the circumstances, but the dear superintendent had been so complimentary . . .

Miss Seeton can never understand that the compliments of the as-yet-unpromoted Detective Superintendent Delphick were by no means empty, and were more than well deserved. Almost without her realising it, she had been the catalyst behind the breaking of a society drugs ring and the capture of the notorious Cesar Lebel, a dope-peddler and killer, whose path had—literally—crossed that of Miss Seeton when they met in a dark alleyway near Covent Garden. Miss Seeton was making for the station after a performance of *Carmen;* Lebel was knifing a prostitute after an argument over her part in the drugs traffic. Delphick, in charge of the case, had asked the little art teacher to draw (in addition to her written statement) her impression of the anonymous young man she had chastised for his rude behaviour to his girlfriend—whom she had chastised by prodding him firmly in the back with her umbrella; and the young man became anonymous no longer, as the features of Cesar were instantly recogniseable from Miss Seeton's swift sketch. In due course, after innocently leading the forces of law and order a merry dance about the byways of Kent, Miss Seeton served up Lebel to Delphick and his colleagues neatly trussed and garnished, on a plate; and the Oracle had commissioned the black silk, gold-handled umbrella as a token of his, and Scotland Yard's, esteem.

Scotland Yard was not the only constabulary force to set a high value on the services of Miss Seeton, who—after a second successful case involving post office robberies and a spate of child stranglings—had been taken on the strength as an Official Art Consultant in order to investigate the sinister Nuscience cult, and a burgeoning popular interest in witchcraft which the criminal element seemed all too ready to exploit. Miss Seeton's appointment had been partly brought about by the good offices of the then Chief Inspector Brinton of Ashford, in whose manor the Nuscientists and devil worshippers had attempted to flourish. Brinton applied to the Yard for Delphick to use his influence with Plummergen's resident artist to coax her to produce some more of her lightning sketches as a help in solving a case that had left him baffled: and solve it, with that help, he had. The chief inspector's name was added to the growing list of those (on the right side of the law) who sang Miss Seeton's praises . . .

Miss Seeton's newest umbrella bore witness to Brinton's

high regard. He had given it to her after an outbreak of crime threatened to run over the recent Christmas holidays and was tripped well and truly up when Miss Seeton thrust her brolly in its path. Like Delphick's earlier gift, Brinton's umbrella was custom-made: and it was with pride that Miss Seeton took it now, a slim shape in royal blue, from the rack in the hall, admiring its furled silken neatness and hand-stitched leather-covered crook handle, embossed with her initials in gold. If—she reflected, with a smiling glance in the mirror—there was time, she might slip into the milliner's for a new hat, since none she had seemed to do her new blue umbrella sufficient justice . . .

Suddenly the cheerful pipping of a car horn outside the front gate warned her that Lady Colveden had arrived. Miss Seeton gathered up her bag, pulled on her gloves, and, locking the door carefully behind her, hurried off to spend an enjoyable few hours pottering from antique shop to auction house in Brettenden.

For anyone but Miss Seeton, this would be a perfectly harmless, uneventful timetable.

For anyone but Miss Seeton . . .

CHAPTER 5

"If anything," said Lady Colveden, changing gear to slow the Hillman round a corner, "I'd say it's raining harder than ever, wouldn't you? Oh, dear, I do hope George will be sensible. I'd rather *not* spend the next week hearing him sneeze his head off all over the house. Having him and Nigel grumbling everywhere is quite bad enough, and then of course there's always the worry it might turn to pneumonia."

Miss Seeton offered the reassurance that Sir George—with dear Nigel to assist, perhaps, in the trickier spots, whatever they might be, for even after seven years in the country she must confess she had very little knowledge of farming—that Sir George was unlikely to come to much harm, no matter how muddy the ditch or how deep the water. She thought. If Lady Colveden didn't mind her saying so.

Meg Colveden smiled. "Oh, if it was just the farm I wouldn't worry, because you're right, Nigel and the others are sure to stop him doing anything silly, like working for hours with leaky boots knee-deep in freezing water. But he's not on the farm. After the fuss over the barometer"—

the smile became whimsical—"he was so apologetic, he made *me* feel guilty—goodness knows why I should—and I suggested he take the morning off for a round of golf. I thought it might cheer him up. George may not be a particularly good golfer, but he does so enjoy all the fun and games and gossip at the nineteenth hole."

Miss Seeton's eyes twinkled. "I have always understood that golf is not so much a game as a—a social event; and social events are always more enjoyable in the company of one's friends, are they not?"

Lady Colveden laughed. "You're being beautifully tactful, Miss Seeton, but we both know—or at least I think we both *suspect*—George's real motives. Of course, he huffed and shuffled and was awfully cagey about it all, so I couldn't be absolutely sure, but he shut himself away to use the telephone before he left, and if you ask me, he rang Admiral Leighton and asked him to go with him." Her ladyship laughed again. "Mind you, if we've guessed right, George has just lost any sympathy he might have won from me, because you know what he and the admiral can be like when they get together."

Miss Seeton, who did indeed know, murmured something non-committal, and thought it diplomatic to change the subject. "Do you know," she remarked, "this will be a new experience for me, if it cannot be repaired. I have never attended an auction before, with renting my flat, you see, furnished; and with dear Cousin Flora leaving me her house with the contents, there has really been no need . . ."

Cousin Flora, Miss Seeton's godmother and (following the death of her mother, Flora's first cousin) only living relative, had been better known to Plummergen as Old Mrs. Bannet. A deaf and arthritic widow, she had been well into her tenth decade before at last fading out of life bequeathing everything of which she died possessed to dear Emily Dorothea: *everything* to include, as well as fixtures, fittings and the cottage—Sweetbriars—itself, the invaluable services of Martha Bloomer, domestic paragon, and Stan, horticulturalist par excellence.

"And I was wondering," continued Miss Seeton absently, her eyes misty as she contemplated her great good fortune in the devoted friendship of Martha and Stan, "whether—afterwards, naturally, and always provided that you were in no great hurry to return home—whether I might slip along to Monica Mary. My new umbrella, you know. Just for a few minutes. It is such a splendid colour that I feel it really needs a different hat, or at least trimming, to set it off to best advantage. But only, of course, if there should be time. Dear Mr. Brinton was so generous, and so very complimentary in his letter—although I believe," she said, turning pink, "the bus runs today, and you have already been most kind. So perhaps . . ."

Flustered, Miss Seeton fell silent with embarrassment. Her wish to change the subject from Sir George's anticipated peccadilloes at the nineteenth hole had led her to commit the grave solecism of asking one who was already doing her a favour to perform another before the first was complete. It seemed so—so ungrateful. Taking advantage . . .

"Oh, you wouldn't be taking advantage of me," said Lady Colveden cheerfully. "It would be more me taking advantage of George, because he does *brood* so whenever I have a new hat. And I shall make him pay for it if I buy one today, which, knowing Miss Brown, I probably will." She smothered a giggle. "Her hats are such a temptation, he never lets me anywhere near the shop if we're in Brettenden together. Poor George—still, it would balance the barometer, don't you think? And if we happen to spot a comfortable easy chair at the auction, then I'll bid for it, to make up for the one I made him put on the bonfire. I've always felt it was my fault, in a way."

Miss Seeton, relieved that her kind chauffeuse would not complain should they pay a visit to the celebrated and exclusive Brettenden milliner, nodded and smiled. She was—

as her ladyship had expected—completely untroubled by
the casual reference to Sir George's late easy chair, though
the circumstances of its demise had been such that the demise of Miss Seeton herself was very nearly accomplished
at one and the same time. Miss Seeton's complete inability
to understand that anyone could ever deliberately mean her
any harm—even when, bound and gagged inside a sack,
her unconscious form had been hoisted by malefactors to
the summit of a Guy Fawkes bonfire to await incinera-
tion—was well known to her friends, who—failing Miss
Seeton's indicating the least worry over whatever might
occur—frequently worried themselves into near nervous
breakdowns on their friend's innocent behalf. One day, they
feared, her luck would run out; but her luck, everyone
knew, was remarkable . . .

Not so much remarkable as (to those not of its number)
incomprehensible is the attitude of the British aristocracy
to change. True blue blood dislikes, almost distrusts, the
new. It prefers—feels comfortable with—the old; and,
given its hereditary nature, feels most comfortable of all
with the heirloom-old, passed down unaltered from generation to generation. Sir George's fireside chair had belonged first to his grandfather. His father had inspired an
outcry when he allowed his wife—a noted needlewoman—
to darn its worn tapestry arms. Lady Colveden, profiting by
the example of her mother-in-law, took no such risk when
the horsehair stuffing once again began to show through:
she left the fabric of the chair untouched and, as her husband muttered of prickles through his sleeves, produced a
pair of loose covers once embroidered by her great-aunt
Eliza, and thus of unimpeachable pedigree. A wayward
spark from an unguarded fire caught the cover of the nearby
arm, burst into flame, and caused irreparable damage to
tapestry, horsehair, and wooden frame alike; sadly, fighting
a rearguard action every inch of the way, Sir George had
in the end to accept the chair's banishment from polite society. Lady Colveden had always meant to make it up to

him; and now her chance had come.

"With the weather so bad," said her ladyship, reversing at an angle into a parking space, "there might not be as many people at the sale as there often are. We could find the most wonderful bargains, Miss Seeton." Her lovely eyes began to sparkle. "It sounds shocking, to say so out loud, but I do hope the jeweller can't fix the barometer. I'm longing for a good excuse to poke about looking for things, and George's chair doesn't really count."

Miss Seeton secretly saw no reason why it shouldn't but, as she'd been looking forward to the auction herself, agreed aloud with Lady Colveden that antique shops and jewellers could be visited, after all, any day, except early closing, whereas her understanding was that Brettenden's two auction houses held sales once a week, at most. Perhaps they should go straight there, rather than take a detour and risk the loss of some truly spectacular bargain?

"Done," said her ladyship, at once. "Only—go straight where? The choice must be yours, Miss Seeton, as you're my guest. The Brettenden Auction Rooms are bigger, but Candell and Inchpin's closer. And it's still raining . . ."

Unlike the umbrella-armed Miss Seeton, Meg Colveden had only a silk headscarf tied over her thick, wavy brown hair as protection against the downpour. "Candell and Inchpin, I think," said Miss Seeton, and saw her hostess smile.

They left the broken barometer, newspaper-wrapped, in the locked boot of the Hillman, and made their hurried way through the rain down narrow alleys and along streets far less crowded than on an ordinary market day, yet still not so empty that Miss Seeton could comfortably share her umbrella with the friend who was several inches taller than she. Lady Colveden repeatedly assured her that this did not matter. They would, she said, be there almost before either of them knew it . . .

And they were. They skirted puddles; they dodged half-blind pedestrians with their heads bowed against the downpour; and within minutes they were squelching side by side up the majestic sandstone steps beneath the legend "Candell & Inchpin, Auctioneers and Valuers, Established since 1782."

Just inside the double doors, a Candell of the umpteenth generation stood to welcome visitors with a smile, a copy of that day's catalogue, and the murmured advice that the sale had already begun. The advice was murmured not because there was any fear that clients of Candell & Inchpin would start yelling at the tops of their voices unless stern hints were dropped to the contrary, but because the young Candell was . . . well, young. Learning his job. A murmur informed without giving the impression that the informer knew more than he did: firm tones implied authority, and until two or three senior generations of Candell had burned themselves out, there must be no chance for lesser lights to shine too bright.

"Through here, isn't it?" Having shaken herself free of raindrops, Lady Colveden smiled her thanks for the catalogue and indicated a second set of double doors nearby. Through the crack in the middle floated the confident voice of a man destined from birth to stand on a podium and wield a gavel.

". . . advance on fifty? Fifty, I'm bid—yes, thank you, madam, sixty. Sixty I'm bid—any advance on sixty? The bidding's with you, sir, at sixty. No? Then it's on sixty. Sixty pounds—ah! Seventy from the gentleman with the red carnation, seventy just entered the bidding. Seventy pounds—and eighty, madam? Thank you, eighty—and is that ninety, sir? Ninety from the red carnation, thank you. Ninety I'm bid. Any advance on ninety? The bidding's with you, madam, at ninety pounds. Care to make the ton? One hundred? Thank you, one hundred pounds I'm bid . . ."

Curious to know what was happening, Miss Seeton and Lady Colveden pushed open the doors and entered the large, high-vaulted chamber with its splendid acoustics. Perhaps sixty people were already there, some plainly experienced in sale-room technique, others obviously not sure what they ought to be doing, but it was better than getting soaked to the skin outside, and they hadn't had to pay.

Miss Seeton, the shortest person present, had to stand on tiptoe, balancing herself with her umbrella, to peer over the central display of furniture, bundles, boxes, and assorted items for a clear view of the podium man with the confident voice. A mounted stag's head caught her eye, its glassy orbs malevolent beneath its twelve-point dignity; she saw a large brass gong, an ornate but rusty wrought-iron bedstead, and something that appeared at first sight to be a china foot-bath, but probably wasn't, balanced on top of a wardrobe with a cracked mirror fixed to one door. The whole idiosyncratic assembly was piled on, around, or occasionally under tables of various sizes laid roughly end to end, or (where they didn't quite meet) linked by precariously balanced planks into a strange sort of continuous shelving.

A closer look at this seeming muddle gave a distinct impression of method in its madness. Large white labels, all numbered boldly in black, had been fastened to, descended from, or were tucked beneath their appointed concomitants; a quick glance at the catalogue suggested that these numbers corresponded to the Lot Numbers listed therein. Further Lot labels could be seen around the perimeter of the room, which like the centre aisle was cluttered with shelving of a haphazard nature, set more or less in rows and piled high with a motley selection of ticketed Household Effects, Furniture and Collectables, as the catalogue described them.

"Miss Seeton!" whispered Lady Colveden, as the confident man knocked down whatever-it-was to the red carnation at a final cost of one hundred and sixty pounds. "I'm sorry, but this might take longer than I thought. There are over five hundred lots listed. Goodness knows how many of them are barometers or easy chairs. If any of them are." She flipped through a couple of pages more, then firmly closed the catalogue. "Not terribly well typed, is it? I mean printed. Don't you think it's going to be much easier just to walk round and look at everything?"

Gravely Miss Seeton agreed. The reproductive quality of the catalogue was certainly poor: nobody could reasonably expect her ladyship to strain her eyes when she had to drive home afterwards—and when it would indeed be so much easier walking round to look at everything . . .

Their consciences now clear, Miss Seeton and Lady Colveden happily set about enjoying themselves.

"It's rather more crowded," gasped Miss Seeton, as she wriggled her way past a large man in a black fur-collared coat, "than I had expected—excuse me—on such a very wet day. Oh, I do beg your pardon," she said to a tall, thin, hatched-faced woman in grey, who glared down her Roman nose as the final drip from Miss Seeton's passing brolly was brushed on her open catalogue, smudging the already-smudged jellied ink. "I am so sorry, but . . ."

Hatchet Face, with a sniff, moved pointedly out of dripping range. Miss Seeton, blushing, subsided into a murmur of continuous apology as she attempted to squeeze in Lady Colveden's wake between two plump, elderly men—no room in the crowded aisle to pass around them—wearing identical tweed hats, plaid jackets, striped woollen scarves, and leather gaiters. Mirror images of each other, the two clutched gnarled walking sticks in their equally gnarled hands, and gripped battered clay pipes (unlit) between their teeth. Whenever the bidding was with the Tweedle Twins, either Dum or Dee—they seemed to take it in turns— would, without troubling to consult his brother, clench his teeth to jerk the bowl of his pipe upwards. The auctioneer was evidently accustomed to this unusual method of signalling a bid, for he accepted it every time without question.

Miss Seeton was entranced by the spectacle. Pausing, ostensibly to admire a set of old "Cries of London" prints, she contrived to position herself by a conveniently large wardrobe with a mirrored door—a gentlewoman does not

stare—and watched with some interest as the Tweedles
tried to stake their claim on what the catalogue advised was
a Box of Crockery, Unmatched, and Kitchen Glassware,
Ditto, As Seen.

Title to this motley domestic assortment was being vigorously challenged by a pink-cheeked woman in a mackintosh of hideous fluorescent green. She had the most
decisive nod Miss Seeton had seen in years. Each jerk of
a Tweedle pipe was countered by such a forceful ducking
of the mackintoshed head that even Miss Seeton, several
yards away, could almost believe she felt the air move. Was
Green Plastic Mac, mused Miss Seeton, the Tweedles' rival
in the bed-and-breakfast trade? A landlady anxious to fur-
nish rented property at the minimum cost? She sighed,
thinking of her former life in London. Or perhaps—

"See them?" The unexpected voice, hard in her ear, with
the accompanying chuckle and nudge in the ribs, made
Miss Seeton squeak with surprise, though the squeak was
drowned out by the clatter of her dropped umbrella. Blushing as every head within earshot turned towards her, she
ducked to reclaim her own, resuming her apologetic mur-
murs as the damp folds sprayed misty drops on nearby feet
and legs.

". . . after the funeral," the voice was saying as Miss
Seeton, breathless, brought herself upright. "Family solicitor made a regular performance of it, they say, insisted on
reading every blessed *being of sound mind* and *devise and
bequeath* th'old girl wrote, and a great whole crowd of 'em,
cousins and collaterals and I-don't-know-whatevers a-
sitting there with their tongues hanging out to see what was
in it for them . . ."

Miss Seeton, quietly sighing for the vagaries of human
nature, smiled politely as she tried to distance herself from
this melancholy narrative. She begged the pardon of a tall
man with aristocratic features as she stepped on his foot—
backed hurriedly away and bumped into a shorter man in

a donkey jacket—blushed, and stuttered—and dropped her umbrella again.

It rattled horribly on the bare wooden boards of the sale-room floor, making the auctioneer pause in his steady vocal ascent from thirty-five to forty pounds. The Tweedle Twins jerked their pipes in unison as they stared. Hatchet Face sniffed loudly and muttered accusations of drink; Green Plastic Mac tossed her head, and her cheeks turned from pink to red.

So, too, did Miss Seeton's, flaming scarlet as, for the second time, she groped downwards for her umbrella, wretchedly aware that in this crowd of perhaps sixty persons, fifty-nine must be looking in her direction. Fifty-eight. Lady Colveden—wherever she might be—was far too kindhearted, and too well bred, to wish to cause her friend any more embarrassment . . .

Fifty-seven. As Miss Seeton, for the second time, rose upright, she realized that her new acquaintance had pursued her in her flight, intent on delivering the punchline no matter how many brollies she might drop.

And deliver it he promptly did, with a gleam in his eye and relish in his tone.

". . . the whole boiling lot to the Cats' Home!" he said as the Unmatched Crockery was knocked down to the triumphant Tweedle Twins for forty-five pounds.

CHAPTER 6

Under cover of the furious protests from Green Plastic Mac and the general interest aroused by them, Miss Seeton was able to make her escape from the Relentless Raconteur. She moved with breathless relief to the opposite side of the aisle, where her attention was caught by a brace of encyclopaedia-sized volumes, their pages gilt-edged between handsomely marbled boards which Miss Seeton, tucking her damp umbrella out of the way, carefully raised. *Knight's Pictorial Gallery of Arts*—she'd thought so. *Illustrated with steel engravings and nearly four thousand woodcuts . . .*

Miss Seeton turned the pages, admired the illustrations, and wondered how much one would have to pay. Need one buy both books together? *Volume One, Useful Arts. Volume Two, Fine Arts.* Sighing, she supposed one need. Consulting her catalogue, she realised one must. Moreover, they were Lot Four Hundred and Ninety, which would be a long time to wait. She shook her head sadly—froze, fearing this might be construed as a bid for the set of golf clubs currently under offer—relaxed, smiled faintly, and moved on.

The golf clubs made her think of Sir George, and she

glanced about her for his wife. Lady Colveden was soon observed in the neighbouring aisle, admiring a large, white, scarlet-combed cockerel, stuffed, on a dark wooden stand. Miss Seeton blinked. She tried to envisage this remarkable fowl on display at Rytham Hall in place of the lost barometer: she failed. Like herself, her ladyship kept hens. She had never voiced the wish to have even the best of her layers, or their mates, preserved for posterity . . .

Lady Colveden patted the bird on the head and passed to the next item, a grandmother clock. Miss Seeton, who had a fondness for the works of P. G. Wodehouse, briefly amused herself with the notion that the diamond necklace of Lady Constance Keeble might have been appropriated and concealed by some Edwardian taxidermist, then chided herself for her folly. Stolen gems—fictional gems, at that: one should keep one's imagination under better control. Perhaps, if one hadn't last night watched *The Treasure of the Sierra Madre,* one would have had more sense.

Across Miss Seeton's inward eye flashed a sudden vision of precious stones and gold, ingots and nuggets and finely wrought chains, heaped high in an open chest bound with iron bands, half buried in sand beneath a tall palm tree. Fierce masculine figures in thigh-length seaboots, with cutlasses in their hands and muscles rippling under their striped jerseys, surrounded the treasure chest and studied it with eyes that glittered, diamond-bright, with greed. Greed . . .

Miss Seeton remembered the Relentless Raconteur and the Cats' Home—and the indignant relatives. She shivered. Dear Cousin Flora. How very, very lucky she had been . . .

Cousin Flora. Moving on, she had reached a little display that reminded her very much of her late godmother. A carved wooden glove-box; a dainty set of opera glasses in mother-of-pearl; a pair of ladies' shoe-trees, hinged, with handles. Elegant wire glove-rests: for those gloves, she assumed, that didn't fit in the box, always supposing these items all came from—she smothered a sigh—the same Deceased Effects, as she'd heard the auctioneer describing his wares. And—good gracious—an album.

An album of the sort that had been so popular in her own young days, when schoolgirls collected souvenirs of their friends for later life. Miss Seeton opened the blue leather cover and plunged into reminiscence. *Mary Helen Becker, Her Memories* was written in elegant copperplate on the title page of smooth, heavy paper: Miss Seeton turned it and realised that each writing page was interleaved with a sheet of drawing paper. Mary Helen's friends had painted landscapes in watercolour, sketched flowers in crayon; had composed witty, or sentimental, or philosophical verses; had written jokes which, after so many years, meant—once more, Miss Seeton sighed—nothing to the one who read them now.

A vivid pen-and-wash study of an elegant couple dancing in evening dress under a chandelier made Miss Seeton catch her breath: Margaret Rose Tilbury, whoever she was, had the artist's eye. If only—

At her shoulder, a cough. "Excuse me." A hand appeared and took the album from her: she was so surprised that her grasp on her umbrella slackened in sympathy, though for once she managed to keep her hold. "It's the next lot," explained the voice behind the hand, which proved to belong to the holder-upper Miss Seeton had noticed—without really noticing him—earlier.

"Oh! I do beg your—" But the holder-upper had gone, leaving Miss Seeton feeling bereft. *Mary Helen Becker, her Memories.* She was not, thought Miss Seeton, alone . . .

"And the next lot," announced the auctioneer, having knocked down an archery set of longbow, arrows, and target to a young woman in a tartan cape. "Autograph album bound in blue leather—thank you," he said as the holder-upper held it up. "Now, who'll start me at ten pounds?"

Miss Seeton's hands clutched the crook of her umbrella. She glanced about her: who else was there who might appreciate the art of Margaret Rose Tilbury?

Nobody moved. "Then we'll say five," said the auctioneer. "Five pounds—anyone bidding five pounds? Thank you, Robin Hood," as the tartan cape twitched a languid eyebrow.

Everyone except Miss Seeton chuckled. Miss Seeton could only blink and remind herself that she had no real need of an album, autograph or—or otherwise. But that pen-and-ink sketch had been—

"Any advance on five pounds? Five pounds I'm bid," said the auctioneer. Robin Hood stroked the folds of her cape and looked smug.

"Five pounds—ten, thank you," as Miss Seeton's clutch became an involuntary spasm that raised the umbrella high in the air.

"Fifteen? Fifteen, thank you," said the auctioneer.

Miss Seeton's heart went thump. She ignored it. As the auctioneer turned with his inevitable question towards her, she waved the umbrella again. Twenty pounds—if a belated Christmas present was good enough for her ladyship, it ought surely to be good enough for Emily Dorothea Seeton—

"The bidding's with Miss Hood there, at twenty pounds." Robin, with a sideways glance at Miss Seeton's face, pale and alert, slowly shook her head.

"At twenty pounds," said the auctioneer. "Anyone give me twenty-five? No? At twenty pounds, then, this autograph album in blue leather. Going—going—gone, for twenty pounds, to the lady with the matching umbrella!"

"Miss Seeton, how exciting." Lady Colveden had materialised beside her. "I never knew you collected autographs," and Miss Seeton, flushed with discreet triumph, explained.

"Then you've had better luck than me. There isn't a single barometer in the place, and I don't like any of the chairs—but I must show you the loveliest miniature violin. It would make a wonderful birthday present for Julia. We

wouldn't have to wait more than half an hour, I imagine—
if you didn't mind.''

Miss Seeton said at once that she didn't in the least. She
was entirely at the disposal of the kind friend who had
brought her into town: as for dear Julia's birthday, she herself might, with her mother to advise, find a little something
among the preceding lots which would suit. There were
several charming pieces of china, for instance—

"Oh." Miss Seeton rocked back at the sight of four huge
black frames, ill made and with peeling varnish, around a
garishly tinted set of biblical scenes. "Oh, dear." She
shook her head at *Adam and Eve Dispossessed, Noah and
His Sons Building the Ark, Elijah Calling Fire upon the
Priests of Baal,* and *The Infant Samuel, Roused in the
Night.* "Dear me. It seems almost irreverent to criticise.
And yet . . .''

Lady Colveden giggled. "I couldn't resist showing them
to you," she said apologetically. "But the violin's just
here." She led the way along.

Miss Seeton agreed that the delicate silver ornament, its
strings so fine one could hardly see them, would make a
most acceptable birthday present for Nigel's sister. For her
own offering, she remembered seeing somewhere a dainty
china dish and matching plate, rosebud-patterned. Would
Lady Colveden think it an indulgence—an impertinence—
on her part to make a bid for these and, if successful, to
give Julia the plate and dear Janie—a sweet and reliable
child—the little dish at the appropriate time?

"I should think they'd both be thrilled, Miss Seeton.
Thank you." Her ladyship's lovely eyes glowed at the compliment to her granddaughter's sense of responsibility in
the matter of fragile and costly gifts. "Only you mustn't
spend too much. Perhaps it's as well for George's bank
balance there aren't any barometers in this week's sale—
it's so easy to get carried away at auctions, isn't it?"

Miss Seeton promised to take the greatest care. It had
not escaped her notice, as she perambulated the room, that

the Tweedle Twins and Green Plastic Mac were far from the only ones determined to outdo each other in bidding for what did not, to her admittedly inexpert eye, seem to warrant the sums eventually paid in many cases. Robin Hood, balked of her blue leather album, had plunged into reckless pursuit of a set of ivory-backed hairbrushes with engraved monograms, in defiance of the Red Carnation. The Roman-nosed Hatchet Face had been determined to prevent the man in the black fur-collared coat from winning the pair of glass scent bottles and powder box (mahogany) on which he had set his sights. Miss Seeton shook her head for these excesses of the competitive spirit, and resolved to show rather more discretion when the time came to bid for the rosebud dish and plate.

If she could only remember where she'd seen them . . .

As Lady Colveden watched the price of a marble splash-back with oak-framed mirror soar to stratospheric heights, Miss Seeton ignored the drama being played out between the Fur-Collared Coat and the Roman Nose. Surrounded by persons all taller than herself, she stood on tiptoe, balanced by her umbrella, and peered about her to refresh her memory.

"Good gracious." She beamed. "Such a surprise, when his office is in Ashford—and what a coincidence, to be using it for the first time today. I hope he'll be pleased to see how much I appreciate his kindness . . ."

Watching Superintendent Brinton bulldoze his way through the crowd, she tried to catch his eye: but Brinton, whose domestic life was still decidedly out of tune, had decided to restore marital harmony by presenting his help-meet with some token of his esteem, and was currently preoccupied with thoughts of his savings account, and his mortgage.

Miss Seeton tried for several moments, but failed to attract his attention: she was, as so often, at a disadvantage in a crowd. Balanced comfortably on the balls of her feet— the benefits of yoga, yet again—she finally raised her umbrella from the floor, and brandished it in the direction of Superintendent Brinton.

And the voice of the auctioneer rang around the room: ''One hundred and fifty pounds I'm bid, from the lady with the smart blue brolly!''

CHAPTER 7

With her umbrella in mid-brandish, Miss Seeton froze as she looked quickly from Brinton to the podium. What bid had her—her foolish carelessness now caused her to make? What was she now duty-bound to buy, if nobody else bid higher? Explanations: so embarrassing. And one could hardly expect people to excuse her folly when one had already been responsible for so much—well, disturbance, with one's umbrella. (Hastily, she brought the brolly down from the salute to rest with its ferrule on the floor.) Dropping it so many times. And now this. Whatever it was.

Still on tiptoe, supporting herself with the umbrella, she stared—and stared again at what stood on the auctioneer's table, far too heavy for the holder-upper to hold up. It was a squat, massive, oblong box of age-darkened wood, carved in curious patterns, criss-crossed with iron bands for reinforcement, padlocked and clasped and fastened by dull, rusting metal which might be who-knew-how-many-hundred years old.

It might almost be a pirate's treasure chest.

"One hundred and fifty pounds the opening bid," said the auctioneer as Miss Seeton continued to stare. "Who'll make it two hundred—you, madam?'' to Robin Hood: who shook her head. ''Anyone else give me two hundred?''

Nobody moved. ''One hundred and eighty, then. Who'll bid one hundred and eighty pounds for this piece of history, ladies and gentlemen? History *and* mystery, because we've somehow or other mislaid the keys. Whoever buys this could find the Crown Jewels inside, for all we know. Left behind by Captain Blood in the seventeenth century,'' he improvised rapidly. ''The ones in the Tower now being forgeries, of course. One hundred and eighty pounds for the Crown Jewels, and a handsome box to put them in!''

His audience chuckled appreciatively, but were otherwise unresponsive. Miss Seeton's bid was still valid.

''Miss Seeton!'' gasped Lady Colveden, as she realised the predicament of her elderly friend. She did frantic calculations in her head. Noblesse must oblige: if she hadn't brought Miss Seeton to Brettenden in the first place, this wouldn't have happened: but would George ever forgive her?

''One hundred and sixty pounds?'' invited the auctioneer. ''Ah, thank you, madam,'' as Lady Colveden, trusting to the Galahad within her spouse, raised a trembling hand. ''One hundred and sixty pounds I'm bid for this mystery box. Now then, who'll make it one hundred and seventy? Everyone loves a mystery, don't they?''

Miss Seeton was quite mesmerised by the man's professional eloquence. How could she deny it? How often had she listened to plays on the wireless, or gone to the cinema to see—and now could watch on television, as she'd been doing over the past few days—the Thin Man films, or Charlie Chan? So entertaining. The Falcon, Mr. Moto . . . One had to agree that, even if ''love'' was certainly an exaggeration, one did *enjoy* mysteries of that sort . . . And she nodded.

''One hundred and seventy pounds,'' said the auctioneer, who never missed a trick. ''One hundred and seventy, I'm bid. And . . . eighty, madam?'' to Lady Colveden. ''One hundred and eighty pounds for the long-lost treasure of Captain Blood?''

Perhaps, if she hadn't watched Humphrey Bogart and John Huston the night before, Miss Seeton might have allowed the box to be knocked down to her ladyship. Perhaps. But she had; and she found herself holding her breath and clutching her umbrella in the suspense of the moment.

''*Do* I hear one hundred and eighty pounds?'' enquired the auctioneer, his eye sweeping the room before it returned to Lady Colveden. ''The bidding's with you, madam. One hundred and eighty pounds?''

Lady Colveden's horrified face was enough to bring him straight back to Miss Seeton. ''Then one hundred and seventy pounds I'm bid, from the lady with the blue umbrella . . .''

And he picked up his hammer.

Lady Colveden suddenly pulled herself together. ''Miss Seeton, no!'' she hissed, tugging at her friend's sleeve. ''We must explain!'' She looked about her: everyone so much taller than Miss Seeton. ''We must! Would you like me to do it for you? Or perhaps if you just kept shaking your head, he might see that it was a mistake and start the bidding again . . .'' On the other hand, he might not. Then inspiration struck. ''I'm sure Mr. Brinton would be able to sort things out—if we could only catch his eye . . .''

She couldn't. Brinton, like everyone else, had his eye on Miss Seeton and her upraised brolly, while Miss Seeton had hers on the auctioneer.

''One hundred and seventy pounds,'' he intoned, his gavel poised above the plate.

Lady Colveden had given up hope of attracting Brinton's attention. ''Oh, wait!''

''Going—''

''There's been—''

''Going—''

''—a mistake!''

Lady Colveden and the auctioneer spoke together: and

his voice was louder than hers.

"—gone! Sold for one hundred and seventy pounds to the lady with the blue umbrella!"

And the gavel came down with a most decisive bang before the banger, turning to his assistant, asked for the next lot to be put up without delay.

"Miss Seeton, I'm so sorry." Lady Colveden hardly knew what to say. "I should have been quicker. I should have shouted. I should have made them realise you didn't mean to bid—Mr. Brinton," she said as the superintendent came looming out of the crowd, "you could tell it was all a mistake, couldn't you? Poor Miss Seeton never wanted . . . never intended . . . I'm afraid it was my fault for distracting her, and when she saw you arriving she . . . That is, what possible use could a locked wooden box be to her?"

Brinton had been about to make some jocular remark concerning hidden treasure and Miss Seeton's good fortune; but now he looked from Lady Colveden's anxious eyes to the hands of Miss Seeton, twitching as they clasped about the leather-covered handle of the blue umbrella; and he realised what had happened.

"More my fault than yours, Lady Colveden. If I'd given MissEss a box of chocolates for Christmas instead of trying to do an Oracle with a swank umbrella, she wouldn't be stuck with the wrong sort of box now. But don't you worry, Miss Seeton. Candell and Inchpin's a reputable firm—the good, old-fashioned sort. They'll have this sort of thing happening all the time, I don't doubt—and even if they're minded to shuffle a bit with your ordinary citizen, well, a superintendent of police ought to be able to get things sorted out in no time. Put it back up for sale right away, and no real harm done . . ."

The superintendent's voice—normally the confident, carrying extension of his robust personality—tailed away as he saw the look on Miss Seeton's face, and the insistent way she was shaking her head. As he fell silent, Lady Colveden hurried into the breach.

"You do see, Miss Seeton? This muddle can be sorted out in no time, with Mr. Brinton's help. You needn't worry . . ."

And then she, too, fell silent as Miss Seeton—her hands restless, her eyes worried, her cheeks beginning to turn pink—shook her head once more, very firmly indeed.

"So kind," she murmured. "But so unnecessary—to take so much trouble, that is, although it was nobody's fault but mine, I assure you, and one does so dislike causing it to others. Trouble, I mean. And—"

"No trouble at all, Miss Seeton," said Brinton hastily, before she could tie herself—or him—in conversational knots. "I told you—an everyday occurrence, this sort of little misunderstanding'll be. So long as they put it straight back up again, I don't—"

"Miss Seeton," said Lady Colveden as her friend blushed still more, and continued to shake her head as she struggled to find the right words. "Are we making a mistake? Are you trying to tell us you . . . don't want the auctioneer to . . . to sell the box to someone else?"

Miss Seeton's blush deepened. Her eyes danced from one side to the other in acute embarrassment. When she spoke, Lady Colveden and the tall superintendent had to lean forward to catch her faltering words.

". . . folly, perhaps," came the murmured explanation, "but my pension—the generosity of the police . . . cannot say it would be an undue financial burden . . . childish fantasies . . . romantic notions . . . intriguing mystery, as the gentleman said . . ."

"Well, well." Brinton straightened; Lady Colveden found herself smiling. Across the top of Miss Seeton's bowed head, their eyes met; and Brinton answered Lady Colveden's kindly smile with one of his own. Who could have guessed that the little art teacher—whose imagination, or lack of it, was a matter for heated debate among those who knew her best—harboured the same dreams of buried treasure that had been dreamed by generations of young-sters? Long John Silver—Blackbeard—pieces of eight, pre-cious stones, Spanish doubloons and gold moidores . . .

And those not so young, as well. "I must say," came the quiet observation from Lady Colveden, as Brinton grinned a shamefaced grin, "I wouldn't mind knowing what's inside, myself. Though that's probably," recover-ing, "because he made such a mystery of it—as you your-self said, Miss Seeton. But as to whether it's really worth almost"—she gulped—"two hundred pounds to find out, goodness only knows, and I do feel . . ."

What she felt was helpless, in the face of Miss Seeton's beseeching look. A lifetime's attempt at the deliberate quenching of every spark of originality in her artistic en-deavours had left Miss Seeton with much in her nature that was but seldom expressed. Only when, despite every effort at suppression, her instincts urged her pencil to run away with her did that spark (which some, though not Miss See-ton, might call genius) burn freely, in those lightning sketches which were so valued by Scotland Yard, and of which Miss Seeton was always a little ashamed. The sketches—swiftly drawn to reveal the hidden truth beneath the outer show—were, to the eye of one who had under-gone an orthodox art-school training, the products of an unruly subconscious. They were . . . undisciplined, when only genius should—or, indeed, could—hope to produce good work freehand. Miss Seeton's innate humility could not envisage genius save in others: such free self-expression on her part was . . . self-indulgent. One went to the work of others for fulfilment and release. It was—as one had so often been told—presumptuous to suppose that one's poor scribbles could achieve release with anything remotely ap-proaching the same quality. One admired the great . . . and the not-so-great, who still were greater than oneself. With-out doubt. In whatever medium they might choose to work—art, music, the theatre, the cinema . . .

". . . so many times," confessed Miss Seeton, looking

up at last into the faces of her friends, and seeming to find comfort there. "Books, in one's childhood, and films . . . Of course, common sense would *suggest* there must be nothing of particular value inside, or the—the heirs of the dead gentleman would surely have known, and opened it before entering it in the sale. But . . ." She blushed again and clasped her hands about the gold tooling of the brolly's blue leather. "But—one cannot help wondering . . ."

"You're absolutely right, Miss Seeton," cried Lady Colveden; and Brinton nodded at her side. "As the auctioneer said, it's a splendid real-life mystery. And"—she eased her conscience with the final happy thought—"the box is rather an interesting piece in its own right, isn't it?"

CHAPTER 8

"What a shame," observed Lady Colveden, edging yard by cautious yard out of the car park, "that the rain's stopped at last, because— My goodness," she said as a hitherto unnoticed vehicle appeared around a corner. "Now where on earth did that come from?"

Miss Seeton, whose eyesight was excellent, was on the point of telling her when she realised, from her ladyship's subsequent mutterings, that the remark had been purely rhetorical. And one had always understood that it was unwise to address the man (or, indeed, the woman) at the wheel unless he—or she—had initiated the conversation. Miss Seeton maintained a discreet silence until the Hillman had nosed its way safely through Brettenden's labyrinthine streets, which were crowded with market stalls, and with shoppers enjoying the first dry hours of daylight for almost a week.

At last they reached the open road to Plummergen.

"Of course, there was plenty of room." Miss Seeton, the perfect passenger, nodded politely. "But George and Nigel would never have let me forget it if anything had happened to the car." Lady Colveden changed smoothly into top gear and stepped on the accelerator. "You know how men can be about women drivers, though after what Nigel did to my MG I'm always amazed he has the nerve." A dented wing, broken lights, and a damaged bumper had been the relatively small price paid by the little red sports car eight years earlier, when it had been commandeered by young Mr. Colveden to play a crucial part in the very first of Miss Seeton's adventures. Sir George's judicial ruling that, if Nigel undertook to pay for all future repairs, his mother should give him the MG in exchange for a more appropriate Hillman, had seemed the fairest solution to the insurance dilemma.

"Dear Nigel," said Miss Seeton, "is equal to anything." Then she blushed: perhaps this had been tactless? "Oh, dear—what I meant was . . ."

"Don't worry, I know what you mean, and I agree. On the whole, he is." Nigel's mother slowed for a bend. "Which is what I meant about being a pity the rain's stopped, because now they'll all be out of doors, trying to catch up, and there'll be nobody handy to help open your box. Nigel's so good with the insides of tractors—spanners and wrenches and things. A couple of rusty padlocks shouldn't present much of a problem—oh. Oh, I'm so sorry, Miss Seeton." An embarrassed laugh. "I'm afraid I was rather taking it for granted that you'd want some help getting it open—it was presumptuous of me. I do beg your pardon. You'll want to make your own arrangements, of course."

"Oh, no, indeed." And then Miss Seeton blushed all the more, partly from dismay that her emphatic denial might have seemed discourteous, and partly with the subsequent effort of explanation. "Indeed not, I assure you. I have been thinking, you see. And there is really only Stan, who will be as busy as everyone else, now the rain has stopped for a while. I would be only too delighted for dear Nigel—if he could spare the time, that is. For I had rather hoped that—as one might argue that there is a degree of . . . of family connection in the mystery, as you were with me when I bought it—if it is not too foolish a concept . . .''

"Not foolish at all.'' Lady Colveden's laugh this time was kindly. "You know I've been longing to see what's in that box ever since the auctioneer started puffing it—and certainly since he knocked it down to you. I'd have been most disappointed if you hadn't let me watch when it was finally opened.''

Miss Seeton was silent for some moments before remarking that whether or not the chest contained anything of particular interest, it was, undoubtedly, a handsome piece of . . . would her ladyship call it furniture?

"I don't see why not.'' Lady Colveden changed gear again as she slowed for the approach to the village. "We have a huge wooden box on the upstairs landing we use for blankets—it's lined with cedar, and smells wonderful, quite apart from keeping moths away—and if you don't mind the knobbly carvings it makes a marvellous window seat. Nigel and Julia used to clamber all over it when they were young, and Janie will sit there for ages when it's raining, looking out at the garden. We give her something to sit on, mind you.'' Janie's grandmother chuckled. "She isn't as well padded as Julia at the same age—and we wouldn't dream of encouraging her to lift up the lid and take out a blanket by herself. It's so very heavy—quite heavy enough to count as furniture, and I'm sure yours will be the same. It looked like it, from the job they had carrying it out to the car.''

" 'The baron's retainers,' '' murmured Miss Seeton, " 'were blithe and gay, And keeping their Christmas holiday.' ''

Her ladyship did no more than blink: after seven years, she had grown accustomed to the sometimes oblique thought processes of her friend. " 'The Mistletoe Bough,' '' she said at once. "Well, yes, though I hope Janie's bright enough not to shut herself inside and starve to death. It always makes me cross that the silly girl didn't shout louder for help, especially on her wedding day, when she ought to have known they'd notice she was missing. There was no need at all to suffocate, if she'd only used a little common sense—not that Janie isn't a sensible child, because she is. No, what bothers me more is that awful Grimm's fairy tale about whoever-it-was and the cruel step-mother letting the lid of the apple-chest chop her head off when she looked inside—ugh.'' Slowing the car in obedience to the speed limit, her ladyship shuddered. ''Really, when you think, it's astonishing that most children in England haven't grown up completely unbalanced, with some of the bedtime stories they've had read to them—yet they don't seem to have done Nigel and Julia any harm, though I admit I'm prejudiced.''

''You have every right,'' said Miss Seeton warmly, ''to be proud of dear Nigel and his sister. They are as much of a credit to their mother as dear little Janie is to hers.''

Discreetly pink with pleasure, Lady Colveden hurried to steer the conversation away from herself. ''Well, if Nigel's going to be on the receiving end of compliments, he'd better start earning them. Would you like to come back with me for tea? My son has an inbuilt clock where meals are concerned. We'll be spared having to wade through oceans of mud looking for him in whichever field he's ploughing, and once he knows what we want he'll fetch the right tools in no time.''

As she spoke, the car was slowing for the right-angled bend where The Street, dividing, narrows to cross the bridge straight ahead, or turns abruptly into Marsh Road—the bend that is overlooked, on one side, by Sweetbriars. Miss Seeton cast a wistful eye in the direction of her dear cottage.

''Tea,'' she ventured, ''would be delightful, of course.'' She hesitated. ''Yet I would hate to put you to any trouble. Or Nigel, if he's busy. It may well take some while for him to decide how best to open it, and when so much time has been lost over the past weeks . . .''

Her ladyship had to acknowledge the truth of this. With sunset barely past four o'clock so early in the year, every minute of daylight counted in a farming community.

"Suppose," ventured Miss Seeton, "he were to come to me? If he didn't mind, that is." She blushed. Had that sounded rude? "You yourself are, of course, more than welcome; but if we telephoned, he might agree to come down when he could and—and, well, lift it out of the boot, to begin with. If," she reiterated earnestly, "he didn't mind."

"What a very sensible idea." Lady Colveden drew the car into the kerb outside Sweetbriars and applied the brake. "I'd love to come to tea, if it isn't putting you out, and I'm sure Nigel would, as well. You know how men love to show off their muscles, and he's particularly good at humping bales of hay and bits of tractors about. The two of us couldn't carry that box of yours into the house—at least, not if we wanted to walk upright tomorrow morning."

"It is certainly heavier," agreed Miss Seeton, "than first impressions would suggest."

"Which means it should be safe enough locked in the boot until Nigel turns up with his toolbox. He can bring *your* box inside, and with any luck he'll be able to open it for you. Goodness, it's like Christmas all over again, isn't it? And Christmas is always far more fun in your own home. I can hardly wait to phone the Hall. If Nigel's indoors having a cup of something, it shouldn't take him more than a few minutes to drive down here, should it?"

To which Miss Seeton happily replied that it shouldn't.

The geography of Plummergen is simple. The village's main thoroughfare, The Street, runs in a long, gentle curve from north—where Lady Colveden encountered the speed-limit sign—to south, where Sweetbriars overlooks the right-angled Marsh Road bend. Directly opposite Miss Seeton's cottage, looking north, on the left-hand side of The

Street one finds the bakery, formerly an independent establishment, but now part of the Winesart chain. The bakery
is run by Mrs. Wyght, who has recently assigned half her
premises to an excellent tea shop which faces, on the other
side of The Street, that popular hostelry the George and
Dragon. Beside the George, to the south, stands the church,
with the vicarage next to it; to the north, looking up The
Street, lies the house of Colonel Windup, renowned for his
leather liver and eccentric epistolary habits.

Yet farther to the north—even more important to Plummergen than bakery, pub, church, or vicarage—is Mr. Stillman's post office.

Plummergen's shoppers are spoiled for choice in the matter of where to buy groceries (fresh or frozen, bottled,
tinned, or dried) and sundry necessaries in the hardware or
haberdashery lines, in those of confectionery or alcohol or
tobacco. Three main establishments tempt a local shopper
to shop locally, rather than in nearby Brettenden or in Rye,
over the marsh. Grocer Takeley, though welcoming and
helpful, carries the smallest stock of the three, and his floor
space for extras is limited; Mr. Welsted the draper has a
wide selection of picture postcards, china souvenirs, Man-
chester goods, and clothes.

But it is to Mr. Stillman and his post office that the palm,
by unanimous consent, must be awarded; for the post office
is situated halfway up The Street . . .

And so is the village bus stop.

Which means that the windows of Mr. Stillman's em-
porium afford (to those inside) an excellent view of whoever might come or go by bus around the village; and, with
this excellent view, these insiders are afforded equally excellent—indeed, almost unlimited—opportunities for speculation as to the purpose of such comings and goings. The
only limit imposed upon this speculation is that of Mr. Stillman's opening hours, which are from eight in the morning
until six at night, without closing for lunch as his compet-
itors do. It can easily be seen that, during those six hundred

minutes, speculation has ample opportunity to run riot.

And not only run. Given the right stimulus, speculation will gallop: and gallop at such a rate that, were there ever to be an Olympiad for gossip, gold medals would be commonplace among the Plummergen contingent. In field events, too, the village scores highly: more highly, indeed, than on the track, for the leaps of imagination to which the liveliest speculators are inclined must rate platinum, at the very least. Speculators are restricted in their speculation by nothing so mundane as a regard for accuracy: enthusiasm is all. Even when the post office is shut, they continue their busy tongue-wagging as they walk homewards up or down The Street, peering over one another's fences ostensibly into their gardens, but in truth into their front windows. The tongues still wag as camouflage while the eyes observe, the brain cells ponder the sights and sounds of Plummergen-in-private; speculation spices mealtime conversation with its preliminary conclusions, easing overnight digestion so that the recipes—suitably, and individually, embellished—may be exchanged next morning, once Mr. Stillman has unlocked his doors. It is a rare occurrence that is reported on the telephone rather than in person: Plummergen likes to savour its scandal at leisure. Moreover, telephone calls cost money. A trip to the shops costs no more than shoe leather—and the occasional grudging purchase of a tin of baked beans, or an ounce or two of cheese.

It was not quite closing time when one of the juiciest titbits in years was served up to those of Mr. Stillman's customers who hadn't yet gone home to prepare a good hot supper. The post office counter was shut: behind the grill, Postmaster Stillman balanced his books. Outside among the groceries, ironmongery, kitchenware, cosmetics, and stationery the last few stalwarts were contentedly shredding the characters of their absent acquaintance with a relish their culinary skills so often lacked.

". . . poor, starved-looking little thing," said Mrs. Henderson, of the Hosigg baby. Young Lily had popped in later than usual for a packet of rusks and a new dummy for her much-loved Dulcie Rose, whose birth had been a difficult one from which her delicate mother had taken too long for the doctor's liking to recover. "I'm sure Len keeps her short, for all that Sir George pays well. She'll be cutting back on the babby's food to save the rent, o' course, while he drinks it."

"*Supposed* to pay well," said Mrs. Skinner darkly. It was as automatic for Mrs. Skinner to contradict Mrs. Henderson as it was for Mrs. Henderson to snipe at Mrs. Skinner. There had been a dispute over the church flower rota which neither lady would ever forget, or forgive: they both enjoyed it far too much. "And *if* he's drinking, there's none have said they've seen him at it in the pub, have they?"

"He'll be buying it off-licence in Brettenden," said Mrs. Spice in support of Mrs. Henderson, though she could never make up her mind from one day to the next which side of the feud she really favoured. "Not as if he can't afford to, is it? With Sir George such a good employer."

"So they say," retorted Mrs. Skinner with a meaningful look. "Has Len Hosigg ever shown anyone his wages slip?"

"No reason why he should," snapped Mrs. Henderson. "Your mum," she said, turning to Emmy Putts at the cheese counter, "hasn't gone about telling all and sundry what they pay at the biscuit factory, has she?"

"Brettenden work's different," said Mrs. Skinner at once. "But if it's here in the village, we've a right to know, I reckon ..." Then she realised she was on dangerous ground, and retreated. "When it's a question of a babby not getting enough to eat, that's to say, and needing to know why so's summat can be done about it once we do. Not in the *normal* course of events, though. After all, we got to respect people's privacy, haven't we?"

This virtuous sentiment must, of course, be approved by everyone: even by Mrs. Henderson, who felt that Mrs. Skinner had taken mean advantage. She was casting about

for some way of levelling the score when there came a
rattle and a jangling behind everyone's back, and all heads
turned in the direction of the door.

In came the Nuts: tall Miss Nuttel—bony of limb and
equine of visage—and Mrs. Blaine, black-eyed, plump, and
temperamentally inclined to flashes of anger followed by
long, brooding sulks. Nutty by name, nutty by nature. The
pair are strict vegetarians, their holistic regime imparting
(so they believe) a certain spirituality that shields them from
the moral contamination of even the worst excesses of village life . . . whatever these might be. The best way to find
out—the easier, of course, to avoid contamination—has
proved to be the keeping of a round-the-clock watch on
their fellow villagers, lest they should indulge in excess
unobserved, and leave the watchers unprepared. Fore-
warned is forearmed. The Nuts live in what Plummergen
wits call the Nut House, more formally Lilikot, a conveniently plate-glass-windowed house of modern design which
stands even more conveniently opposite the bus stop, on
the other side of The Street, affording that clear view of
arrivals, departures, and all intermediate activities essential
to moral self-preservation. Opinion in Plummergen is di-
vided as to which of the pair has the more energetic tongue:
it is generally agreed that—for all Erica Nuttel's
abbreviated mode of speech—the honours are about equal.

The turned heads, having nodded to the Nuts in greeting,
seemed on the point of turning away again as the shoppers
went back to their shopping.

"Oh, Eric, please, I must catch my breath!" Mrs. Blaine
held a dimpled hand to the middle of her coat, beneath
whose respectable woollen check it must be assumed that
her heart palpitated with the horror of whatever shock she
had just received. "Too, too awful," moaned Mrs. Blaine,
having first assured herself that her audience, for the moment at least, consisted of more than one. She closed her
eyes, shuddering, and somehow contrived to turn pale.

"Glass of water, Bunny?" Miss Nuttel directed a forceful look upon the gaping Emmy Putts as she stood with the cheese wire in her hand. "Can't have you fainting all over the place, old girl. Should really have taken you straight home, but . . ."

Bunny's black eyes snapped open. A soulful expression appeared on her face as she said bravely, "You know I never like to burden you with more than your fair share of the chores, Eric, no matter how my nerves have been— oh!" A too, too awful remembrance made her shudder once more. Miss Nuttel patted her on the shoulder, and glared again at the slow-witted Emmy.

"Mrs. Blaine feeling a bit poorly, Miss Nuttel?" It was Mrs. Spice who spoke. "Emmy, luv, how about a quick glass o' water for Mrs. Blaine? And then you can serve me my half of Cheddar before you shut—if you don't mind," she added to the Nuts, "us carrying on, seeing as you've only just come in, and Mrs. Blaine most evidently not up to it at present."

This was very clever of Mrs. Spice. The other shoppers, following her lead, crowded close about the counter with a distinct air of urgency, their shopping lists in plain sight, their bags and baskets ready to be filled. It was well known in Plummergen that to ask the Nuts a straight question about whatever news they seemed minded to impart almost always made them change their minds about imparting it. Let the village, however, ignore even the most tempting of hints, and no amount of holistic self-control could stop the Nuts from spilling the beans.

"Oh—no, thank you, Emmy." Mrs. Blaine, feebly waving the water away, allowed a note of plaintive martyrdom to enter her voice. "Too ungrateful of me, you'll say, I know, but with our own well just across The Street—and so many dreadful chemicals in tap water—and what a second shock would do to my system when I'm barely starting to recover from the first . . ."

"Over-imagination, Bunny, that's your trouble." Miss Nuttel shook her head, mock-scolding. "Be honest now.

Not as if you saw it clearly, is it?''

Mrs. Blaine, sighing, acknowledged that she had not; then added that, for one as sensitive to such things as she was, a glimpse had been more than enough.

"Mug of chamomile tea, and you'll feel better in no time. A good night's rest, and you'll be a new woman.''

The prospect of a new Norah Blaine intrigued every member of Miss Nuttel's audience save that one for whom the remark had been ostensibly intended. Bunny, quaking, bleated that she didn't see how Eric, of all people, could possibly dream of suggesting she could have a good night's rest, when *she* knew she could never sleep a wink. "I'd be terrified to close my eyes," said Mrs. Blaine. "Too *sinister* in the dark. I shall have nightmares about it, I know I shall—should, I mean, if I even *tried* to sleep, so naturally I shan't try. You, being so much less highly strung . . .''

The highly strung insomniac here broke down completely, burying her nose in the handkerchief she had pulled out of her coat pocket to make her waving away of Emmy's aquatic offering a truly dramatic gesture. Miss Nuttel, patting her on the shoulder again, struggled for soothing words.

"Cheer up, Bunny. No good looking on the black side. Besides, two of us with imagination wouldn't do, scaring each other into fits all the time. I'm sure," said Miss Nuttel with rather less conviction than compassion might require, "you must have made a mistake." Mrs. Blaine intimated, with a wordless but eloquent moan, that she had not. "Well . . . hope you did, anyway." Now it was Miss Nuttel's turn to shudder. "I mean—only out for a breath of fresh air. Not as if you saw a raven or anything, was it?''

"Harbingers of doom," responded Mrs. Blaine in hollow tones. "But you can't tell me a . . . a coffin's not just as bad when you see one.''

"Worse," said Miss Nuttel. "If that's what it was.''

"Oh, it was!" Mrs. Blaine, in her emphasis, was oblivious to her fascinated audience as it crowded, open-mouthed and panting with curiosity, close about her. "*Far* worse, to see it come *looming up* out of the dark that way, carried by those—those ghostly white hands, *right by the church* . . ."

Nigel Colveden, in dark jacket and trousers, carrying the treasure chest into Miss Seeton's cottage, would have been insulted that anyone should consider him—a hardy, weatherbeaten son of the Kentish soil—white and ghostly; but Nigel wasn't there.

A chorus of gasps had greeted Mrs. Blaine's revelation. Spectral sarcophagi, it was evident, rated high as harbingers of doom in Plummergen opinion.

"Right by the church? Mark my words," said Mrs. Spice, as the rest could only shudder, "a haunting at that end of The Street can mean nothing but ill luck for the village—and worse for them as saw it . . ."

"Death," Mrs. Blaine corrected her bravely. "Death— oh, Eric!"

"Death," repeated Mrs. Spice, not to be outdone. "Death—and disaster for all concerned . . ."

And everyone shuddered once more.

CHAPTER 9

Brettenden, though deep in the heart of Kent, lies no more than forty miles from the nation's capital. At around the same time that Lady Colveden and Miss Seeton were driving home through the first dry weather for days, in London, likewise, the rain had finally stopped.

In the basement of a tall Georgian house in the middle of an up-and-coming street of Georgian houses, a little grey cat, roused from his slumbers by the longed-for sounds of silence, uncurled himself luxuriously from the cushion on which he had just spent a most comfortable week. He yawned, stretched, and padded purposefully to the door. His claws raked the clean white paint as his mouth opened in a yowl; his master, immersed in classical music on the fireside sofa, leaped at once to obey the command.

"So the forecast was wrong for once. Aren't you lucky? Off you go, then. Make the most of it—and have fun."

Fun? Did the man think he'd asked to be let outside for *fun*? It was almost a week since he'd felt like spending more than the necessary few ablutionary minutes in the open air; almost a week since he'd been in the mood to go on patrol. He took his duties seriously, of course, in the normal run of things—but it wasn't normal for a cat to have soaking wet fur and whiskers drenched with rain the moment he popped his nose out of doors. He hated having to paddle through puddles to his private bathroom; he hated feeling cold and clammy, and having his beautiful fur plastered flat against his body instead of fluffing out round it in the soft, warm haze his man loved to stroke by the hour. He hated being wrapped in a towel—never mind it was the man's best terry—and rubbed, no matter how gently . . .

But these pet hates—the little grey cat flicked his tail with pleasure at the pun—could be forgotten now. The rain had stopped. It was high time he checked on how his kingdom had survived during his absence: there was a lot of catching up for him to do.

He ran lightly up the area steps to ground level, where he paused, his nose twitching. Grey, rain-laden clouds had smothered the evening sun from sight; the air was heavy and damp, and the world was a riot of smells—enticing, disgusting, intriguing. Dogs on routine tours of inspection had marked their appointed lampposts; oil and leaking petrol, washed from the road into the gutters, swirled there gently in the gleam from wakeful lamps and the breeze from passing cars. Twigs and small branches from the trees that lined the road lay, smashed by the weight of rain and traffic, exuding a rich, green, dying scent.

Dying? No. His nose twitched again. Not dying: dead. The breeze had strengthened suddenly, wafting a whiff of death in the direction of the little grey cat: and it wasn't death of the kind to which he was accustomed, the kind he himself so often caused. No mouse or rat or bird, this dead creature: larger, he thought. The scent was so much stronger . . . Stronger—and familiar, somehow . . . But wrong, in the natural order of things . . .

And where things were out of order in his kingdom, it was his duty to see how they could be put right.

And when he came clawing at the basement door with something in his mouth, it took the man only a few seconds to realise that this was no mouse, or rat, or bird that hung limply from the small, but powerful, jaws. Yes, there was skin: but no bone, or fur, or feather.

And the skin was—or had been—tanned, and dyed, and shaped by skilled hands . . .

Into the wallet which the little grey cat had nosed from the pocket of a dead man's coat.

"Screwdrivers, nil: treasure chest, four." Nigel Colveden sat back with a weary sigh, dropped his assortment of tools beside him on the carpet, and rubbed a hand across his brow. "I think anyone would have to call that a pretty conclusive result, Miss Seeton. I'm sorry."

"Oh, no, it is I," said Miss Seeton at once, "who must apologise, for putting you to all this trouble when I know how busy you are on the farm."

"Not after sunset, thank goodness." Scrambling up from his knees, with a smile of thanks Nigel accepted the cup of tea—his third—that his hostess had poured as his mother handed him the plate of chocolate biscuits for the fourth (or possibly fifth) time. "I do hate admitting I've been beaten by anything mechanical, but umpty-centuries-old padlocks are a bit out of my league. If it had been a tractor engine, or the MG . . ."

"You did your best, Nigel," Miss Seeton assured him, "and nobody can do more than that. Please don't think I'm not grateful for all your hard work. Would you rather have some of Martha's fruit-cake than another biscuit?"

Mr. Colveden was far too well bred to hint that he would, for preference, have both. "Well, if you twist my arm, I could force down a slice or two. If you can spare them, of course."

"I don't know how you do it." Nigel's mother regarded her son with envy as she nibbled daintily on what was still her first digestive. "One hint of a calorie, and I have to diet for a week, whereas you . . ."

"A finely balanced metabolism, tuned to perfection with

regular exercise and fresh air." Then Nigel grinned. "Now, there's an idea, talking of air—or rather hair. Mother, do you have any grips or pins about your person?"

Her ladyship shook back from her face the thick, wavy brown locks that had drifted forwards in the excitement of the moment. On the point of uttering a scornful reply, she recollected herself just in time and smiled apologetically at Miss Seeton even as she frowned at her son. "No," said her ladyship, "I haven't. As you really ought to know by now, you unnatural child."

There was a twinkle in Miss Seeton's eye as she admitted that she, too, must disappoint her visitor in the matter of pins: she, like dear Nigel's mother, was fortunate in that her hair had a strong natural wave, and held its shape well without, as it were, artificial aid.

Nigel, after a moment's resignation, volunteered with a faint grin that there always remained brute force and Miss Seeton's poker, if—

"Nigel, really." His mother favoured the future baronet with an exasperated glance, but Miss Seeton, having taught for many years, was accustomed to the younger genera-tion's sense of humor, and replied cheerfully that she had, of course, given due consideration to what she feared one must call the more violent approach. If all else failed, com-mon sense would indeed suggest a poker as the last resort, but on the other hand . . .

"On the other hand, if a *hat* pin would be of any use, I have several you could try—do excuse me while I slip up-stairs—and there are always, of course," said Miss Seeton, her hand on the doorknob, "the refugees." Her eyes twin-kled still, even as she sighed. "I'm sure they would never miss one or two, if they came in handy for the purpose—yours, that is—for though, naturally, I have done my best, I am, I fear, no great loss, unlike dear Martha, or Miss Armitage, or dear Miss Treeves, for example. And while I agree with you, Nigel, that it is . . . disconcerting, to say the least, when one is forced to admit to failure, there are times,

I feel, when common sense does require that persistence should yield to realism. Don't you agree?''

"Why—yes," said Lady Colveden on her son's behalf, as Miss Seeton, smiling again, vanished into the hall. Nigel's attempt at a reply was mercifully muffled by cake crumbs.

Mother and son regarded each other in a puzzled silence which was broken only by the sound of their hostess's feet hurrying hatpinwards up the stairs—and then by a quiet choking, as the last of Nigel's crumbs went down the wrong way. His mother reached hurriedly for the teapot.

"I'll take a chance on the twins," she said, struggling to keep her voice steady, "if you'll only promise not to ask about the—about the refugees when she comes back." And, with a shaking hand, she poured.

Miss Seeton returned to find Nigel with flushed cheeks and watering eyes, as Lady Colveden thumped him maternally on the back. She uttered a startled little gasp, and her ladyship turned quickly to greet her.

"Don't worry, Miss Seeton, it was just a crumb, and I took the liberty of giving him some more tea to wash it down." She smiled. "I thought it worth risking ginger twins to save Nigel's life, but I'm afraid I may have emptied the pot. Shall I make amends by clearing away for you while he has another try at the lock?"

Miss Seeton, no more superstitious than Lady Colveden, had always been quietly amused by the country belief that the second person to pour from a pot is destined to give birth to a brace of redheaded infants. Smiling back, she begged Lady Colveden not to bother about plates and cups, which could wait: would she not find it of far greater interest, if dear Nigel was fully recovered, to watch him picking—if that was the correct word—the lock? She had brought as wide a selection of likely implements as she could find, if he cared to look . . .

"Your knitting needles!" Lady Colveden swooped on the fine metal rods as their owner tumbled them, together with an assortment of still finer rods—sharp at one end, decorated at the other—on the crisp white tablecloth. "And your hatpins—oh, it does seem a shame. But then . . ." Miss Seeton was by no means the only member of Plummergen Women's Institute who had struggled to complete even one of the six-inch knitted squares destined to be sewn into blankets for an international relief organisation. The airy comments of Nigel and his father about birds' nests and manic wool spaghetti had rather annoyed her ladyship, who was in general resigned to the knowledge that her talents lay in other directions than those of stitchery and fancy needlework. But when it was for charity . . .

"As I mentioned earlier," said Miss Seeton, with the faintest of sighs, "my contribution is likely to be so—so insignificant, compared to that from others more gifted, that it will be little missed, I fear. And I hoped—that is, thought—that if by any chance hatpins should prove unsuitable, then knitting needles—depending on the size, of course—might well do instead."

"They might, indeed. In fact, they'd probably be better," came the quick response from the gallant Mr. Colveden, who strongly suspected that it had been only her inability to fulfil her guest's request for hairpins that had prompted the conscientious hostess to volunteer for crib-cracking duty the treasured collection of hat ornaments inherited from her godmother. "I'd certainly hate to bend one of these"—he rattled the exotic pieces with a thoughtful finger—"beyond repair—they're . . . magnificent. You couldn't hope," he said, his voice commendably steady, "to buy replacements nowadays—but if anything should happen to your knitting needles—why, we've heaps to spare at the Hall." He grinned at his mother.

Lady Colveden hastened to give rueful confirmation of this irreverent remark, and Miss Seeton, much relieved, smiled, then nodded as Nigel made a random selection from the knitting needles and gave her an enquiring glance. Observing the nod, he returned her smile, squared his shoulders, excused himself from the table, and prepared to address his attentions once more to the battered, iron-banded wooden box in the middle of the sitting-room floor.

"I'll have one more crack at the fastening staples, just in case the oil's finally condescended to do its stuff with the screws," he told his audience, which hovered discreetly behind him, peeping curiously over his shoulders towards the treasure chest where it squatted on protective sheets of newspaper, surrounded by discarded tools. "Lucky you keep hens, Miss Seeton, or we'd have had to waste time popping back to the Hall for some of our own feathers." He substituted for his knitting needle the stoutest among the screwdrivers. "Or we could have risked Martha's wrath"—he set metal to metal and began the hopeful application of force—"by dismembering one of her—your—dusters— Ouch! Oh, damn and blast the stupid thing!"

The future baronet was seldom so free with his speech in the presence of ladies, but in moments of acute stress even Jove must nod. He soon recovers himself, however: noblesse will always oblige. Nigel's apology came swiftly, muffled through tightly clenched teeth as he sucked his gashed finger.

Even had it not been muffled, the apology would have been drowned out by the remonstrances of his mother and Miss Seeton. Enough (they insisted) was enough. He had done his best: he could do no more. Not without running the risk of considerable damage—

"And not just to you," said her ladyship sternly. "What about poor Miss Seeton's carpet, with you bleeding to death all over it?"

"Oh, dear," said Miss Seeton hurriedly, "I assure you that careful sponging with cold water—not that there seems any particular need, of course. Dear Nigel is so considerate—but that cut looks deep, Nigel. I will fetch bandages and plaster while you cleanse it thoroughly with plenty of soap and hot water. Thoroughly, mind," she added, reverting automatically to her pedagogic persona, and sounding even more stern in this crisis than his mother.

Nigel grinned a feeble grin as Lady Colveden applauded the good sense of her hostess and dragged her son—above his protests that it was only a cut—out to the kitchen, where she supervised his ablutions at the sink to an accompaniment of scolding that if he hadn't kept his tetanus jabs up to date it was nothing to do with her, and if he and his father chose to risk death by lockjaw it was all very well, but she had better things to do with her time than take care of invalids who'd brought their illness on themselves, and neither of them need expect any sympathy from her—

"I *am* up to date," Nigel managed to interject as his fond parent finally drew breath. "And so's—ouch."

"The more it stings, the better it's working," came the callous reply. "You need to be sure every single germ is dead—that rust could be hundreds of years old." Lady Colveden looked up and smiled as Miss Seeton appeared, carrying a small metal box, painted white. "Do you really want to make medical history by dying of some rare blood poisoning that became extinct hundreds of years ago?"

As Nigel grinned again, Miss Seeton was just about to protest the illogicality of what his mother had said when she recollected herself with a start, and a blush. She set her first aid box quickly on the table, opened it, and began to rummage inside for scissors, lint, and disinfectant . . .

"I am so very, very sorry," said Miss Seeton, as, with the final inch of sticking-plaster safely stuck, the party repaired once more to the sitting room. "That anyone, and most of all a friend, should have been—been injured in the cause of my—my foolish box. I fear that the—the mystery of the affair blinded me somewhat to the realisation that, though the task of picking a lock is always made to appear comparatively easy in films, or on television, in real life such matters are sadly different. Or possibly," she added in reflective tones, "not. Sad, I mean, if it serves to deter people of a—a less honest nature than one ought to approve—not," said Miss Seeton with a blush, "that I wish for one minute to imply—oh, dear . . .''

She subsided into an embarrassed babble of apology, gratitude, and ethical confusion.

Nigel and Meg Colveden were long accustomed to Miss Seeton. Her ladyship assured their hostess that they entirely understood her meaning; her son insisted that so slight a laceration couldn't prevent a little judicious prodding with one or other of the knitting needles procured for that very purpose. In the inevitable curiosity of the moment, Miss Seeton's cheeks soon paled to her habitual shade of modest rose. Neither she nor Nigel's mother raised any objection as the intrepid mechanic inserted the tip of the first slim, shining metal shaft into the obstinate black mouth of the padlock, and probed. And twisted . . . and probed again, and again, in a silence broken only by the breathing of three attentive souls . . .

Whose pent-up breaths were released in a collective sigh as Nigel threw down the last of the needles, and shook his head. ''You don't need oil and feathers and screwdrivers for this, Miss Seeton. You need a blow-torch, or a hammer and chisel—you'll have to get tough, I'm afraid. It's beyond me. They don't build tin-openers strong enough.''

''But they do,'' said his mother, as Miss Seeton struggled to suppress her disappointment, ''have people who could make them, if they were asked. People like Dan Eggleden, for example. If he isn't the strongest man for miles, then I'd like to know who is.''

And the delighted sparkle in her hostess's eyes showed Lady Colveden that Miss Seeton more than approved the idea of seeking assistance from Daniel Eggleden, Plummergen's own captain of that band of mighty men much celebrated in verse: the village blacksmiths.

CHAPTER 10

London has been described as a series of villages, joined companionably together. In one of these villages, in the basement of a tall Georgian house in the middle of an up-and-coming street of Georgian houses, a cat-owning music lover bent to pick up the leather wallet dropped at his feet by an agitated feline friend.

"You've been raiding the dustbins again, you revolting creature." Philosophically the man retrieved his trophy from the floor. "If I let you eat this, your insides will turn navy blue." He made for the kitchen and his flip-top, cat-proof waste bin. "Which I suppose would serve you right for— Good heavens!" He stopped in his tracks. "Well, someone's going to be sorry he emptied his pockets without checking . . . I wonder how much—oops."

The rain had soaked right through the protective leather, turning the contents of the wallet to a sodden, papier-mâché mess of wadded notes and blurred ink, pink and green and blue and brown. The man contemplated the kitchen range with a calculating eye. "Well, that's torn it. We haven't a hope of knowing who owns this lot till it's been properly dried out—hey!"

The grey cat had leaped from the floor to the table, and was skidding across the surface, lashing his tail in the manner of a propeller to increase his speed. He skidded to a halt at the table's edge, reached out a paw, and swiped at the wallet in his owner's hand.

"That's not funny. You know you're not allowed—I said that's not funny!" he insisted as there came a second, more vicious swipe from the swift grey paw, and the wallet was dashed to the ground. The man bent to pick it up again, and a hissing, growling complaint rang out from above his head.

"You're having haddock for supper," said the man, "and no arguments, all right? This," he added, seizing the wallet, "gets dried out and identified and returned to its owner—hey!"

The grey cat sprang. The wallet flew from the man's startled hands to a corner of the room. The cat flew after it, twisted somehow in the air, and landed beside rather than on top of it, facing the man, and spitting. Flattened ears and narrowed eyes showed above sharp, pointed teeth as the spitting became a snarl. The plumy tail lashed to and fro across the floor in a nervous, lopsided arc that did not include in its sweeping embrace the damp blue leather bundle in the corner.

"What's got into you?" The man's tone had softened. "I've never seen you like this before. Don't tell me you really wanted to try banknote goulash as a change from fish. Something's wrong, isn't it? You don't like it when I talk about the chap who owns this—ah!" The tail ceased suddenly to lash. The snarl became a warbled squeal, and the fur rose all along the spine as the little grey cat almost doubled in size.

"You're going psychic on me," said the man after a few moments' frantic thought. "You're trying to tell me something—and I'm going psychic, too. I've the nastiest feeling I'm not going to enjoy the answer to all this once I've found out what it is."

Pleased that his message had finally begun to penetrate his man's less speedy brain, the little grey cat allowed his nervous stance to relax. He stopped growling, smoothed his fur, and uttered as emphatic a chirrup as he could achieve in the stress of the moment. He rose to his feet and chirruped again. He padded to the door and glanced over his shoulder to where the man stood scratching his head.

On the doormat, he stopped. He mewed. He stretched a paw as high as he could reach. The doorknob rattled.

The man sighed. "You win. I know I won't have a minute's peace until we get this sorted out—but if you're having me on . . ."

He snatched his hat from the peg, shrugged on a battered mackintosh, and opened the door. The little grey cat danced outside and up the area steps. The man made a quick assessment of the likelihood of further rain, decided not to take his umbrella, locked his door, and set off as quickly as he thought prudent along slippery pavements in pursuit of his eager guide.

Five minutes later he returned, twice as quickly, with no thought at all of prudence. All his attention was focused on the telephone in his kitchen, and on those three vital numbers on the dial:

Nine, nine, nine.

"I was afraid of this," remarked Chief Superintendent Delphick. He and Bob were, for the present, no more than onlookers in a mean and noisome passage, standing as close as they were allowed to the spot on which lay, where the little grey cat had found it, the body of a man. A body now surrounded by those busy and inevitable attendants upon any sudden, violent death, the medical, the photographic, and the forensic officers. "If my instincts don't deceive me, Sergeant Ranger, this is only the first in what could well prove a long and bloody series of gangland killings."

For a reply, Bob merely nodded. He intended no discourtesy: with his attention, like Delphick's, fixed on all the activity around the body, he didn't need to speak. He was in complete agreement with his chief . . .

Who sighed. "We suspected some time ago that Rickling might be poised to set out on the war-path. We heard rumors to the contrary, of course, which were not altogether convincing; and we may now, I believe, not unreasonably suppose our suspicions to have been correct. Unless . . ."

Gazing over the heads of his preoccupied subordinates, he sighed once more. "We have, our best endeavors notwithstanding, entirely failed to discover even the least trace of the missing Cutler. We have assumed, however, that he did not break out of prison for the fun of it. Should we perhaps also assume that it is his hand, and not that of Rickling, which has directed some felonious cohort towards ridding the underworld of Artie Chishall?"

"But, sir, if that *is* what happened, I don't see why he couldn't have fixed it up just as well from inside. I mean, Cutler's got influence. He wouldn't exactly've had to stand there on the spot supervising the blokes who did for poor old Artie, would he? If he told 'em by postcard or something to do him, they'd do him, no question."

"When your Majesty," muttered Delphick—prompted, despite the gravity of the circumstances, to quote—"says, 'Let a thing be done,' it's as good as done—practically, it *is* done—because your Majesty's word is law." He coughed. "You're right. Cutler has, as we know, a depressingly large number of loyal henchmen all too eager to oblige the boss—even more obliging now, so close to the date of his release." Bob shunted his weight from one massive foot to the other; Delphick coughed again. "His official release, that is. Yet, had he fewer than half the number—and all of them unwilling—I would find it almost impossible to credit that he would become directly involved in Chishall's demise. Face-to-face violence isn't Cutler's style."

"One of the best informers in the business," said Bob, one professional paying tribute to another, as he contemplated the sorry corpse of Artie Chishall. "Played both sides against the middle a little too often for comfort, but he came up with a lot of good stuff. Could be he got hold of something a sight too good for his health, sir—or perhaps he overdid the double-dealing. Whatever it was, when Cutler found out, he was so cheesed off about it he decided he had to get stuck in for a spot of . . . of personal revenge."

Delphick frowned. "*Pour encourager les autres?* There's always that aspect, of course—and yet . . . I won't explode your theory out of hand, Bob, but I'm afraid I can't put it at the top of the list, either. I repeat, such face-to-face violence is not Cutler's style."

"More Rickling's, sir, I agree. Artie worked for both of the blighters—we know that, and you bet they did, too. Most likely for a whole lot more we don't know about, as well. So, then, one or other of these characters will've used him for—what's the word? Misinformation purposes. And once he'd told whoever-it-was whatever-it-was they wanted him to tell 'em, they . . ."

"Disposed of him," supplied Delphick as Bob came to a thoughtful pause. "Yes, that's also a possibility—and a grim one, Sergeant Ranger. If only we could believe that this was a commonplace backstreet killing with robbery as the motive . . . but the killer's indifference to the acquisition of his victim's money, wristwatch, and other valuables suggests otherwise."

"He could've been interrupted," suggested Bob without much conviction. The alley in which Chishall's body lay was hardly a main thoroughfare. As a shortcut, even in such heavy rain as had earlier been falling, it was inhospitable, to say the least.

Delphick acknowledged with a nod his subordinate's professional willingness to act as Devil's Advocate, but did not rise to the challenge. He shook his head and sighed. "No . . . I fear that we simply cannot afford to ignore the dangers Artie's death appears to signal. He could be, at the

top of his form, one of the best informers in the business—
you said it yourself. Whatever the proposed crime in which
you have postulated his involvement, it must be of
considerable magnitude for the criminals to be . . .
unconcerned by this permanent loss of his services.

"Which means that *our* concern has to be to discover
the crime before it occurs, and prevent it. As soon as we
can."

"If we can, sir," said Bob; and Delphick nodded again.
"If we can," he echoed. "If, indeed, we can . . ."

"I thought, you see," said Miss Seeton, "knowing how
busy you so often are, that it might perhaps be a little inconvenient, when by coming in person to see how you were
placed I could be quite sure that it would not interfere too
much with your usual work to discuss it. The telephone, I
mean. Dear Nigel volunteered—so very kind, as always—
to bring it here, but as he had already carried it into the
house for me—and though he is, of course, accustomed to
such heavy work as lifting bales—I felt it would be far too
great an imposition on my part to ask him to bring it even
the short distance to your forge, Mr. Eggleden, when you
are a recognised expert in these matters."

Blinking against the heat from the blacksmith's glowing
fires, Miss Seeton shifted her umbrella from one arm to the
other, and in so shifting contrived to turn herself towards
the current of cooler air coming in through the large double
doors. "And with the rain, for once, easing off," she went
on, quite failing, as she turned, to observe the farrier's puzzled frown, "it would surely be an even greater imposition
for me to expect a friend to take time from his work, when
in your case, as a professional, you would of course be paid
the going rate, whatever that might be. As indeed I am most
happy to do."

Dan, scratching his head, opened his mouth to speak, but
lost his chance as Miss Seeton smiled up at him, and nodded. "I do appreciate, of course, that until you have seen

it you are unlikely to know just how long it will take, but, if you would not think it impertinent of me to enquire in advance, I should be most interested to know what you normally charge for jobs of this nature. Or is that''—her eyes twinkled as she saw his blank expression—''a trade secret? With each one being different, that is, so that different rates must apply, and until you've seen it you won't know which.'' She nodded, more to herself than to the smith, who continued to stare at her in bewilderment. ''Yes . . . On reflection it was perhaps a little foolish of me to have asked before you had seen it. I beg your pardon.''

She shifted the umbrella again, so that she looked out of the forge down The Street towards her own dear cottage, and the sitting-room windows behind which waited such an intriguing challenge for the blacksmith's skill. ''While I should not wish, Mr. Eggleden, to take you away from anything *urgent*, I fear I must confess to''—Miss Seeton blushed—''a slight—though I believe you will agree not altogether unnatural—impatience—that is''—blushing still more—''curiosity, I think, might be a more apposite term—and, though I do not seek to excuse myself, I am, you know, not the only one. The Colvedens, of course, are also interested in the outcome—and in view of their kindness I should prefer, if at all possible, not to leave it too long—although whenever you feel able to come, I will be delighted to see you. It is always such a pleasure to watch an expert at work,'' said Miss Seeton with a final nod and an admiring smile.

The smile of Dan Eggleden was more mystified than admiring. He scratched his head again, cleared his throat, and, as it seemed that Miss Seeton had fallen silent, prepared to address himself to her problem—whatever she thought it was. For his part, he had absolutely no idea: but village etiquette demanded that neighbours should do their utmost to help solve the problems of others less fortunate, in anticipation of any future spins of fortune's fickle wheel.

''It's not that I ain't willing to oblige, Miss Seeton,'' he began slowly. "For if what you mean by expert's that I'll set my hand to many a task others'd refuse as soon as look at, why, that's true. Iffen you was to have your garden barrer a new wheel made, or a brazier for Stan's bonfire, I'd tackle them and welcome the challenge. Not," he said hastily, "as wheelbarrers and braziers'd present much of a difficulty, in any case, to a man of my calling with an honest pride in the name of smith. But telephones, now, they're another matter entirely."

Miss Seeton blinked. Dan, warming to his theme, ignored her faint cry of alarm. "Telephones," he went on, "I'd be fearful even of touching, with all them wires and electricals. And if young Nigel couldn't fix it for you, with him understanding the working of most things under a bonnet near as well as Cousin Crabbe at the garage, I have to say I've my doubts why you're so sure *I* could do it—yet allus willing to oblige, like I said, though you'd have to take the risk I'd mebbe do worse damage nor's already occurred. Such as," he reminded her, "you've not yet told me, so I'm no true judge. Though I do wonder that if it's too heavy to be fetched," he continued, as in her turn Miss Seeton stared, "then it's a type of phone I've never seen. You're really best, if you ask me, to find one trained properly to the job. And don't the Post Office people cut up rough if folk not qualified in such matters takes their telephones to bits? If you was to get into trouble, say, for having asked me . . ." He was too much of a gentleman even to hint at the trouble which might be wished upon Dan Eggleden, should he interfere with their delicate communications equipment, by the GPO.

Miss Seeton's second cry of alarm was rather less faint than her first. Dan, who had in any case come to a tactful pause, regarded her with a courteous interest, which quickened to smiling relief as the realisation was brought home to him that he had—as better men than he had done on more than one occasion—mistaken Miss Seeton's meaning. As she stumbled to the end of her apologetic explanation, his smile broadened to a grin.

"Open an old box? Glad to do it, Miss Seeton. But you don't need to fret over fetching it here, I'll be along to your place just so soon as I can safely leave the fire. And my guess is I'll be able to carry what's wanted, and do the job on the spot." His eye fell upon the stout canvas bag hanging from its hook on the wall, and on the long bench of assorted tools that rested underneath. "Say in half an hour or so? Then with luck I'll be able to sort things out well before dinner time . . ."

And Miss Seeton, smiling and nodding her thanks, hurried home to possess her soul in patience until the mighty tread of the blacksmith should be heard on her front path, and his hand should smite the knocker on her door.

CHAPTER 11

Nigel Colveden, despite every encouragement from on-lookers with a decided enthusiasm for experiencing, in both book and film form, the myriad convolutions of mystery and crime—but who lacked (as did Nigel) the expertise necessary for successful passage through the convolutions of real-life crime—had failed in his attempts to pick the convolutions of the lock of Miss Seeton's iron-bound box.

Dan Eggleden, expert in metalwork if not in criminality, didn't make even one attempt to pick it.

"Loosen 'em?" He shook his head as he contemplated the massive screws, still glistening with the haloes of last night's oil, which affixed the heavy fastening-plate of the lock to the oaken body of the box. "Take years to loosen, they would, so rusted in as they are. And that padlock—well." He chuckled, though not unkindly, and shook his head again. "Well, as a burglar I reckon he makes a good farmer, does young Nigel."

Blushing, Miss Seeton discreetly removed from sight the collection of bent knitting needles which, now that she came to think of it, she really should have known dear Mr. Eggleden would not need. As to what he *would* need, she couldn't begin to guess . . .

"A pity," opined the blacksmith, "to go cutting through the hasp, when for all the rust it's a fine piece of work, that padlock. I'm not saying as I couldn't mend it after, mind you, but it'd show, no matter how careful I might be—and you'd know 'twas modern work, what's more. Something so old as this, you want to see it aright whenever you look at it, now don't you?"

Art teacher Miss Seeton thoroughly approved this sentiment. The importance, as she so frequently tried to impress upon her pupils, of *seeing* things properly should not, could not, be ignored. She herself always tried her best to see, to notice, to observe . . .

And it was with considerable surprise that she now observed Daniel Eggleden remove from his canvas bag of tools a large, sharp-toothed hacksaw.

At her muffled exclamation, Dan grinned. "Don't do as I do, do as I say—that what you're thinking, Miss Seeton?" He paused in his approach to the wooden box, and chuckled as she blushed and murmured that she was sure he knew what he was doing, and that it was hardly her place to question the actions of an expert.

"Except," she added, recovering herself as her interest was quickened, "that I should, indeed, rather like to pose a question or two—if you would not regard such questions as an impertinence, that is. But only," she hastened to assure him, "in a—a spirit of enquiry, you understand. I have never seen anyone breaking into anything before, apart from films, of course, and then it is usually safes, or strongboxes. Gelignite," she enlarged. "Petermen, I believe they are called, and most expert many of them appear to be, which as they are following the—the script, of course, is really no more than one would expect.

"Like detective stories," continued Miss Seeton, "which are frequently most informative, when the author writes with any degree of expertise on what can be a wide variety of subjects. When one reads, for example, that the missing . . ." After the briefest of pauses, her own expertise

supplied the example . . . "The missing work of art is . . ."
Here deference to the metalworking expertise of her guest
supplied the courteous conclusion . . . "A signed Degas
bronze, then when the detective explains why this must be
a forgery, one believes him. Except," she added honestly,
"that in this particular instance one would have known in
any case, because he cast none during his lifetime apart
from the little dancer, I believe. But as a general rule, one
may say that it is possible to learn a great many most interesting facts from detective stories—as, indeed, one can
from other books as well, of course, but it was one of the
Lord Peter Wimsey books that reminded me that one can
learn, as it were, how to pick a lock. Except, of course, that
he couldn't. Nigel, I mean, not Lord Peter, although it was
in fact Miss Murchison who . . ."

Blushing with the sudden recollection that by her chatter
she was distracting a busy man from his business, Miss
Seeton smiled apologetically, and fell silent.

Dan Eggleden, as he listened with half-attentive ears to
his hostess, had focused most of his attention on her mys-
terious box—and not on the front of that box, but on the
back. He seemed pleased with what he saw, nodding to
himself, and tapping the hacksaw gently on the palm of his
huge hand; as Miss Seeton, pink-cheeked, ceased speaking,
he nodded once more, and cleared his throat.

"An old newspaper's what's wanted now, if you've any
to spare you don't need for laying the fire. Or an old sheet,
mebbe, or a tablecloth—a blanket, a rug—summat to catch
the filings when I start to cut. This here's too hard a job
for pliers, as I suspected all along it'd be."

Miss Seeton at once produced the papers used by Nigel
the previous night, and with surprised admiration watched
Dan lift the box from the carpet in an effortless, one-handed
movement. She slid the protective pages underneath at the
smith's instruction, then moved out of range, though not
out of view, as he addressed both himself and the saw to
their task.

"These hinges, now," he said, tapping at the elaborate metalwork with the hacksaw handle, "they're much the sort of design you'd expect. They pivot open on these here pins, or spindles—see?"

Dutifully peering, Miss Seeton saw.

Dan nodded. "When they open in the normal way, that is. But with the locks holding it shut at the front, they're not about to open in the normal way, believe you me. We're not beat, though, not by a long chalk, we ain't. What do you do if the electric fails?" He didn't wait for a reply. "Light the house with candles, that's what you do. There's allus another way of solving a problem, if you've your wits about you—and more than one, if you've sufficient ingenuity."

"Indeed there is," said Miss Seeton fervently. Like every female of her generation, she had vivid memories of ingenuity's wartime apotheosis in the matter of Make Do And Mend.

"The man who built this box," Dan continued, "you'd call him an ingenious bloke, I don't doubt, and so would he have done. It's a grand piece of work he's made, and a pity to damage it more than needful—still, like I said before, once I've finished the job you'll hardly know it's done. What one man can invent, never mind how ingenious, there's another man can beat—and that man's myself, Miss Seeton, concerning this box of yours. Not to boast, but if it ain't open before dinnertime, I'll—I'll eat my apron, darned if I won't!"

This was indeed a boast. Daniel Eggleden's apron was of the design traditional for a working smith, being of thick, heavy leather with a wide fringe at the bottom for the safer sweeping of red-hot metal particles from the surface of the anvil to the floor. Even had the apron been sliced, minced, marinated in herbs, and casseroled in an exceedingly slow oven, the dish thus created would have required jaws—and a digestion—of top quality steel to consume, and the stomach of a dozen Gargantuas combined.

"My goodness," breathed Miss Seeton. A sudden vision of a tormented blacksmith desperately downing pint after pint of effervescent liver salts flashed across her inward eye. "Oh, dear, I do hope it won't come to that . . ."

Dan never heard her. He was leaning over the box, the saw in his hand, pondering the best place for his first stroke. "The lock," he said, "you could call the electric, Miss Seeton. And these here hinges we'll say are the candles—the other way of doing it. Once get them open, and you'll open the box from the back every bit as well as you'd normally open it from the front, see? But they're fixed to the wood with screws quite as powerful as the lock. You'll shift them no more easily—so what you do is shift the spindles instead. Then top and bottom halves'll come apart as if they was two locks instead of two hinges. And the lock turning into a hinge, o' course, at the same time."

He made it sound so easy; so obvious: which was the mark of the true expert. Miss Seeton, hanging on Dan Eggleden's every word, nodded without speaking as she waited with growing excitement for the first scrape of the hacksaw against the ornate knobbed end of the spindle, wondering whether the noise would be as unpleasant as, one had to say, the working of metal—even when heard from outside, when peeping inside to watch Mr. Eggleden at work—so often proved to be.

As it proved now. Even more unpleasant, perhaps, in so confined a space as the little sitting room: but Miss Seeton didn't grudge the smith a single screech as the saw worked its way back and forth across the spindle in a steady, rasping rhythm. Fine powder began falling to the newspaper beneath, darkening the printed page from distant, muzzy grey to sombre, spreading black. Headlines were slowly smothered by a blanket of funereal hue; assorted worthies, photographed smiling, disappeared in gloom despite their smiles. Miss Seeton put her fingers in her ears, and watched, and waited.

A light perspiration bedewed the brow of Daniel Eggleden as he straightened for a moment from his sawing to rub the small of his back. "Not till I'm done, thanks," he replied in answer to Miss Seeton's enquiry about a cup of tea. "Hot work this is, and thirsty, too—but I'll finish it first. This iron's not so hard as I feared it might be: I'm a good halfway through already, see?"

Once more, a fascinated Miss Seeton saw, and nodded, and murmured a polite response which was drowned out by the renewed screech of metal against metal, higher and still higher in pitch as what remained of the spindle requiring to be severed grew gradually smaller in diameter.

A descant screech—a clang—a clatter. Spindle and knob had at last parted company. The knob bounced up from the floor, then recoiled from the age-old oak to rest, rolling in a gentle arc, on newspaper which shivered with its movement, and scattered iron filings into strange shapes.

Miss Seeton, thrilled, uttered cries of congratulation.

Dan Eggleden wiped his steaming brow with his forearm, and grinned. "Now, didn't I tell you? We'll hope the other comes as easy . . ."

And, to his relief and great delight, it did.

Breathing hard, he met Miss Seeton's admiring gaze with a weary twinkle in his eye. "Need ear-plugs for this, too," he warned, yielding the hacksaw to the canvas embrace of his tool bag, and rummaging within for a mighty hammer and a tapering steel rod about twelve inches in length. "Punch," he said as he rummaged, and across Miss Seeton's wayward imagination danced a belligerent hook-nosed hand puppet, in hot pursuit of a ruff-collared dog with a string of stolen sausages in its jaws.

Things were just starting to look bad for poor Toby when Dan, having applied the business end of the punch to the sawn-off spindle where it lay within the curving clutch of the hinge, made a minor adjustment, picked up his hammer, and smote mightily, driving the point of the punch against the spindle . . . and the spindle, accordingly, partway out of the hinge.

"Oh," breathed Miss Seeton as a shower of rust flaked down on the iron filings, creating shapes and patterns yet more strange. Visionary sausages, hound, and hook-nosed vengeance vanished at once. "Oh, Mr. Eggleden, it moved! How very, very clever of you to—"

With a hasty clang, Dan drowned out her words of praise until he should properly deserve them, pounding away at the punch in slow, resonant time. Miss Seeton was so entranced as the spindle edged its rusty way out of the hinge that she almost forgot to put her fingers in her ears. The blacksmith's hammer thumped merrily on . . . and on . . .

Until one final blow sent the second spindle shuddering from its hinge to the floor. And the box—as Dan Eggleden informed her with pride—could now be opened.

"Oh," said Miss Seeton, pink-cheeked with excitement. "Oh, how splendid! And now . . ." Then she recollected herself. Excitement was checked by the need to pay tribute. "And so quickly, too, although that is only to be expected, of course, from an expert. Thank you so much, Mr. Eggleden, for all your hard work and kindness, when you could have had no idea how long it would take. To have taken you from your normal work . . ."

"Pleasure, Miss Seeton." Dan grinned at her over his shoulder as he began packing his tools into the canvas bag. "A bit of a change to have a job so out of the normal run as this, once in a while. A challenge, you might say—and a pity I couldn't have made you new keys instead, but with so much rust and the padlocks jammed, I doubt I could've got 'em to work in any event. But now, well, from the front you'd never know it'd been opened, would you? Except," he added slyly, "as it ain't exactly been opened yet."

Miss Seeton, suppressing a sigh, agreed that it hadn't but her natural curiosity wrought with her innate courtesy, and courtesy prevailed. "You must be thirsty, Mr. Eggleden. It won't take long to boil the kettle for a cup of tea, if you would care for one." She turned her back on temptation, and headed for the sitting room door. "Whatever is inside the box—if, indeed, there is anything at all—has been waiting, or so one gathers from the state of the hinges and lock, for many years. Another ten minutes,'' said Miss Seeton heroically, ''can make no real difference, can it?''

Dan Eggleden's mid-morning summons to Sweetbriars, his lengthy sojourn beneath Miss Seeton's roof, and his subsequent cheerful return to the forge had not escaped the notice of the village.

It was Mrs. Spice, popping into the bakery for one of Mrs. Wyght's celebrated chocolate cakes and a bag of buns, who on her way out had paused on the doorstep to tickle one of the tea-room cats beneath his chin. While thus bending to pay her respects, she had observed at her back the brisk passage up The Street of a pair of well-shod, size four feet in sensible grey stockings. The shoes, hose, and nimble tread could have belonged to many an honest citizen: the swinging tip of a defendant umbrella crooked over a tweeded arm could belong to only one—a citizen concerning whose integrity and respectability Plummergen never ceased to argue.

"Miss Seeton? At the smithy?" Mrs. Spice, busy fingers coaxing, had been followed north by all four feline Wyghts as she drifted to a convenient halt outside the residence of Miss Cecelia Wicks. Miss Wicks lived right next door to the forge; her cottage, decorated by a wrought-iron balustrade, was often pointed out to potential clients by Dan Eggleden as the perfect setting for one of the finest examples of his work. Mrs. Spice had been forced to rest against the ornate black curlicues as she stroked as many cats as demanded her attention, such attention being far too dangerous to give while in motion. She must, for safety's sake, remain where she was . . . and this she did, while her ears strained to hear what was being said indoors, and her eyes did their utmost to penetrate the shadowy gloom.

"At the smithy," said Mrs. Spice, as she at last presented her report to an eager post office, and quite took everyone's mind off phantom caskets. "You could've knocked me down with a feather, you really could—to think Dan Eggleden, of all people, 'd let himself get talked into plotting goodness knows what *against the Queen . . .*"

The gratifying sensation aroused by this intelligence more than made up, in the opinion of Mrs. Spice, for the ache in the small of her back. Absently she smirked as she massaged her restive fingers, then quickly replaced the smirk with an expression as serious as the tone in which she continued her story.

"Yes—plotting, they were, the pair o' them! And after what happened on Bonfire Night, you'd think Miss Seeton'd be the very last person, wouldn't you? There's some folk as have no gratitude for their lives being saved—and a fine way to show gratitude, to pay it back with treason!"

Further sensation. Mrs. Spice nodded sagely. "Treason, yes—and worse, for all I know, though what I *do* know's bad enough. For ain't it treason to go interfering with the Royal Mail? And ain't it the post office as takes care of the telephones?"

All heads turned as one towards the grille behind which Mr. Stillman, postmaster, performed his official duties. Mrs. Stillman, supervising Emmy Putts on the grocery counter, let a quick cry of warning escape her before emitting a furious remark that turned all the heads back again. Mr. Stillman—one of the cricket team's star bowlers and, like

the less projectile Elsie, a staunch admirer of Miss Seeton—at his wife's warning reluctantly loosened his grasp
on the red-inked stamp embossed with the loyal legend
OHMS. He would leave Elsie to fight this particular battle
on her own, as he knew her well able to do. Against all
official policy, he slammed down the grille with a vicious
clang, and sat back to listen as his loving spouse let rip.

"Well, really! If you ask me," said Elsie Stillman before
anyone did, "I think a far worse thing than treason is
slander. And if it wasn't so ridiculous nobody with half
the sense they were born with would believe it, if you ask
me Dan Eggleden and Miss Seeton should think
about . . . about *suing* anybody who goes around repeating
such rubbish."

Feet shuffled with embarrassment. Throats were cleared;
eyes met, then darted away. Even Plummergen opinion—
swift as it is to build on the slimmest of foundations the
firmest of prejudices—can be influenced, if the voice of
influence is sufficiently forceful; and, while Mrs. Spice had
spoken with no small authority, Mrs. Stillman, with the
greater authority vested in her as the wife of the licensed
postmaster, on her own territory must necessarily speak
with an almost irresistible force.

Mrs. Spice, indignant at the loss of her thunder—not to
mention the slur on her mind, morals, and judgement—
after a moment's startled pause opened her mouth to protest: but too late. Mrs. Stillman's righteous wrath was urging her on to yet higher flights of eloquence.

"And I'm sure I wouldn't be the only one glad to—to
bear witness to their good character, when you think of all
the wonderful things Miss Seeton has done over the years,
helping the police the way she has. The whole village, too,
for that matter. If there's any talk of *gratitude*," concluded
Elsie Stillman caustically, "it's as plain as the nose on my
face there are a sight too many people around here who
don't even know the meaning of the word!"

She gave the handle of the bacon slicer a vengeful turn,

sending the wicked steel blade screaming through the air. Everyone remotely within range jumped out of it.

"You were asking for cheese, Mrs. Henderson." Mrs. Stillman prodded young Miss Putts sharply in the ribs and indicated the rich yellow wedge—almost the end of the truckle—that rested on the white marble slab. With an eloquent gesture, she handed her assistant the wood-toggled wire, glared at Mrs. Henderson, and folded her arms in a dignified manner. "Now, Emmeline, I want to see you cut Mrs. Henderson's cheddar just the way she wants it, d'you hear?"

The matter might have ended there: but Plummergen society, like many another, has its undercurrents against which even Elsie Stillman would find it difficult to swim. The Skinner-Henderson Flower Feud was never far from the minds of the ladies concerned; and Mrs. Skinner was not slow now to seize her chance. She, like Mrs. Henderson, had come to the post office intending to buy a pound and a half of cheese. Her rival had somehow slipped ahead of her in the queue. A distracted Mrs. Skinner had been unable, in all the welter of gossip that had preceded the breathless arrival of Mrs. Spice, to redirect her thoughts to the concoction of an alternative menu for that night's supper. Eat anything the same as Mrs. Henderson Mrs. Skinner simply would not! And with a little care she might not need to. By encouraging Mrs. Spice to enlarge on her story— which was, in any case, one of the most promising snippets she'd heard all week—she'd be doing no more than her neighbourly duty. If anyone was to take objection—if Mrs. Stillman, supervising Emmy Putts, chose to be so busy interfering that Mrs. Henderson's order didn't get served; if anyone else, naming no names, decided to shove her oar in—well, you couldn't blame a body for that, could you?

"So what manner of treason would you say they were plotting, Mrs. Spice?" Mrs. Skinner managed to suggest, by a sly sideways look at Mrs. Stillman, that she did no more than humor a friend, and was willing to be corrected in any false assumptions into which she might be led. "You aren't saying as they want to blow up Buckingham Palace, are you, or kidnap the Royal Family again?"

Mrs. Skinner's expression, if not her tone, hinted once more at a humorous interpretation of the news brought by Mrs. Spice. Mrs. Henderson, queueing for cheese, had her back to Mrs. Skinner. Abruptly she turned round to pour scorn on the import of what she'd overheard.

"I'm not saying Miss Seeton ain't queer in her ways, as nobody with even half the sense they were born with"— she turned back to hurl a scornful look at the grim-faced Elsie Stillman—"could deny, but"—turning again—"after Guy Fawkes and everything, well, it'd be more than *queer* to go plotting treason in the open air where any old Tom, Dick, or Harry"—she deliberately looked in quite the opposite direction from Mrs. Spice—"could hear them: it'd be downright crazy. Besides, for all you can say Miss Seeton's sometimes—sometimes a *bit* crazy, Dan Eggleden—"

"Sometimes?" broke in Mrs. Spice, her voice shrill. "You just tell me a time she wasn't! From the very first day—"

"What absolute rubbish!" This from Mrs. Stillman, above a rising babble of concurrence and—from a few rare specimens—contradiction. "Miss Seeton—"

"Dan Eggleden—"

"—never have thought it, but they say it's always the quiet ones—"

"—can't deny there's some funny things happened—"

"—what about that coffin the Nuts saw last night—"

To judge by the clamour that now arose about her, Mrs. Stillman, for all her authority, was clearly outnumbered. The rare specimens—understandably, perhaps—began to fall silent; and their fall was not slow. Within a minute or two at the most, Mrs. Spice had the floor. It was a position she was determined to enjoy to the full.

Neither she nor Mrs. Henderson—on this occasion willing to accept the Spiciest speculation as gospel—nor, indeed, Mrs. Stillman, her supervisory attempts forgotten—observed the serpentine progress of Mrs. Skinner past everyone else to the front of the grocery queue, or the smug way in which she advised Emmy Putts that she wouldn't trouble her to use the wire, but just give her all that was left on the slab, and not to worry if it was a bit more than usual: if she didn't finish it for that night's supper, she was sure it would come in handy for tomorrow's dinner. Mrs. Skinner did not admit, even to herself, that while Mrs. Stillman was busy defending the reputation of Miss Seeton, she would be unable to oversee her less experienced assistant's attempts to start the new, fifty-six-pound truckle of cheese that waited in its sacking wrap at the side of the counter. Greater skill than Emmy yet possessed was needed, Mrs. Skinner well knew, to take the first slice from so daunting an example of the dairyman's art . . .

"So if talk of treason and plots is—is *ridiculous*, and *rubbish*," said Mrs. Spice, glaring at those of her visible detractors who hadn't ducked their heads out of range, "then I should very much like to know what business people think Miss Seeton's got to be—to be bugging the telephones!"

Sensation. Even the lips of Mrs. Spice's strongest detractors gave forth little cries of alarm. Mrs. Spice tossed her head and smirked: the attention of her audience, almost to a woman, was now fastened upon her with a most gratifying intensity. "It's nobbut the one, mind you, to start with, but set between her house and the forge as it is, it's plain as the nose on your face," she said, ignoring the evident indignation of Mrs. Stillman, "she'd try that one first. But you can be sure she won't stop there, if it's as easy as Dan Eggleden made it sound. Do the job on the spot, he said he could, and be along to sort things out well before dinnertime—*this* dinnertime, as ever is! Oh, I tell you, there won't be a secret safe in Plummergen, once that precious pair have set their wicked electricals in the village's one and only telephone box . . .''

The box, with whatever long-lost mysteries it contained, brooded on its newspaper bed as Miss Seeton brought tea and biscuits to the sitting room, did her hostessly duty by Dan Eggleden, then trotted back to the kitchen for a dustpan and brush. Dan quenched his thirst, munched a chocolate digestive, and voiced only a faint protest as Miss Seeton fell to sweeping up the debris produced by his recent endeavours. It had been, for all his boasts, a more difficult job than he had anticipated; and crouching, for a man of his inches, was cramping and wearisome after a while.

Miss Seeton had brewed up in her everyday earthenware pot rather than her best bone china, and had brought a pair of the sturdy mugs she used whenever Stan Bloomer dropped in for his elevenses in preference to popping back home or bringing a flask. It was, of course, only to be expected that the delicate and dainty, while aesthetically pleasing, would be of no use to a working man—not, that is, while he was working. And dear Mr. Eggleden had worked so hard: even if the treasure chest should prove to contain nothing whatever of any interest, it had been most interesting to watch an expert displaying his expertise.

"Some more tea, Mr. Eggleden?" Miss Seeton hopped up nimbly from the floor and, not for the first time, blessed the years of yoga that enabled her so to hop without her knees emitting those embarrassing cracks common to many persons of her age. The result, as she understood it, of a gradual stiffening of the tendons, although it was not a phenomenon entirely unknown to persons far younger than herself, as well. In the young, of course, it could be accepted as no more than a mildly amusing—if one's sense of humor was so inclined—physiological trait: she had on several occasions heard Nigel making jokes about rifle-shot and fireworks . . .

"Oh, dear." Miss Seeton paused with the teapot in mid-pour, and blushed. "Oh, dear. I wonder . . ."

There was more than a hint of misgiving in the quick look with which Dan Eggleden favoured his hostess. Had he broken some hitherto unknown taboo of the gentry by saying he'd welcome a second draught of tea? Should he not have asked for three heaped spoons, when Miss Seeton didn't take sugar on her own account? Was the poor little body too polite to tell him to his face and wondering what to do?

But it was no question of tea-table etiquette that now troubled the mind of Miss Emily Dorothea Seeton: anything so simple would have been almost a relief. What worried her far more than second helpings could ever have done was a sudden memory of Nigel, and his mother, and their assistance—unavailing, of course, but none the less welcome—in the matter of the treasure chest. Did not the Colvedens deserve some share in the excitement of the official—as it were—opening of the chest, quite as much as Mr. Eggleden? Admittedly, it was his job, while the part played by Nigel and his mother had been no more than kindness to a friend; but kindness ought surely to merit a more courteous return than being overlooked in—again, she blushed—the merely selfish satisfaction of one's own curiosity. Except—Miss Seeton stifled a sigh—that Mr. Eggleden, also, had expressed some curiosity as to the contents of the chest. It hardly seemed right to ask him to wait, when he had already been—like the Colvedens—so very kind . . .

That sigh (the blacksmith, despite the near-perpetual clangour in which he worked, had quick ears) convinced Dan Eggleden, who rose to his feet before the pot could begin its proper pouring. "You know, Miss Seeton, I think mebbe I've left the forge a bit longer than I really did ought, in the middle of the day as it is, so I'll say thank you kindly for the beaver and be off, if it's all the same to you."

A few startled drops splashed from the spout as, despite

her having known for years that Plummergen folk often referred to their elevenses as beavers, Miss Seeton's attention was distracted by the vision of a furry-faced, bewhiskered little animal gnawing away at the obstinate old oak of her chest. She blinked; the beaver, with a flirt of its flattened tail, vanished. Miss Seeton set down the teapot, trying to hide her relief at Dan's decision. She must remember to round up by another five pounds her cheque for whatever sum he would write on the bill . . .

So Daniel departed and left Miss Seeton, the beating of her heart just a little louder than usual, to close with heroic resolution the sitting room door on the sight of that tantalising carved oak chest, and to hurry instead to the telephone, to dial the well-known number for Rytham Hall.

CHAPTER 13

Lady Colveden informed Miss Seeton, with genuine regret, that she had a meeting straight after supper, and wouldn't be able to come. Nigel, however, she felt fairly certain had nothing planned.

"And even if he had," said his mother, "I'm sure he'd be only too happy to cancel, unless it was something absolutely vital. He'll be thrilled to be one of the first people for goodness knows how many years to know what's inside your box—and are you positive you don't mind waiting until tonight? I really don't believe I could be so noble."

Miss Seeton's assertion that she was indeed happy to wait soon became tangled with courteous references to the aristocracy, of which the Colveden family were so shining an example. She paid particular reference to the good sense and character of her ladyship, and Lady Colveden, embarrassed as the English always are at the compliment direct, was quick to divert the confused tributary flow by laughing her thanks, promising Nigel's attendance upon Miss Seeton at the agreed time, and firmly ringing off.

Miss Seeton ate her lunch, washed the dishes, darned a slight tear in the sleeve of her cardigan while she digested, and then forced herself out into the crisp January air for a spell of gardening. Not that the garden—dear Stan, even in winter, worked so hard—needed it; but she did. With her border fork, she pricked over the bulb beds where the pale spikes of daffodils, tulips, and hyacinths had crept their first quiet inches through the earth. This aerating task complete, she pruned the few straggling stems Stan had left among the roses; hoed the ground destined for the first spring flowers; peered at some of the softer shoots, looking for early greenfly; and finally, captivated by the yellow stars cascading down its dark green stems, picked a large bunch of winter jasmine as the light was fading, and hurried indoors to find a suitable vase.

"Jolly flowers," said Nigel, observing the graceful arrangement in the centre of the table. "Mother's up to her ears in cyclamens and hellebores and things. Lenten roses, you know—silly, isn't it? I'd have thought Christmas rose would be a more suitable name for them, considering the time of year."

Miss Seeton smiled. "Christmas roses, indeed, come into flower rather closer to Easter than to Christmas—but this may be due to the calendar change, perhaps. When everything was brought forward by eleven days, in the eighteenth century . . ." She frowned. "Or perhaps not. When one comes to consider the names, they do seem somewhat . . . illogical—though that, of course, is one of the charms of the English language, isn't it?"

"I could always," came Nigel's impish reply, "disagree with you. And then we could spend the rest of the evening in—dash it, what's it called? Learned philological discourse, that's what. Which sounds splendid—but I'd far rather spend my time looking inside here," he said, tapping the lid of the waiting wooden box, "and solving the mystery. And I bet you would, too."

Miss Seeton twinkled at him and agreed that she would. From what she had been told by Mr. Eggleden, opening the lid backwards, as it were, on its makeshift padlock hinge, would be far easier with two pairs of hands than with one . . .

His expert eye honed by years spent humping sheaves of harvested wheat into stooks, Nigel gauged the likely weight of the lid and suppressed a grin. Miss Seeton might well stand only five feet high and weigh no more than seven stone wringing wet, but even she shouldn't have found it an impossible challenge to part the ancient hinges and tip back the iron-bound lid without assistance. Nigel knew his Miss Seeton. She was making excuses, as she generally did, for being caught out in any act of kindness: she'd known he'd been really keen to learn the contents of the treasure chest, having spent so long the night before trying to get into the thing, and she'd saved up the fun on purpose until the working day was over, so that he could share it.

Not for the first time, Miss Seeton seemed to read the thoughts of another. ''It would be selfish of me, wouldn't it?'' she went on, twinkling again, ''not to share the fun of this little adventure that chance—and my own careless-ness''—here she gave a faint smile—''has placed in my way—when you consider how very uneventful is the life I normally lead.''

She said this last with a perfectly straight face. The face of Nigel, as his jaw dropped, was convulsed. If Miss Seeton really saw her life as uneventful, she was the one person in the world who could. ''Whether or not,'' she continued calmly, ''there's anything inside, it will be a most delightful change—not, of course, that I'm complaining,'' she said with a blush. ''I have been, I know, very fortunate. And afterwards it will, in any case, make a charmingly unusual box for storing blankets and pillows, as your mother sug-gested, once it has been cleaned and polished.''

She nodded at him, smiling. Nigel nodded back. ''What does Martha have to say about it?'' he enquired with a grin. The invaluable Mrs. Bloomer came to Sweetbriars twice a week, in normal circumstances, but a shocking head cold had kept her away for some days past. Nigel supposed that the efficiency of Plummergen's grapevine would have advised this domestic paragon of every detail of her employer's accidental purchase, even if Miss Seeton herself hadn't told her all about it on the phone. Nigel was genuinely curious as to the Bloomer view on carved wooden blanket boxes. He had heard Martha (who also obliged on a regular basis at Rytham Hall) hold forth many times—and at some length—on the problems associated with the polishing of old oak, with particular reference to parquet floors and the heavy boots worn by working farmers.

Miss Seeton, who'd heard similar grumbles when Martha's irritation with the boots had lasted overnight, nodded, then smiled again, rather ruefully. "I fear I haven't told her very much just yet—with such a dreadful cold, you know—but at least, because it *is* oak, there's no need to treat it for woodworm. Which is a relief, as I dislike the smell. It would be so ungrateful of me to allow dear Cousin Flora's inheritance—the furniture, you know, and the floorboards—to become riddled with holes, which seems strange when you remember that I have spent much of my life working with turpentine. Dear Martha would rightly be very vexed with me. And most irresponsible . . ."

As she spoke, Miss Seeton had drifted, followed by Nigel, from the doorway to the box, where she was now absently running her hand across the massive, rusty iron bands and the battered panels with their worn, though still intricate, carving. She hesitated, took a deep breath, and turned to address Nigel in a voice that barely trembled.

"Which side will you take? It makes little difference to me, and there seems to be plenty of room—as Mr. Eggleden never needed to move it from where you left it in the middle of the floor—but . . ."

Nigel realised she didn't so much need his muscular as his moral support. For ladies of Miss Seeton's generation, gentlemen made all the decisions. If he didn't start, in the nicest possible way, to organise his hostess, they could be here half the night before anything was accomplished. "I'll take the left," he said, "if you're sure you'll be happy with the right. Let me just bring this chair across to lean the lid on once we've got it open . . . Here . . . And now if you kneel sort of sideways on, like this . . ."

It never occurred to him that Miss Seeton would be incapable of kneeling: and of course she wasn't. Not for the first time, her yoga, which she regarded as the most private of pursuits, proved its public worth. She tidied her skirt out of the way, bent her ankles and knees at the same time, and without a single click or creak almost glided down to the newspaper, settling herself a convenient distance from the eager young man at her side.

She watched him closely. As he moved, so did she, copying everything he did with the mirror exactitude only to be expected from someone with a trained eye. He checked that the pin was indeed missing from its double cradle: Miss Seeton checked hers. He seized his corner of the lid and shook it. Miss Seeton, likewise, shook.

"Not wedged solid," said Nigel, "by the feel of it. We shouldn't have too much trouble—touch wood." He grinned. "Which is what we're doing anyway, so three cheers for us—and now let's have it up, shall we?"

"Oh," breathed Miss Seeton. "Oh, yes, let's . . ."

The whisper died away. In a spellbound silence, Miss Seeton tightened her grasp on the lid as Nigel tightened his. They met each other's glance, and nodded.

Another shake; a tug—tentative at first, then more forceful; a jangle, as the pinless hinges began to separate, top half from bottom; a sprinkle of ancient wood dust, mingled with flakes of iron, on paper and cloth-covered knees alike, though by this time neither Nigel nor Miss Seeton could have cared less. A slow, steady creak; a growing mustiness in the air accompanying the screech of metal as the dark mouth of the box gaped gradually open, pivoting on its unaccustomed, improvised hinges to rest at last against the back of Miss Seeton's chair.

"Whew." Nigel released his burden to wipe a hand

across his brow and shook his hair back from the forehead over which it had fallen in the heat of the moment. "Jolly well done us, Miss Seeton, don't you think?"

Miss Seeton, beaming, could only nod. Nigel, beaming back, emitted a sudden splutter. "Ugh! I beg your pardon. But when you think how that air's been lurking inside your box for heaven knows how many hundreds of years, and we've gone and let it out, no wonder"—he coughed—"it's feeling a bit . . . a bit lively."

Miss Seeton blinked and sat back on her heels in dismay. "Germs, you mean? Oh, dear, I do hope not. If you should fall ill, Nigel, it would be dreadful—and all my fault. How could I ever face your parents? One hears of such diseases as—as anthrax . . ."

It was the smothered grin, and the ill-concealed gleam in young Mr. Colveden's eye, that alerted Miss Seeton to the fact that her leg might be being pulled: pulled, moreover, in that manner peculiar to the British aristocracy, even if (to one long accustomed, as was Miss Seeton, to teaching) the social status of such youthful humorists as over the years had crossed her path was probably immaterial. Miss Seeton—who in her secret soul possessed a certain dry wit of her own—hid a smile as she continued:

"Of course, we may be worrying unnecessarily—let us hope so, although if you are at all anxious, Nigel dear, I would be only too happy to prepare a—a mustard inhalation for you." His sudden horrified spluttering seemed to surprise her. "You think not? It's no trouble, I assure you, and won't take long. The kettle is always ready to boil, and one cannot take too much care, in the circumstances—which are unusual, to say the least." She hid a smile as he continued to splutter. "Yes, the air from inside the chest is—or rather was—undoubtedly stale—though one wouldn't call it damp, or mouldy . . ."

Then, all at once, enough was enough. Good manners had required that Miss Seeton follow her guest's conversational lead: but she could suppress her curiosity no longer. She knelt up—leaned forward . . .

And finally allowed herself a glimpse of the contents of the old oak chest.

Nigel, even while raising the lid, had contrived, in the most gentlemanly fashion, to keep his eyes turned away from what that lid concealed. It was Miss Seeton's box: she must have the first fun of seeing inside: but at her excited little gasp he allowed himself to turn slowly back to gaze at . . . what?

The shadowed inner surface of the lid seemed curiously carved about the edge, but even the eye of an artist wasted little time in studying under electric light what would be far easier to see in the daytime. Miss Seeton spoke.

"Papers," she said very softly. "Such beautiful, old-fashioned writing—printing, too—and clothes, I think."

She sounded doubtful about this last. "Looks more like somebody's old curtains," said Nigel, "all that brocade and—and embroidery—and . . . paint?"

"Painted, certainly." Miss Seeton reached out a tentative finger. "Theatrical costume, perhaps. And these could be scripts," she added, remembering the recent production of *Cinderella* at which she had acted as Prompt. "Although," she said, touching one of the pale bundles, "this feels rather too . . ."

Nigel touched, as well. "Good quality," he agreed. "D'you think it's parchment? I say, Miss Seeton, do let's look underneath—we might find one of Shakespeare's lost manuscripts, or something!"

Miss Seeton smiled: enthusiasm always pleased her. And, of course, they might, though it was most unlikely, even if the appearance and style of the chest were decidedly Elizabethan, or at least Jacobean. A lost Shakespeare man-uscript—*Love's Labour's Won,* perhaps . . .

She smiled again.

She sobered. "Oh. Oh, dear, Nigel . . . It has only just dawned on me, but . . ." A quiet sigh escaped her. "So great a responsibility, you know, I'm not entirely sure . . . From the little we've so far seen, the documents—those underneath may of course be quite different—but the ones we can see do appear to be of—of considerable antiquity, and are possibly of great value—historically speaking, that is, if not in financial terms, when one considers what I paid for them. Except, of course, that the persons who entered the chest in the auction must have been ignorant as to the contents, with the locks being jammed . . . but ignorance can be no excuse where you and I are concerned.'' She gently took up the topmost paper, unfolded it, and gazed pensively at the neat, ornate black writing. ''We, you see, have seen it—that is, them,'' she said with a wistful glance back to the open chest, and the unexamined treasures therein. ''One cannot help but wonder whether perhaps we ought not to—to wait for somebody more suitable . . . some member of the local history society, such as Dr. Braxted . . .''

It was Miss Seeton's house: she could invite into it whom she chose; and Nigel, the ever courteous guest, had—in the abstract—no objection to the presence of Euphemia Braxted. The renowned historian and archaeologist, though somewhat eccentric in her manner, had a jolly enthusiasm for her subject which had won young Mr. Colveden's heart on the occasion of her recent excavation work at Rytham Hall: but youth, too, is enthusiastic, and enthusiasm often breeds impatience.

Euphemia, as Nigel knew, lived several miles on the far side of Brettenden. He didn't grudge the petrol—or the engine wear and tear: but the time was quite another matter. He calculated silently how long it would take to collect her in the MG—even Euphemia, a noted fresh-air fiend, didn't ride her bicycle after dark, especially in January—and winced at the conclusion. And as his hostess had so clearly wished to have her tentative suggestion rejected, Galahad Colveden promptly and firmly rejected it.

''Oh, I don't think so, Miss Seeton. Not if we're careful taking the stuff out. Order and method, and all that.'' He tried to remember what he'd seen of the Rytham Hall dig before it had been closed for the winter. "Suppose we make a list as we go along? You fish 'em up, and I'll write 'em down—nobody could have any objection to that, could they? Besides," added the tempter, as Miss Seeton, still feeling guilty, wavered, "until we know just what's in there, how will we know if it's worth bothering a busy woman like Dr. Braxted with coming all this way to see? She wouldn't thank us for showing her a load of theatrical props, would she? Why, we'd be doing her a favour!" said Nigel in his most persuasive tones.

Miss Seeton had asked Nigel for his opinion. What else should she, having asked, do now but accept it? Especially when it married so happily with her own secret wishes . . .

She found a clean newspaper for the floor, and for Nigel a pencil and a pad of paper.

With eager hands, she began to lift, one by one, the papers and documents and lavish garments from their place of long concealment in the old oak chest.

CHAPTER 14

The first paper Miss Seeton unfolded proved to be a theatrical handbill. It was faded, but presented little challenge to a trained artist, despite the quaintness, to a modern eye, of the lettering. " 'The Celebrated Players of Mr. Colley Kemble,' " Miss Seeton informed Nigel after no more than a moment, " 'will today present a stirring narrative of Charlemagne, *Les Quatre Fils d'Aimond, or, The Four Valiant Brothers,* in which the part of Charlemagne is to be taken by Mr. Augustus Pottipole. With diverse Interludes as; Mr. Franklyn, an Ingenious Exponent of the Dance, with a dozen Bells; Monsieur Baudoin and Signor Radicati, fighting with broadsword, small sword, javelin and battle-axe according to the custom of Ancient Chivalry; and an Elizabethan Egg Dance brilliantly perform'd by Sieur Daigueville over a dozen Eggs laid out upon the stage, blindfold.' "

The vision which this last intelligence brought to mind made Miss Seeton pause in her reading.

Nigel gurgled at her side. "The eggs, or the brilliant performer? Can you imagine what my mother would say if I raided the hen house and started practising? Or what Stan

Bloomer would say if you did,'' he added.

"It sounds a shocking waste, unless they were addled, no matter how brilliant he might be. There is always the risk . . . and the smell. Quite dreadful. From the style of printing, I would guess this dates from the eighteenth century. Georgian buildings were not, I believe, noted for the fresh quality of their air after dark. Candlelight and over-crowding—but then it was hardly a hygienic era, was it? Powder, and scent, and sadly inadequate plumbing . . .''

"Give me cows and pigs any day,'' muttered Nigel as Miss Seeton delved into the chest again.

There were a great many playbills, celebrating such long forgotten spectacles as *The Rival Cavaliers, or, Betrand and Matilda*, in which combat was waged with *mace d'arme, poignard* and sabre as well as with swords of various sizes. Nigel was much struck by the eccentric spelling and florid descriptions of *The Devil to Pay, or, The Wives Metamorphos'd*, where the part of Sir John Loverule was taken by Mr. Pottipole. " 'The better to entertain the Gentry, Mr. Lee has engag'd a Company of Tumblers, lately arrived, who perform feveral furprizing tricks; particularly, one throws himfelf off a Scaffold twelve Foot high; another throws himfelf over 12 Men's heads; He likewise leaps over 6 Boys, sitting on 12 Men's Shoulders; another tumbles over 16 Swords, as high as Men can hold them; and feveral other diverting Things too tedious to mention.' Don't we just wish they had!''

"Mr. Pottipole,'' observed Miss Seeton, "appears to have been a versatile actor, to play both heroic and comic parts. Here he is again,'' she said, unfolding another bill, "in *The Inconstant, or, The Way to Win Him*, as Young Mirabel.''

Nigel was peering rather glumly at a crumbling yellow newspaper. "Gosh, it must be my age. They say the print tends to get smaller as you grow older. I think I need a magnifying glass for this.''

"May I try?'' Miss Seeton, whose eyesight was excellent, studied the tiny letters with some care. After a while, she nodded. "Here he is," she said, pointing. " 'Several of Mr. Pottipole's Friends being pre-engaged for Monday 23 March, advertised for his benefit, and Mr. Kemble having kindly given him Saturday the 14th, he humbly hopes (the shortness of the Time not permitting him to wait on his Friends as usual) those Ladies and Gentlemen who desire to favour him with their presence, will be pleased to send for their tickets and places, to his House next Old Slaughter's Coffee House in St. Martin's Lane.' "

"I think we may surmise," said Nigel with a grin, "that your box used to belong to Mr. Pottipole, Miss Seeton."

He was even more inclined to this view when a number of elegant engravings of a handsome gentleman in various theatrical costumes were unearthed. "Mr. Pottipole in the Charecter of the Roman Father—they spelled things differently then, I suppose. *Mr. Pottipole as Hippolytus* . . . as Hodge . . . as Sir John Brute—Miss Seeton, are any of these chaps—the ones who engraved these prints, I mean—famous?" He was too much of a gentleman to suggest that they might be worth hard cash.

Miss Seeton confessed herself sadly ignorant of William Holland, Mr. Sherwin, and the Sylvester brothers. "But there is an excellent library in Brettenden," she said. "I intend to find out all I can—tomorrow." She smiled. "There's more still to find tonight, isn't there?"

There was. Following the playbills and assorted likenesses of Augustus Pottipole, there were letters written in ink which were difficult to decipher under electric light. Miss Seeton promised to let Nigel know as soon as she had made some sense of them on the morrow. They then began to uncover items that could only be theatrical props, wrapped in a variety of garments. A Persian dressing gown, a pair of baggy breeches, and a length of patterned cloth Miss Seeton believed must be a turban. A pair of boots, a close-cut tunic, and two gloves, unmatching; a pair of battered shoes, with buckles that might be diamonds (Nigel) but were probably paste (Miss Seeton). A rusty scimitar, a feathered headdress (Nigel made another joke about hens), and a remarkable wig, with traces of powder still clinging to it.

"From the very little I have read," said Miss Seeton, "I know that it was only around this time that actors began to wear what we would call costumes on stage. In Shakespeare's day, I don't believe they did. The current vogue for Shakespeare in modern dress is, you see, really rather an old-fashioned concept."

"Because doublet and hose was modern for him?" Nigel had pulled out another tunic and a pair of puffed breeches of slashed design. "You'd need good legs for these." He chuckled as he recalled his role as Buttons the pageboy in the recent production of *Cinderella.* "Wonder how I'd have looked in this?" He made to stand up and let out a yell as he stretched his cramped knees.

"Nigel, I'm so sorry. I hadn't realised we'd been working so long. Should we rest for a few minutes?" With one graceful movement, Miss Seeton uncoiled the stockinged legs on which she'd been sitting, and rose to her full height, smiling now instead of blushing.

No sign of a twinge, no hint of a yell. Nigel, stamping out the prickles in his sleepy feet, regarded his hostess with some respect. If that was what yoga did for you, he'd have to think hard about trying it himself—if he only had the time.

"Time to put the kettle on, I think," said Miss Seeton in that uncanny echoing way she sometimes had. "Will tea suit you—that is, tay," she said with a further faint twinkle for the historical jest. "Or would you prefer coffee?"

"Well," said Nigel, "thanks, but I'm in no hurry, unless you are, that is. Wouldn't you like to get right to the bottom before we stop?"

Miss Seeton cast a brief and eager look towards the waiting chest, then shook her head. "The rest will do us both good, especially our eyes. And your pins and needles," she added with a smile. "If you would be so kind as to help

me bring the tray, I think you'll notice a distinct improve-
ment.''

"Slave driver," groaned Nigel, grinning despite himself.
"Okay, you're on—but let's make it coffee, if you've got
instant. Then we won't have to wait for it to brew.''

They didn't. They topped up the cups with cold water
and took biscuits from the tin instead of wasting time with
cake knives and crumbs. Within five minutes, they were
back in the sitting room.

"A book!" cried Miss Seeton, spying the leather-bound
corner beneath a roll of purple silk which, unrolled, proved
to be a cloak.

Nigel waited hopefully, in case it turned out to be a First
Folio; but it wasn't. It was a small, slim volume in a stiff
leather binding, embossed with interlinked initials in flaking
gold leaf. "B, A, F, H," murmured Miss Seeton, her fingers gently tracing the letters as she spoke. "An album,
perhaps?" She opened the cover, and with a little straining
made out the faded writing on the flyleaf. "No, it's
somebody's diary. *Benedicta Adeline Florence Hedgebote,
her journal and commonplace book, 1749.*"

"Oh, well.'' He hadn't really expected . . .

Miss Seeton closed the diary without reading further: it
would seem, she felt, almost like prying. Like the letters.
Later, perhaps, when she had emptied the chest completely;
but not yet.

"The theatre curtains!" suggested Nigel, as Miss Seeton,
exclaiming over its soft smoothness, reached into the shadowy depths of the now half-empty box to stroke the dark
red velvet that lay there. "Or Mr. Pottipole's dressing
gown," he went on. "And maybe the family silver's
wrapped up in there," he added when the stroking hand
met knobbly resistance, and she gave it a tentative prod.
"You and Martha could be in for a lot of polishing, Miss
Seeton, if I'm right.''

Miss Seeton smiled. "Dear Martha might have
something to say about that, I think, although of course one

would hardly expect to *keep* anything in the nature of a—
of an heirloom, which must surely have gone to the auction
by accident. Anything so valuable as silver would have to
be returned—to the Pottipoles, I assume, if it indeed belonged to them. Or to their descendants, if one knew who
they were. After two hundred years . . .''

Nigel was helping to lift out the dusty dark folds. ''I
can't say I recognise the name as local, but the auction
people're bound to know where it came from. If it turns
out to be—oh, I say.'' With a little puff of dust, and a sigh
of drifting fabric, the velvet bundle was raised from the
historic shadows into the yellow glare of the twentieth century, into a light very different from the mellow candle
gleam that must have last illuminated its soft magnificence.
''I say, this is rather swish.''

''The material,'' said Miss Seeton thoughtfully, ''appears
to be of remarkably fine quality. And hardly worn.''

''You know,'' said Nigel, quite as thoughtful, ''that fur
looks awfully—awfully *real*. Did they have fake fur in
Georgian times? What I mean is, I somehow don't think
it's your average coney.''

Miss Seeton bowed to the superior knowledge of a pest-
plagued farmer who had, on occasion, to rid his growing
crops of assorted vermin.

''Not vermin exactly,'' said Nigel. ''When you look at
those black tails—try *ermine*.''

''The stoat,'' said Miss Seeton blankly. ''The winter
coat—velvet and ermine—Nigel, surely not! There must be
some mistake . . .''

''Look out!''

A slither, a tumult of unfolding fabric, a clatter as
something fell to the floor and rolled a little way across it.
Something that gleamed bright and untarnished in the electric light.

Something that was not silver, but . . .

''Gold,'' gasped Nigel, ''or I'm a Dutchman.''

''A tiara,'' said Miss Seeton, trying desperately for the

common-sense solution. "Gold-plated. An unusual design,
of course, with that—that cloth centrepiece, and no jewels,
but those ornate metal flowers around the edge are—"

"That's no tiara," broke in Nigel, too excited to care
about the courtesies. "Technically that's a circlet, Miss
Seeton. And they aren't flowers, they're—they're leaves."
The voice of the future baronet was hoarse as he began to
describe in heraldic language the object he held in his incredulous hands. "A gold circlet around a cap of maintenance—a chapeau—decorated with"—and he choked—
"with *strawberry leaves,* Miss Seeton."

Nigel stared at his hostess: she, quite as incredulous as
he, could only stare back. He drew a deep breath. "A coronet," he croaked, "with eight strawberry leaves, wrapped
in a crimson velvet robe with an ermine cape, as worn—
as worn on state occasions . . . Miss Seeton, this could have
belonged to—to a duke!"

"Gosh, no. Not really," said a still-agitated Nigel some
time later, once he and his equally agitated companion had
calmed down just a little. Miss Seeton, her yoga training
once more proving its worth, had been first to recover, and
was quick to praise her young friend's breadth of knowledge on so arcane a topic as heraldry. Mr. Colveden, whose
practical skills far outshone his academic qualifications,
was just as quick to disclaim such praise. "I mean, I'd
hardly call myself an expert—time enough to learn all that
when I need it, and Dad's going to be with us a good few
years yet, thank goodness . . ." He coughed, embarrassed
by this display of emotion, and hurried on:

"Filial feelings apart, mantlings and achievements and
helmets and crests honestly aren't my idea of fun—but you
can't help picking up a bit here and there without noticing,
if you know jolly well one day it'll happen to you. Coats
of arms and things, I mean." Nigel, in the best traditions
of the aristocracy, did not care to seem in any way boastful
about his inheritance. "My mother's more the one to ask—

and even she doesn't bother all that much. No crested soup spoons, I mean, or plaques on the wall, or embroidered table napkins—not that she's much of a hand at embroidery,'' he said with a wicked gurgle as he recalled the tapestry firescreen kit he had once given her ladyship for Christmas. Her ladyship, like a certain other personage of undoubted blue blood, had been decidedly Not Amused.

''Somewhere,'' said Nigel, his imagination running riot, ''there could be some owner of a stately home who'll be jolly glad to have these back for his ancestral museum, I bet.'' He shuddered. ''Poor blighter, whoever he is. Probably a cadet branch, by now—if he's real.'' He grinned. ''Well, whoever he is, it should make good publicity, if he needs it: thank goodness we haven't been like so many others and had to open up the Hall to trippers. One advantage of being a viable working farm—and I shall make dashed sure it goes on working, believe me.''

Miss Seeton, who had never known her young friend to be so forthcoming about his ultimate destiny, trusted that he would not consider it indelicate were she to enquire if he, too, would have to wear coronet and robes for ceremonial occasions. Dear Sir George, as she understood it, did not, on the bench: which had always seemed strange, when she knew that judges did. And would he—Nigel, that was to say, and many years from now, she most fervently hoped—have to take his seat in the House of Lords one day?

''It'd be rather splendid, don't you think?'' Nigel eyed the heavy spillage of crimson, white, and black with some admiration. ''Nigel Phillip Raymond, Duke of Plummergen—Miss Seeton, I don't seriously believe all this, but may I try them on anyway? Just for fun. I promise I'll take the greatest care.''

Miss Seeton, who had been secretly longing to know how the robes and coronet, genuine or not, would appear when worn by someone of patrician birth, gave her delighted permission. Together they gently shook out the velvet folds.

"Hey!" Nigel instinctively dropped his share of the drapery to retrieve two more pieces of paper, which had fallen out of the crimson mass to the ground. "These," he said, handing his prize to Miss Seeton, "were pretty well hidden inside there." He grinned, his imagination running riot once again. "One of them will be the map with the spot marked X, you see if it isn't."

Miss Seeton proceeded to do so. More carefully than Mr. Colveden, she set down her half of the fabric burden, and unfolded the first heavy linen document with care. She read it. She was silent.

Nigel said, "May I?"

"Oh—I'm so sorry. It was just . . ."

"Marriage lines." Nigel accepted the paper that had caused Miss Seeton to become lost in thought, and himself studied it closely. "A marriage in the Fleet, performed under licence, between Benedicta Adeline Florence Hedgebote and Augustus Pottipole on February the fourteenth, 1750/51." He scratched his head. "Married on Valentine's Day, two years running? And they say I'm a romantic!"

The teacher in Miss Seeton could not let this pass. She explained that up until a time she could not exactly recall in the eighteenth century, all dates between the first of January and the twenty-fifth of March were written in this duplicate style because the legal, if not the calendar, year began on Lady Day and not in January.

"First quarter-day," said Nigel, son of a landowner. "Lady Day, Midsummer, Michaelmas, and Christmas. Yes, of course. But it's still romantic," he said with a grin. "Valentine's Day, I mean—though it's sad, too, that it's been bundled away in here for so long. I bet it's real, even if the rest . . . I should think the family will be glad to have it back."

Miss Seeton sighed and nodded. She opened the second document, which was large, creamy-grey in colour, and rich to the touch. "Surely this can't be parchment!" she exclaimed.

"If it is," said Nigel, sobering, "I'd say that's taking authenticity a bit too far, for theatrical props. Isn't parchment fearfully expensive? But perhaps it wasn't in seventeen something."

Miss Seeton did not reply. She was gazing at the broad expanse of ornate, closely written script, with flourishes and curlicues erupting from the top row of lettering, and in the centre of the lower edge a red ribbon, with a small box attached. Miss Seeton warily opened the box.

"A seal," said Nigel. "Real wax, from the feel of it, and rather a splendid design, don't you think? Chap sitting on a . . ." He gulped. "On a throne . . ."

Dumbly Miss Seeton shook her head. Nigel decided that a heavy dose of metaphorical cold water was by several minutes overdue. "Well, I don't believe it for a minute," he said. He tried to sound convincing. "Dukes, indeed, and royal seals—Augustus, or at least his ghost, is playing tricks on us. Pottipole was an ordinary actor, and Benedicta had a tidy fit one day after he'd retired, and made him pop everything in this chest of yours out of the way. We'll lay the ghost right here and now. Would you help me on with the gear, please, Miss Seeton?"

Miss Seeton helped to rearrange the white fur cape with its sable decoration before draping it carefully about the future baronet's broad shoulders.

"He wasn't as tall as me." Nigel contemplated the foaming sea of ermine-bordered crimson on the carpet about his feet, then looked up to set the gold coronet cautiously on his thick, wavy brown hair. "And his head was a bit smaller than mine—but these fit *round* me, all right." He flung out his arms in an expansive gesture. "Short and tubby, not a bit like the pictures, but—hey, what's that?"

A final, far smaller piece of paper fluttered to the floor. Miss Seeton, this time better placed than Nigel to pick it up, bent and did so. She held it to the light, and after a moment's study gave a little gasp. She studied the paper again, then read its inscription aloud, in a voice deliberately calm.

"The ceremonial robe and coronet of my dear and much lamented father, Bennet Adelard Florence Hedgebote, fourth Duke of Estover. Last worn by him at the crowning of our gracious sovereign lord King George the Third, and put aside upon the occasion of his death by his sorrowing and dutiful daughter until such time as circumstance shall require that she wear them . . .''

Miss Seeton paused. She cleared her throat. Her voice was husky.

"And it's signed Benedicta Adeline Florence Pottipole, in her own right and by God's grace the second Duchess of Estover.''

CHAPTER 15

Whatever phrase is used to describe them—keeping company, walking out, going steady—the courting habits of the young do not alter greatly from generation to generation. Comfort and privacy, preferably in the dark, are desirable; shelter, when the weather is wet, is essential.

Some hours after Nigel Colveden, bubbling over with the thrill of recent discoveries, had left Sweetbriars to report to his parents the astonishing contents of Miss Seeton's old oak chest, it began to rain. In nearby Brettenden a pair of youthful lovers, less far-sighted in the matter of umbrellas than the current owner of the Hedgebote inheritance, had perforce to desist from their starlit spooning, and sprinted hand in hand for the shelter of that narrow alleyway into which opens the rear entrance of the noted auction house, Candell & Inchpin.

"Ooooh." Chrissie squealed and wriggled at the water trickling down her neck. "That's horrible! Can't we go somewhere where it's dry?"

Terry glanced up to the top of the tall fence beside which they had huddled against the wind. "Stop fussing, stupid, it's only dripping off the overhang. Anyone'd think you was made of cotton wool."

"Well, I ain't, I'm flesh and blood, which if you don't know by now you never will, Terry Mimms—and never you mind *hot stuff*," as Terry interpolated a lascivious compliment, "I'm freezing to death out here, as well as drowning. What you going to do about it? And I don't mean *that*."

She slapped away his wandering hands and achieved a pitiful sneeze. "Catch my death, I will, if you don't look sharp—come on, let's move. I'm sicker this."

Accepting that her reluctance was no longer feigned, Terry took command and began leading the way down the darkened alley towards a remembered corner, out of the rising wind. He held Chrissie encircled in one arm, while with the other hand he groped along the fence.

His groping suddenly stopped: stopped as suddenly as his footsteps. "Here—what's this?"

He released his willing prisoner and turned to rattle something on the other side. "This here gate's open, Chris. It ain't locked—it moved when I touched the handle—and if I push it, like this . . ."

He pushed. Creaking, the gate swung open. Chrissie let out a muffled squeal, more excited now than complaining. "Terry! We going in there? That's surely Candell and Inchpin, and they're dead posh. We don't want to get into no trouble . . . but I could fancy a bitter fun on one o' them four-poster beds, mind you." She giggled, and reached out to squeeze his hand. "Pull the curtains tight round, and nobody'd know we was there . . ."

"No harm in looking," said Terry, but he said it with less enthusiasm than Chrissie thought fitting. She would have pouted, but in the rain-swept darkness it was barely light enough for him to see; she muttered something sulky and hung back when he began to move slowly forward.

Terry's wits were rather quicker than those of his girlfriend. His attention had been caught by that unfastened gate. Once inside the shadowy yard of the auction house, he peered about him to get his bearings, then began edging between the parked pantechnicons and the side wall towards the double doors through which Candell & Inchpin took discreet delivery of their High Class Antiques, Household Effects, and Bankrupt Stock.

As Chrissie squealed in genuine fright at having been left alone in the empty alley, Terry froze abruptly. Nigel Colveden, knight-errant, would—on hearing those squeals—have rushed back to rescue the lady: Terry Mimms did not. Terry hadn't heard the squeals; and even if he had, he would have hesitated before acting. He knew his Chrissie, always one for creating when things didn't go just the way she wanted . . .

It looked to him now as if things weren't going the way Candell & Inchpin'd want, if they'd known. Anyone with a half-decent reason to be in that downstairs room would've switched the light on, not go prowling about with a torch in the dark, with the gate unlocked and—Terry drew near the weathered brick building, and stared—a window smashed, as if he didn't know a smashed window when he saw one.

What to do? Dial nine-nine-nine for the cops, and not give a name because he'd only spotted whoever-it-was through trespassing?

Catch the bloke coming out, and risk having 'em moan about trespass if there was a reward? He could certainly do with the money: who couldn't?

He frowned as he stood watching the torch flicker in the illicit dark. There was money in antiques, no question. So maybe he should catch the bloke coming out, and get just a bit heavy with him until he agreed to go shares in whatever he'd nicked?

Or maybe—

"Terry!" This time Chrissie shrieked aloud. "Terry, where are you?" The torch was extinguished. Terry cursed. "What you playing at, leaving me here?"

Furious, Terry didn't answer. His eyes, more accustomed now to the darker night of the high-walled yard, repeatedly darted from the broken window to the double doors, and back. He'd have to come out, one way or another: and when he did, Terry Mimms'd be waiting—

"Terry!"

But Terry never heard that final shriek. With a rush of fugitive feet, a body came bursting through the wicket door he hadn't noticed in the dark, and hurled itself upon him with unexpected force.

And, after a few seconds' desperate grappling, smashed his head savagely against the wall.

And left him lying senseless in the rain . . .

And was gone.

"Whoever he was," said Superintendent Brinton, "and whatever he wanted, the blighter wanted it badly enough to kill for it. And don't even try telling me it could've been an accident," he added, as Foxon stirred at his side. "When I put my hand on chummie's collar, the charge'll be murder, not manslaughter—there was no need at all to hit young Mimms as hard as he did, poor little beggar."

Foxon, shuddering, nodded his agreement. Although by the time Chrissie's screams had raised the alarm the rain had been falling more heavily than ever, it had not been heavy enough to wash the horrid traces of blood and brains and splintered bone from the rough bricks of the yard wall, and from between the cobbles of the paving.

"He was a vicious devil, all right. Young Mimms didn't stand a chance, did he, sir? And he wasn't exactly a seven-stone weakling . . . but you can see from the traces chummie left that he must've been built like a tank, the way he waded into poor old Terry. Young Chrissie's lucky all he did was knock her down when she came running to see what all the fuss was about. If he hadn't been in such a rush to get away . . ."

He observed Brinton's frown and his thoughtful shake of the head. He promptly shut up. He'd done his best to get the super's brain into gear, the middle of the night as it was, and the whole team still more than half asleep: now it was up to the old man.

Brinton, after a pause for yawning and to rub a hand over his stubble, finally delivered his verdict.

"I've . . . I've got a feeling about this one, Foxon." He dared his subordinate to speak: but Foxon was silent. "Yes, well. The violence, and the hurry, and the shambles he left behind do suggest an amateur . . . but I think chummie was a professional. And not just because he wore gloves—every tuppenny-ha'penny hoodlum in the country knows enough for that, thanks to television and the films—I doubt if many of the blighters have the brains to read, so I won't go blaming the types that give away trade secrets in detective stories—but there's . . . there's something about all this that smells of somebody being just a bit too clever for their own good. Somebody trying to make us think he was an amateur when he wasn't . . . and I'd like to know why."

Foxon wasn't going to argue, but couldn't resist slipping into his habitual role as Devil's Advocate. "The up-and-coming generation of villains is better educated than their dads, sir—think of our old friends the Choppers. Would you exactly call 'em pros? Could be it was one of them trying to act clever, then panicking when he heard the kids outside, and going out the way he went in instead of making a break for it through the front, where nobody would have seen him."

"Could be," returned Brinton in tones that suggested he thought this unlikely. "If he'd come popping out of a door he'd no business to be using, the local beat bobby would've noticed him—he's a good man. Doesn't patrol to some blasted timetable the villains know as well as we do. And even if he did, in all the kerfuffle I doubt if chummie would've kept his head enough to remember who was supposed to be where, and when . . . Don't wriggle like that, Foxon. If you've something to say, lad, spit it out."

Foxon stamped his chilly feet again, pushing his hands into the pockets of his leather jacket for added warmth. "It was something *you* just said, sir—about him having no business to be using the front door—and what you said before. How about if he *is* being a bit too clever for his own good? How about if he had every business in the world to be using that door, and he's tried to throw us off the scent by—by not?''

''An inside job, you mean.'' Brinton didn't make it sound like a question: after so long in the force, very little about the depths to which human nature could sink surprised him. Besides, he prided himself on being a good copper. A good copper always tries to keep track of what's going on in his manor; recently he'd started to pick up the odd, very faint—almost inaudible—whispers about the financial concerns of Candell & Inchpin . . .

''In which case—in whatever case,'' he amended, ''there's no point in hanging around out here any longer, never mind it's getting colder by the minute and I'm not as young as I was.'' Foxon, again, was mute. ''We'll take it the burglary came first, and the murder was a . . . an afterthought. So, find our burglar—professional or amateur, hired for the job or off his own bat—and we've got our murderer.'' He glowered in the direction of the murder site, still frantic with the bustle of preliminary forensic work. ''While this lot's finishing up out here, the others should be almost done in there with their blasted photos and fingerprints and measuring tapes. Time to get on with some honest question-and-answer detection, the way I like it. Wouldn't hurt to find out just what it was he got away with, for a start—*if* we can, for all the clutter.''

''And what he didn't,'' supplied Foxon, hurrying in the wake of his chief past the tarpaulins and floodlights and ominous chalk marks towards the scene of the original crime. ''*If* he didn't, I mean, because from the mess it's hard to tell one way or the other. But if he wanted whatever it was badly enough to kill for it, sir, would you care to give me odds he won't have another try for it, if he didn't get it, once he thinks things have calmed down?''

To which Brinton's only response was a rumble of acknowledgement, followed by a world-weary sigh.

The steady patter of the pouring rain against her bedroom window murmured its way into Miss Seeton's subconscious, making her dream of bees, and summer, and apple-tree shade. Elegant theatrical figures in colourful dress floated across her inward eye, and made her smile in her sleep: which was untroubled, deep, and long—unusually long, as suited her unusually late night.

She had stayed up for some hours after Nigel's departure, admiring the props and costumes, marvelling at the coronet—*could* it be real?—and Benedicta's note; poring over the other papers, whether printed or written by hand: trying, yet again, to decipher the more fanciful script . . . until even her trained eye could take no more of such close work at such an hour, with only artificial illumination to help her. It seemed an age until morning and daylight; but she must wait. There was nothing else practical she could do; it would be foolish to allow oneself to become impatient over what common sense told her was inevitable.

To calm herself, she carried out—despite the hour—her complete yoga programme before climbing into bed. She doubled the length of time she spent in each of those postures intended to assist relaxation: she almost fell asleep on her travelling rug while in the *Savasana*, or Dead Pose; and she later escaped, by the narrowest margin, an unpleasant experience when she yawned in the middle of cleaning her teeth, and the toothpaste tried to wrap itself around her tonsils.

She fell asleep as soon as her head touched the pillow; she remained asleep well past the hour at which the alarm should have woken her. In last night's confusion, she had forgotten to set the clock; nor did the rattle of letters through the box upon the mat, or the diesel roar of postman Bert's van, the screech of his tyres, or the tootle of the horn, disturb her dreams in that comfortable, eiderdowned cocoon in the upstairs bedroom.

With Martha's cold still not completely cured, there was nobody to rouse Miss Seeton from her dreaming. Sunrise— at the start of January no earlier than eight—was in any case darkened by the relentless storm-clouds that had poured forth rain for most of the night, and looked set to continue pouring for most of the day. Oblivious to the sight, lulled by the sound of the weather, Miss Seeton slumbered on . . .

Until the telephone woke her at half past nine.

"Good gracious!" Miss Seeton, blinking at the visible crack in the curtains, realised that it was rather later than she'd thought. Reaching for the bedside extension—one could hardly call the additional charge an extravagance, when one never knew when she might not, given her age, be ill, and unable to negotiate the stairs to the phone in the hall—she blinked again, smothering a yawn as she greeted whoever it was on the other end of the line.

"Miss Seeton? I do hope I haven't rung too early. It's Meg Colveden," came the cheery voice of Nigel's mother. "You're not in the middle of breakfast, are you?"

Miss Seeton, still half asleep, had a strange sense of déjà vu, but soon brought her brain into focus and assured her ladyship, with perfect truth, that she was not at that moment breaking her fast.

"Oh, good, then we can chat. If I don't have someone sensible to talk to soon, I think I shall scream. George is being an absolute bear today—and Nigel's not much better, prowling and growling around the place as if it's all my fault the rain's come back," she said with a laugh. "Not that it ever really went away, of course, or at least not for as long as they'd like. You know how farmers always grumble about the weather. Which doesn't exactly make for a cheerful morning, even if in Nigel's case it's tiredness as well as temper—oh, goodness, that sounds terribly rude, Miss Seeton. I'm sorry. I'm not blaming you and your mystery box for an instant, truly I'm not. It's just that after he left you last night and told us all about it, George and I went to bed and left him looking through half the history books in the library, I should think.'' Nigel's mother laughed again. ''And I imagine the last time Nigel opened a non-fiction book from choice, unless you count checking up on diseases of wheat, or car maintenance manuals, was when he was at Wye—and you know how long ago that was.''

''Indeed I do,'' said Miss Seeton as Meg Colveden temporarily ran out of breath. ''Dear Nigel—so very *practical,* but perhaps not precisely what one would call *academic.* And while history is undoubtedly a fascinating subject, it is not, perhaps, as practical in its application as . . . well, as a knowledge of diseases of wheat, or car maintenance.''

The smile in her voice was echoed by Meg Colveden's mischievous giggle. ''You could say that. I'm amazed at how your Hedgebotes and Estovers and Pottipoles seem to have caught his fancy—or I suppose, if I'm honest, I'm not, because they've rather caught mine, too. Which is why I rang, as you might guess.''

Her ladyship paused politely. Miss Seeton, with another smile—this time of incipient relief—said that she rather believed she might; and, in an expectant silence, waited for the speaker's next words.

''You'll tell me at once, won't you,'' began Meg Colveden, ''if you think it horribly inquisitive of me? But after what Nigel told us last night, I would so much like to see your theatrical costumes, and the coronet, and everything— if you didn't mind a morning visitation, that is. When I think I was with you when you bought it . . . even if we didn't actually buy the barometer.'' She giggled again. ''Though if we had,'' she added with a sigh, ''I expect it would have gone the same way as the first, the mood my menfolk are in. So until it stops raining, it's probably just as well we didn't.''

''One could almost call it providential,'' assented Miss Seeton, whose ability to find the bright side through the darkest blanket of cloud was the envy (and sometimes the despair) of her friends. "Except, of course, that it is so very, very different from an umbrella."

The telephone clattered in her ladyship's hands; Miss Seeton, giving vent to her worries, was oblivious to any disturbance. "One might argue, indeed, that providence could have chosen a far more suitable . . . instrument, if that is the word I require, than myself. Not, of course, that one would shirk one's duty," she hurried to explain, as Lady Colveden could vouchsafe in reply nothing but a nonplussed silence. "Finding them on the bus, or in the tube, one knows at once where to take them, and what should be done. But the peerage—the aristocracy . . . Which is why," she concluded, sighing, "it is such a weight off my mind that you—and your family—have shown this interest in my little problem. I am so pleased that you called, because your advice, believe me, will be most welcome . . ."

And Meg Colveden—although not a member of the peerage, undoubtedly an aristocrat—was only too happy to assure her anxious little friend that she would be with her, to offer what advice she could, within minutes.

Miss Seeton promised to have the kettle boiling; and, as soon as her ladyship had rung off, hopped out of bed to see to it, realising that for once she would have to forgo her yoga practice for matters far more urgent . . .

And, for once, not minding in the least.

CHAPTER 16

Miss Seeton's innate courtesy could not allow her visitor the least inkling that an early beaver for one might be a most belated breakfast for another. As Nigel's mother sighed and shook her head to the offer of a second chocolate biscuit, her hostess nibbled thankfully at the slice of rich fruit-cake—baked by the skilful hands of Martha Bloomer in pre-infectious days—which was far too great a risk to a susceptible waistline. Lady Colveden intimated that she would be only too happy to sit and watch Miss Seeton enjoy cake or biscuits in abundance: for herself, if Miss Seeton didn't mind, she would forgo both biscuits and cake in favour of another cup of tea—whenever this should be convenient to Miss Seeton, who wasn't, please, to hurry—because paperwork always gave George a tremendous thirst, and now she rather felt the same way about it, too.

"Though it does sound frightfully disparaging to call it paperwork," her ladyship concluded. "Rude. When everything's so interesting, and so old—and all so beautifully written, even if we couldn't read half of it. Besides, there's parchment as well, isn't there?"

Miss Seeton's twinkle over the last mouthful of plummy crumbs hinted at her appreciation of the wordplay; and she did more than hint that, like her guest, she would welcome a second cup of tea. She suspected that studying documents—of whatever vintage—would always make one feel dusty. And thirsty. Not to mention the sad deterioration of so much of the fabric—always excepting the chest, of course . . .

"Yes, it's a magnificent piece of work." Meg Colveden had slipped, with Miss Seeton's smiling nod across the teapot, from her chair back to the chest in the middle of the floor. Her fingers again caressed the carved wood, the curlicues and ornamentation of rusting metal that must, in its prime, have looked so proud. "The lid fits so closely to the bottom. It's pretty well an airtight seal, I think. The robe and the coronet cap have almost no moth, and they're hardly faded at all—it's only the cheaper costumes that haven't survived so well. And unless you've been busy with the vacuum cleaner, which I'm sure you haven't because it might cause goodness knows what damage, there's very little dust, considering."

She ran an admiring finger around the lower lip of the chest and tilted the lid back to inspect the inside bite.

"Our forebears," agreed Miss Seeton, "certainly enjoyed great practical—"

"Oh!" Miss Seeton jumped. Lady Colveden, normally the essence of courtesy, ignored her. "Oh, my goodness—Miss Seeton, do look. Wouldn't you say," she said, peering at the inner surface of the lid, "this fancy carving round the edge is really letters?"

Miss Seeton hopped down from the table. In her turn, she knelt on the floor and peered. She jumped up, hurried to the window, and twisted the curtains out of the way.

In the brighter light, there could be no doubt. She and Lady Colveden, side by side, stared at the letters around the inner edge of the lid; and marvelled.

"That's not English," said her ladyship at last. "Apart

from the names, I mean. It looks like Latin, though I suppose it could always be some sort of historical French.''

''*Fils* is French for son, of course.'' Miss Seeton frowned. ''*Fil, fils* . . . and *fille* is daughter—*filia* . . . but I do agree that this is Latin. The dear vicar would be able to tell us for certain, but . . .''

''Molly Treeves wouldn't thank us for dragging her brother out of bed,'' supplied her ladyship. ''Even if it *is* only just across the road, knowing how colds always go to his chest if he's not really careful. She'll have the phone off the hook and visitors banned until his temperature's been normal for forty-eight hours—I know Molly of old. We're on our own with this, Miss Seeton.''

''*Hoc*,'' read Miss Seeton aloud, in a doubtful tone, and with decidedly shaky pronunciation. ''*Hoc op fiebat Ao Dni*—that must be *Anno Domini*—goodness . . .'' At the long list of capitals, she hesitated. ''*Anno Domini*,'' she continued, leaving a prudent blank, ''*ex suptu Adelardi Hedgebote filii Adelard fil Florentius fil Adelard fil Bennet viri Adeline filia et hered Adelard Turbary qoru aniabus prpicietur De*.''

''M,'' said Lady Colveden, ''is a thousand, I remember that—and isn't C a hundred?''

Pencil and paper were fetched. After much calculation, it was triumphantly decided that MCCCCCXXV could be translated into 1525. As to the rest of the inscription, without a dictionary it was impossible to translate it fully, although one or two words did seem familiar to both ladies from their school-days.

''*Hic, haec, hoc*,'' chanted Lady Colveden. ''*This*. I'd no idea I still remembered it.''

''And *op* is probably *opus*—musical, you know,'' murmured Miss Seeton as she scribbled. ''*This work*,'' she announced after a pause, ''something *in the year of Our Lord 1525* . . .''

''Dates from?'' suggested Lady Colveden. ''Belongs to? That long list of names is virtually a pedigree for your box.

Almost as if half the family was . . . well, trying to stake its claim to spite the other half.''

Miss Seeton thought back to the auction: to the Relentless Raconteur's dispiriting tale of the Tweedle Twins, and the Green Plastic Mac, and the ultimate bequest to the Cats' Home. ''I fear,'' she said, ''that you may be right. If, of course,'' she added as common sense prevailed, ''all this is—can be—authentic. But surely it can't?''

''Authentic?'' Lady Colveden was once more examining the heavy parchment with its ornate, impenetrable script and the boxed, beribboned seal at the lower edge. ''I just don't know, Miss Seeton. I somehow find it awfully hard to think this isn't real. It looks far too . . . well made to be just another theatrical prop.''

''As dear Nigel said of the coronet,'' said Miss Seeton.

''And the robe.'' Lady Colveden stroked the crimson velvet with a gentle hand. ''It sounds so fantastic, doesn't it? I mean—that note . . .'' Her ladyship, the wife of a mere baronet, couldn't help sounding impressed as she unfolded the paper again. ''Benedicta Adeline Florence Pottipole, second Duchess of Estover and daughter of Bennet the fourth duke . . . Miss Seeton, you're right. Can we really believe in all this?''

Miss Seeton, after a pause, admitted that, like her friend, she simply had no idea. ''Since the crowning of King George the Third,'' she recalled wistfully.

''A long-lost dukedom—if that's what it is—I've never heard of the family or the title, though I certainly don't claim to know Debrett by heart from cover to cover—but the idea is almost irresistible, isn't it?''

Miss Seeton pulled herself together. ''Which was, perhaps, the intention. To be irresistible, I mean, which one gathers is how confidence tricksters achieve their success. Except that . . .'' She sighed. The romance of more than two centuries appealed to her red plebeian blood just as strongly as ever it could to the Colveden blue. ''Except that if this *is* a—a confidence trick—even a practical joke—it seems to have been remarkably . . . well prepared. To have falsified the documents and the costumes is surely all that most—most reasonable, as it were, charlatans would bother to do. But to take the trouble to inscribe this—this legend inside the lid, where it is far from obvious . . . Considerable care, I would suggest, has been taken with every detail to—to give an appearance of verisimilitude . . .''

"To an otherwise bald and unconvincing narrative?" Lady Colveden smiled. "Oh, I agree. To my inexpert eyes, the whole . . . arrangement looks utterly convincing, with the obviously fake stage props in contrast to what seem to be the genuine things—the coronet, the robe, the marriage lines, the parchment and seal . . . But then any hoaxer worth his or her salt would, wouldn't they? Take proper care. And of course, if it *is* a hoax, who did it?"

"And for what purpose?" A pucker appeared between Miss Seeton's brows. "One finds it hard to imagine why— or, indeed, how—such a scheme, whatever it might be, could have been set in motion—whether two hundred years ago in the Georgian era, or more recently—on the off chance that an ordinary bystander such as myself, making a simple mistake at an auction, should find the chest, and act upon its contents. If such was in fact the intention. Except, of course, that I have as yet no idea how to, so I haven't.''

In this one brief speech, Miss Seeton accidentally contrived to convey the very essence of her singular being. *She found it hard to imagine?* The quality of Miss Seeton's imagination, or lack of it, has been for years a topic more than moot for discussion among those into whose professional ambit she and her umbrella have unwittingly strayed. *An ordinary bystander?* Bystander—of her own choice, and in her own eyes—yes . . . perhaps, if the point is stretched: but ordinary? Imaginations of rather more ordinary quality than Miss Seeton's understandably boggle here. *A simple mistake?* Where Miss Seeton is concerned, mistakes may

well abound, but they—and their aftermaths—are very seldom simple . . .

Lady Colveden allowed nothing to show in her face as
she replied that, though Miss Seeton might have no idea
what to do next, she believed she had one or two sugges-
tions. "The first thing," she enlarged, as Miss Seeton
begged her to continue, "is to find the previous owner of
your box—well, one of the first. Of course it's going to be
an enormous help to have everything translated, papers and
all, but that will take time, and we—you—don't want to
let the trail go cold, do you?" Miss Seeton shook her head.
Lady Colveden smiled. "Candell and Inchpin are only a
quarter of an hour away, so I would suggest a preliminary
trip to Brettenden, and a word with the head clerk or
someone, as soon as you can. The catalogue only has the
basic description, but they'll have the rest in the files, I
should think, though you could sketch it, just in case they
haven't . . ."

Privately her ladyship felt it unlikely the sale-room staff
would need their memories refreshed: one glimpse of the
umbrella should be enough: yet one could never be absolutely sure. "Who entered the box in the auction? Where
did it come from? They might not have owned it, you see—
they could have been acting for friends, or relations. Or
doing it to spite them," she added cheerfully.

"The provenance," said Miss Seeton, who sometimes
surprised herself with the extent of her knowledge—although when one considered the time one was able to spend
reading, since one's retirement, and the many most informative programmes on the television and wireless, it was,
perhaps, not so very surprising after all.

"Fine arts people like Sothenhams insist on goodness
knows how much written information before they'll handle
a piece, I know—almost a pedigree—but I doubt if Candell
and Inchpin are quite so thorough. Or need to be, in many
cases," added her ladyship loyally. Large London establishments couldn't possibly match the intimate, personal

knowledge of their clients—should that be customers?—possessed by local firms, which might be smaller but which had decided advantages.

"Such as," she concluded, "knowing not just who's put up what for sale, but sometimes even why, as well. And if they don't know, they can hazard a good guess. And it doesn't always have to be money—not exactly. There were quite a number of Deceased's Effects that day, weren't there?"

"Some descendant of the Pottipoles," suggested Miss Seeton, "ignorant of his—or her—inheritance, and lacking sufficient curiosity to have the box opened before sending it to be sold . . ."

"His," repeated Lady Colveden thoughtfully, "or hers. You could have hit the nail right on the head, Miss Seeton. Assuming it's *not* a hoax, then from what Benedicta wrote the dukedom can descend through either the male or the female line, which could make it tricky. There's no law, you know, that says wives have to change their surnames when they marry. Nearly all of them do, though it's less likely they will if there's a title or estate in the family that would otherwise be lost—but you can't be sure, even then. They might assume the title and take the husband's surname to keep him happy, as Benedicta seems to have done—but would her descendants necessarily do the same?"

She laughed suddenly, her cheeks turning pink. "Oh, dear—I'm sorry, Miss Seeton. You can tell who's married to a magistrate, can't you?"

"The points you raise," returned Miss Seeton, "are surely pertinent. Which is no more than I would expect, having asked the advice of an expert—"

"Goodness, I'm no genealogist! Nor's George, if it comes to that, though I agree he knows something about the law—but a justice of the peace doesn't deal with peerage claims. They're dealt with by the House of Lords, I think, once the College of Heralds has done the preliminary checking—not that it's come to the Lords yet, and if it does I don't envy them. Imagine how complicated two hundred years of distaff and collateral inheritance would be! But until there's been some preliminary checking in Bretten-den . . .''

Her ladyship paused. She smiled enquiringly at Miss Seeton. Miss Seeton smiled back, though behind the smile her eyes held a hesitant gleam.

Lady Colveden nodded: her earlier instinct had not failed her. The little art teacher, charmed by the romance of the situation in which she found herself—romantic indeed, and for once, in the nature of true romance, how very, very different from many of the situations into which she so frequently stumbled—would prefer to enjoy the excitement of the chase (so to speak) alone, yet felt morally obliged to offer a share in that excitement to those who had rendered her some assistance.

"It all sounds tremendous fun, Miss Seeton—almost like a real-life detective story, or a crossword puzzle. Such a challenge—and so interesting. I'd love," said her ladyship, "to invite myself along to help, if you'd let me, but with so much happening at home—George and Nigel on the rampage, for one thing—unless you desperately need me, if you wouldn't mind, I'm afraid I'll really have to leave you to it for now. Though I'd be fascinated to hear what-ever you manage to find out," she added, as hesitancy gave way to a guilty delight in Miss Seeton's still-smiling eyes. "Candell and Inchpin might tell you whoever-it-is lives miles away, and this is hardly the weather for riding a bike," she said with a speaking look out of the window. "I'm sure I could leave people to their own devices for long enough to give you a lift in the car—or Nigel would, if I had a committee—but that's the second stage." She smiled again. "The first, Miss Seeton, is up to you! Shall you start this afternoon?"

Miss Seeton's glance had followed that of her guest, and she now shook her head. "I don't think so. The bus, as you know, doesn't run today . . . and I would, in any case, be glad of—of one final chance just to—to peep at the contents of the chest." She gave a faint sigh. "Before having to hand them back to their rightful owners. If, that is," she added quickly, "you do not consider this would be too great a—an impertinence on my part. I should not wish to be thought of as—as prying into matters that were none of my concern. Private family papers . . ."

Blushing, she tailed into silence. Lady Colveden blinked then hurried to reassure her. "Miss Seeton! Nobody in their right mind could call you impertinent or prying—and as for the rightful owner, it's you. Didn't you pay for the chest fair and square in open auction? Possession is nine-tenths of the law—just ask George. Or perhaps," she said with another glance at the steady downpour outside, "you'd better not. I wouldn't like to say what sort of mood he's in just now, and you need peace and quiet to enjoy a nice legal argument—but if it will make you any happier about things, I'll be terribly rude and invite myself to a picnic lunch, if I may, and we can look through everything properly. I've been longing," confessed her ladyship with a twinkle, "for a good excuse . . ."

And Miss Seeton, relieved by the encouragement of the magistrate's wife quite as much as by the promise of her presence, twinkled back.

"Everything" proved so intriguing that lunch was followed by tea and biscuits at an hour neither of the ladies could believe she had reached, and which they promptly forgot again as they plunged back into their historical research with the clearing of the cups. Slowly, with frequent recourse to Miss Seeton's lamentably inadequate library of reference books, the two ladies read letters, and checked dates, and studied fashions; and began to guess at something of the history of Benedicta, nee Hedgebote, Duchess of Estover. A runaway match (they guessed, under age) with Actor Pottipole; her family's disapproval, their ostracism of the young couple; Benedicta's early death—

in childbed (Lady Colveden) or from the plague (Miss Seeton); her husband's heart-broken decision to lock away all mementoes of their life together . . . and their descendants' failure, generation upon generation, to realise the importance of these mementoes.

"And if it isn't true," said Lady Colveden happily, "it makes a marvellous story anyway, doesn't it?"

"It does," agreed Miss Seeton with a sigh.

It was Nigel's tactful telephone call, just before supper, that finally woke his mother to the passage of an entire day in the perusal of the Estover inheritance, and brought her leaping to her feet babbling with horror of men in her kitchen, and burned saucepans, and smashed plates, and indigestion remedies.

She drove off in her little blue Hillman with Miss Seeton waving from the lighted window, more than half willing to believe her ladyship's affirmation that she'd had more fun in the past few hours than she would have thought possible. She'd bought things at auction on several occasions and had never made such a fascinating find: she'd be looking out for old oak chests everywhere she went, after today.

"And tomorrow, remember, you must come to supper—Nigel will fetch you—and tell us what happens at Candells. And whether you want either of us to give you a lift to—to wherever you need to go."

Which left Miss Seeton nodding and smiling in her wake, grateful for her good fortune in having such kind and helpful friends. Noblesse, where the Colvedens were concerned, could always be relied on to oblige.

CHAPTER 17

Next morning's customary deluge was easing all too slowly into drizzle as Miss Seeton, with her umbrella over her head and a new pair of galoshes over her outdoor shoes, hurried from the high-street bus stop in the direction of Candell & Inchpin. Spiteful gusts of wind drove still-heavy drops of rain into her face, and whipped the skirts of her waterproof coat about her legs. Miss Seeton tilted her brolly against the most consistent blasts, and made her way along the pavement as best she could with her head down, and her handbag bumping rapidly at her side.

Canvas awnings, snatched from their normal bonds by the storm, slapped repeatedly above shop windows. Passing cars in bottom gear, their headlights on, their wipers brisk, grumbled their way through puddles in the road, splashing unwary cyclists and pedestrians who strayed too close to the kerb. Miss Seeton clicked her tongue, readjusted her umbrella, and trotted on.

At the foot of the sandstone steps, she paused for no more than a moment before mounting. She saw the double doors closed above her, and approved this precaution against the weather: she remembered the weather of the past

few weeks, and shook her head for the ridiculous fancy that
it might never be fine again. Or—was it so ridiculous? Just
now she didn't only feel out of breath, she felt cold and
uncomfortably damp: as was the doorknob, cold and damp
and slippery. Miss Seeton had a struggle to turn it, with the
umbrella over her arm and her handbag determined to wander. She felt rain trickle under the cuff of her mackintosh,
and dribble up her sleeve. She made one last effort, opened
the door, and darted thankfully inside.

She drew a relieved breath and looked about her. There
was not, of course, a sale that day: yet somehow one had
expected more of the routine bustle of a busy establishment
to greet one's ears: doors slamming, telephones ringing,
voices of people moving to and fro. If, that was, they
would, on days when there was no auction. Perhaps they
wouldn't. But in shops there were always shelves to tidy,
stock to check, displays to dust . . . although could—
should—one compare auctioneers to shop assistants?

So tiring, she had always thought. A rewarding job, one
couldn't deny, finding out first what people wanted—which
apparently they often didn't know—and then helping them
to buy it; but so very hard on the feet, having to stand all
day, and the uniform not as flattering as it might be. And
in those large London stores, with their unpredictable central heating and the air-conditioning, in summer, even more
so . . . it was, perhaps, no wonder (concluded Miss Seeton,
with a faint but charitable sigh) that people might be glad
of the chance for a few hours' peace, when the chance was
there . . . except that this was Brettenden, in the depths of
winter, not Oxford Street at midsummer.

Miss Seeton pulled herself together. Having shaken off
the worst of the rain on the mat, she rapped politely with
her umbrella for attention, as she'd so often had cause to
do in her Hampstead days. For the phantom floors of assorted city emporia she substituted the well-worn wooden
boards of a country auction house: boards on which, in
time, she heard the patter of approaching footsteps.

Miss Seeton, still slightly breathless, looked towards the sales assistant—she begged silent pardon, the lady auction-eer—now drawing near. She saw a thin, faded woman of medium height and middle age, with sunken eyes around which dark circles had been drawn, perhaps by lack of sleep; perhaps by worry. Her mouse-brown hair was scraped back in a pleat, emphasising the gaunt bones of her face and the furrows between her black-pencilled brows—furrows that deepened as she came to a halt in front of Miss Seeton.

Before she could speak, Miss Seeton begged her par-don—though she had no idea why—and felt herself blush-ing as the auctioneer then demanded in a hoarse but penetrating voice what on earth she thought she was doing there, and why she had knocked.

"I—that is—oh." Miss Seeton blushed still more: one must remember that, having come to live in the country, one should expect to adapt to country ways. To have rapped in such a—such an imperious way had been . . . rude. It was hardly her place as a newcomer to criticise . . . And she begged a second pardon of the startled auctioneer.

"I'm so sorry, Mrs. Candell. I'm afraid I wasn't think-ing—or rather I was, but of something else. And—"

"I'm not Mrs. Candell." The voice was no longer hoarse, but flat: yet still penetrating.

"Oh!" Miss Seeton's quick eye fell upon the speaker's left hand, with its ring on the third finger. "Oh, how very foolish of me. I mean, Mrs. Inchpin—"

"I'm not Mrs. Inchpin!" This denial was less flat than shrieked in a strange, muted fashion. "My name is Stane-bury. Nothing to do with the family *at all*." The paleness of her face now gave way to a blush rivalling that of Miss Seeton. "I may well have worked in the office since I was a girl, but that's the nearest I've come—and it's not *Mrs.*," she explained as she saw the inevitable mistitle hover upon Miss Seeton's lips. "It's *Miss* Myra Stanebury. And before you ask, my—my mother suggested I should buy this ring"—her fingers knotted themselves together—"at one of our sales—I'm allowed, you know—in case of any *Bother.*"

The last word was spoken with a wealth of white-knuckled emphasis which darkened the rosy hue of Miss Seeton's maiden cheek. Bother of the sort to which Myra so clearly referred had never been a particular problem for Emily Dorothea Seeton. While many of her art college acquaintance, resolved to Enrich their Art by a due broadening of their Experience of Life, had joyfully embraced the wildest tenets of Bohemianism, free thought, and free—the rose crimsoned—love, such embraces (whether in theory or in practice) had failed entirely to attract one whose nature, conventional though it was, found some conventions totally without charm. And with hindsight—not hers, but theirs—perhaps a little unwise, unless one had the good fortune to be a genius. In which case the normal rules need not apply . . . although she had never been able to see why not. And perhaps somewhat weak-minded, as well; and a little foolish, meekly following the fashion when it might be (indeed, in her generation undoubtedly was) against every principle and precept of one's upbringing, and when one would, she felt sure, feel embarrassed for one's weakness, in later life . . .

Miss Seeton shook her head for the folly of her contemporaries. "Fashion," she murmured, "sometimes has much for which to answer, I fear."

Myra gasped, then glowered. "What I choose to call myself has nothing to do with fashion." She uttered that strange, muted shriek once more. "It's a matter of principle!"

Miss Seeton blinked at this unexpected echoing of her thoughts, but rallied swiftly. "And not at all against the law," she said with a nod. Lady Colveden's little lecture on the surname habits of the aristocracy had left its mark. "A matter of custom," said Miss Seeton, all awkwardness now forgotten in her pleasure at the coincidence, "no more.

Unless, of course, there should be something to inherit. And
even then it is not absolutely necessary.'' She smiled. ''One
may take the estate with the money or without—it is entirely up to you . . .'' And then she frowned. Perhaps that
last statement had been inaccurate. Certainly it sounded
rather different from her original recollection. Or so she
now thought: perhaps she had, after all, misunderstood
what she had been told—which in the unusual circumstances of the telling surely came as no surprise . . .

Miss Stanebury seemed surprised, if not startled. The
look she turned upon Miss Seeton was at first wide and
dark, then narrowed into a fixed, quizzical regard. Miss
Seeton's gaze fell to the far less accusing sight of her umbrella handle, hooked about the strap of her bulky leather
bag. She felt herself turn pink again, and she sighed.

''Look,'' said Myra after a pause. ''What are you doing
here?'' She unknotted her hands and stabbed in the air with
one long forefinger. ''And what do you want?''

Miss Seeton responded to the less-than-faint challenge
by clutching with one hand at the familiar leather-twined
crook. Clearing her throat, she began:

''I—I don't know whether you remember me?''

''Should I?'' That flattened tone again.

Miss Seeton's glance drifted back down to the umbrella
which had begun what she couldn't help but see as her little
adventure. ''At last week's auction. I—I bought an old
wooden chest.'' She looked up. ''It was padlocked, and
with iron bands, and—and most delightfully carved.''

''I—we—can't help you.'' Myra seemed to be making
an effort to keep her voice level. ''I work in the office, not
the sale-room, but I can tell you we take nothing back once
it's bought, whenever it was, if that's what you're asking.''
Miss Seeton, confused by the unexpected turn of the conversation, shifted uneasily from one foot to the other. ''And
if you're thinking to put it in for this week . . . we'll
want . . . the usual commission.'' She paused. Miss Seeton,

hesitating over the best way to explain, said nothing. "Well, do you?"

In her turn, Miss Seeton stared. Did she? "Thank you, I have no need," she replied, "for any money." Myra's ill-disguised gasp made her add hastily, "No more than anyone else, that is. Quite possibly less, since my life is very quiet now that I have retired."

"Then what," demanded Myra, "do you want?"

The demand was so indignant that Miss Seeton's response came almost without thinking. "To find out where things in auctions come from. How one puts them in, that is, and how to find out who owns them—or rather," she added, recalling Lady Colveden's words on possession and the law, "used to own them." Myra uttered one of her queer little shrieks as indignation seemed to give way to exasperation. "The—the provenance," Miss Seeton concluded hurriedly, yet with a hint of doubt. Was this a correct application of the term? Should she have used another, such as pedigree?

Myra turned white. Her black brows, and the dark rings about her eyes, were the only colour in her face as she drew a deep breath and spoke in a shaking voice through pale lips. "If you're suggesting that the provenance of anything we sell here is doubtful—if you're trying to say we—we handle stolen goods—then you're wrong. We don't. Candell and Inchpin's honest as the day, and always has been—and there has never a complaint been raised against the firm in over two hundred years!"

Miss Seeton, still confused, gave a little start at her mention of those critical two centuries that had posed the original problem. Myra observed this reaction, glared any attempt at speech into silence, and rushed hoarsely on:

"If things aren't bad enough already, having the—the police around asking their horrible questions—messing up my files even more than he did, whoever he was—poking and prying—and that boy—no better than he should be, I don't doubt, he and his girlfriend—dead as mutton on the back doorstep, and now you—you . . .''

And Myra burst into tears, above the noise of which Miss Seeton's shocked exclamation passed completely unheard.

But not for long. As tears gave way—to Miss Seeton's horror—to hysterics, there was a movement at the end of the corridor, and a figure appeared around a corner. Quick eyes took in the scene; quick footsteps heralded the arrival of that young Candell who had done door duty on the day of the auction. To the great relief of Miss Seeton, he took Myra firmly by the arm and shook her. When she failed to respond, he administered the sharp but gentle slap Miss Seeton—for all her teaching experience—had herself been hesitant to deliver to this overwrought stranger.

Additional feet, hurrying from different parts of the building, converged upon the now-sobbing Myra, the remorseful Miss Seeton, and the young man with the difficult task of trying to soothe two distracted ladies at one and the same time. Matters were soon cleared up. Still sobbing, Myra was led away for tea and sympathy. Miss Seeton, apologising profusely for whatever it was she had said that had so upset poor Miss Stanebury, learned from the Senior Partner himself that she had, in fact, said nothing—or, if she had, it had been (he must suppose) by accident. She had not (he ventured) heard of the recent tragedy on the premises of Candell and Inchpin? He had thought as much.

Mr. Candell expressed no surprise that the Brettenden grapevine—as notorious for the wide spread of its branches as that of Plummergen—had left his visitor apparently unaware of the events of the night before last. Anyone who rose to the heights of a senior partnership, family firm or not, could keep his post in the current business climate only by knowing when to speak out and when to shut up. He might privately suspect this little old lady of being a sensation-seeking snoop, breaking into a closed building on the chance of some gossipy titbit to score over her neighbours—but he wasn't going to say so. And when, having heard her ostensible purpose in questioning his employees, he replied, he was courtesy itself—even though courtesy was tinged with a certain malicious glee as he said:

"I'm sorry, Miss Seeton, I don't think we can help you. The police haven't quite finished their investigations yet, you see. They haven't just sealed our back yard—most inconvenient—but," he added hurriedly, "it's a shocking business, of course. Perfectly understandable . . . only they've sealed the office, too. Why, they won't let Miss Stanebury across the threshold to tidy things up, and that filing system is her pride and joy. You could see she was a bit upset about it all, couldn't you? Yes, I thought you could. Understandable, as I said—but there it is, and there's nothing to be done about it. All I remember of the sale in which you say"—he added the very slightest emphasis on his last word—"you're interested is that we had half a dozen house clearances go through that day—deceased's effects, they're called in the trade. And then, of course, we don't put confidential information like who it was in the catalogue for anyone to know there's a house empty—encouraging burglars and squatters and so on. I'm sure you can see that, can't you?"

"Oh, indeed I can," Miss Seeton said, gathering up her belongings and preparing to retreat. "One may regret, but sadly one cannot deny, that there is bound to be a degree of temptation to—to certain weaker members of the delinquent classes . . ."

"Juvenile delinquents? Have a heart, sir." In an office on the umpteenth floor of New Scotland Yard, Detective Chief Superintendent Delphick stared in disbelief at Sir Hubert Everleigh, Assistant Commissioner (Crime), superior officer to the Oracle's own superior, and as a person of such rank not normally given to the pulling of people's legs. "You don't seriously suggest that this—this internecine strife the capital's underclass is currently undergoing is due to no more than a rush of over-enthusiastic post-festive-season youthful high spirits?"

"As a matter of fact, I'm not." Sir Heavily's tone was dry as he regarded his junior colleague with a steady gaze. "We may be fairly confident, however, that such will be the opinion of the assorted headshrinkers and trick cyclists the defence puts forward once—or, alas, if—the perpetrators are brought to trial."

Delphick, after a moment's further pause, accepted his superior's remarks in the spirit of kindly warning in which they had been intended. Social workers (he opined with some vehemence) had a lamentable—to police eyes—habit of perpetually pleading broken homes and disadvantaged backgrounds when the poor, misguided, misunderstood villains of their professional acquaintance hit harmless bank clerks over the head, or broke into jewellers' shops and terrorised young females, or mugged old men in back alleyways for sixpence ha'penny and a wristwatch, if they were lucky.

Sir Heavily's brows rose in pained surprise. "Arthur Chishall, if memory serves, is—that is, was—by several years my junior. Yes," he said as Delphick nodded, "I thought my—ahem—increasing age had not as yet affected my powers of recollection—and I would advise you, Chief Superintendent, that any plans you may have to succeed me—"

"Perish the thought, sir!"

"—should be set in abeyance for some time to come." Sir Hubert contrived to disregard the interpolation with rather more than his usual urbanity. "Neither I, Delphick, nor my masters, consider that I am approaching even the foothills, as it were, of my dotage. And I trust that this opinion is one with which you would not disagree?"

"No, sir—I mean, yes." The Oracle sighed. "I wouldn't have said that Artie was exactly doting, either; but a clump on the head from something heavy, applied with force, would finish off someone twice his size and—ahem—half his age. And Artie was merely a—a random example. He's by no means the only one, remember.''

The Everleigh eyebrows arched still higher. ''These continuing slurs upon my mnemonic powers are quite unnecessary, Chief Superintendent. I have not forgotten that Chishall is, according to your report—which I must assume to have been both accurate and thorough—''

''Sir, this *slur* upon my professional competence—''

''—that Chishall is, or I should say was, the only member of the fraternity whose, ah, presence is, ah, forever lost to us.''

Delphick abandoned his protest and sobered completely. ''So far, sir. At least, the only one we know of—but he's by no means the only one to have suffered some form of attack. Most of which have been pretty unpleasant, to put it mildly. Razors, knives, bicycle chains . . .''

''Spare me the repeated details, Delphick. One reading of your report was enough. I am fully aware that there are some particularly unsavoury activities being prosecuted with considerable vigour among the criminal classes—a vigour that has dramatically intensified since Cutler's departure from Pentonwood Scrubs. I do not forget that Chishall was, at one time, a trusted informant—within the limitations of this phrase—to Cutler. And also,'' he added before Delphick could remind him, ''to Rickling, at the same time—''

''And before it,'' supplied the Oracle. ''Likewise, afterwards. The man had the morals of a slug. Plus the tight-rope skills of Monsieur Blondin, who achieved four crossings of Niagara Falls in safety—''

''Delphick, one more impudent insinuation about my fading memory, and—''

''—but who wisely quit while he was ahead,'' proclaimed the Oracle, as deaf to the protests of his chief as ever Sir Hubert had been to his own. ''A fifth crossing was beyond the bold monsieur. Now, Chishall was not so much bold as foolhardy: and one would rather call him cunning than wise. If it is known even to the police that he turned his coat on four separate occasions . . .

"Then I think we should consider the proposition that he made a fifth attempt—and his luck, at last, ran out."

Really, one had to agree that Sir George and dear Nigel had some cause for complaint. The hours during the past two or three weeks when it had *not* been raining must by now number very, very few. It came as no great surprise that farmers everywhere sounded, when one heard them interviewed on the television, or the wireless—there was that most interesting and informative programme, *Farming Today,* of which one sometimes caught snatches before breakfast . . . it was no wonder that they were so gloomy. As gloomy, in fact—a faint chuckle escaped Miss Seeton as she wrought with button and strap—as the weather . . .

"Miss Seeton! Whatever are you doing here?"

Miss Seeton, putting up her umbrella before descending the front steps of Candell & Inchpin, was quite as startled by this situation as the speaker—from his tone—had evidently been startled by her presence.

"Why, Mr. Foxon, what a pleasant surprise." Miss Seeton halted in mid-unfurl to stare, then to beam, at the young man who came bounding up the steps towards her. "And would you think it too late," she went on as he reached her, "for me to wish you—as this is the first time we have met since Christmas—a happy new year?''

''Well, thanks, MissEss. And the same to you, of course—though it's not so much happy as *soggy,* wouldn't you say? I reckon it's the super's fault, giving you that brolly for Christmas—even if you haven't got it with you today.''

Miss Seeton smiled and murmured that it had seemed a shame, when the weather promised to be so damp, to make too much use of Mr. Brinton's generous present all at once, when she had, as Mr. Foxon knew, several others.

''That's how I guessed it was you.'' Foxon nodded down the steps to the street from which he had erupted. ''Though I shouldn't really have been all that surprised to see you, even if old Brimstone—the super—never said he was going to ask you—but you should've let me know. Checking statements or not, I'd've been happy to fetch you in the car, and I know nobody else did because they'd've told me. I bet you didn't like to cause any bother and came by bus, didn't you? I can't believe you rode your bike. But on a day like this, you could end up with pneumonia if you aren't careful.''

''It's very kind of you to be concerned, Mr. Foxon, but I assure you there's no need. The bus service is generally most reliable, as it was today. And if I had entertained any serious doubts about the weather, dear Lady Colveden would have brought me, had I asked, though normally one does hate to impose. But she and Nigel have expressed almost as keen an interest in the outcome as my own—and, now you mention it, it is of course only natural for Mr. Brinton to be quite as interested, since he was present at the time.''

Foxon goggled. ''Old Brimstone? Come off it, Miss Seeton—with all due respect. While I'll agree with you he's got a temper, and might just bash someone a bit too hard if things got out of hand, you'll never make me believe he's a—a closet burglar. He's too fond of his creature comforts, and prowling around in the middle of the night in the pouring rain, when he could be tucked up nice and warm in bed, wouldn't be his scene at all, believe me.''

It was Miss Seeton's turn to goggle: which she did with ladylike restraint. ''I cannot imagine—if you will pardon my taking issue with you, Mr. Foxon—that Mr. Brinton would ever—*could* ever—strike anyone . . .''

Foxon recalled various high-velocity peppermints, hurled in the heat of the moment, but said nothing. He gulped once or twice, however, and felt himself turning red.

''And as for his being a—a burglar . . .'' Miss Seeton favoured her scarlet-faced young friend with an anxious, appraising stare. ''It has, of course, been a decidedly wet few weeks, and even when there was no rain, the sun was more often than not obscured by clouds. Nevertheless,'' she said as Foxon returned her puzzled stare with a look of slowly dawning comprehension, ''are you sure, Mr. Foxon, that you are feeling entirely yourself today?''

''Apart from being incredibly short of sleep, I'm fine, thanks for asking.'' He grinned at her in the way she knew so well. ''And don't worry, the super isn't suffering from sunstroke, either. That was just my little joke.''

Miss Seeton, whose sense of humour was as restrained as herself, smiled politely, but with a doubtful air that made Foxon feel guilty for having confused her.

''Oh, don't mind me. Put it down to overwork,'' he said apologetically. ''The pair of us—the whole team, come to that—are rushed off our feet right now, you know—well, of course you do. I don't suppose,'' he enquired, lowering his voice as he spoke, ''you've had any ideas yet, have you? If you could give me even a slight hint, I'd be awfully grateful. Might even come up with a brolly of my own when it was your birthday. I like my eight hours,'' he said in heartfelt tones, ''as much as the super does, and until this is sorted out there won't be too many of us getting 'em. Take pity on a weary copper, Miss Seeton! Spill the beans—I mean, let's have a quick look at your sketchpad. Please?''

"My sketchpad? I didn't bring it with me, after all."
Miss Seeton sighed. "The one or two I attempted didn't, I
feel, do it proper justice. But I have the catalogue in my
bag . . ." Her eye gauged the strength of the rain-lashing
wind as it eddied about the corners and crannies of the old
brick building. "Perhaps we should move back inside, to
more adequate shelter . . . with, of course, the full written
description. It all happened so"—here she blushed—"so
quickly that Mr. Brinton really had very little chance to pay
the close attention he would no doubt have wished."

Foxon goggled again. What bee was it she'd got in her
bonnet (and what a bonnet—even at such a moment, he
had to grin at the sight of that godawful hat) about Old
Brimmers being on the spot the night Terry Mimms was
murdered? Talk about a one-track mind. Talk about her
thinking *he'd* got sunstroke—he'd the nastiest suspicion the
boot must be on the other foot.

Or maybe it was visiting the scene of the crime that'd
done it. The body wasn't still there, of course, and things
were chugging slowly back to normal: but they all tended
to forget she wasn't getting any younger, and there'd be
bound to come a time when she cracked up: so, maybe it
had finally come. Brinton had pushed her too far, for once,
and her subconscious had guessed it was coming and made
her leave her sketchpad at home, so she'd tried to put it
down in words instead—never anyone more conscientious
than MissEss—and she was offering him the written description as the best she could do, poor old girl, and looking
guilty as hell about having let everyone down, because normally they didn't come much more conscientious than Miss
Emily Seeton . . .

Miss Seeton, politely waiting for Detective Constable
Foxon to endorse her proposal (one could hardly, of course,
insist on his seeking shelter—but how fortunate that the
squall appeared to have died down) was suddenly dis-
mayed. How foolish of her not to have realised before! Mr.
Foxon must be in Brettenden on official business. Here she

was, wasting his time in idle chatter—

Or was it indeed so idle? Had he not been asking about her recent sketches and speaking of Mr. Brinton's interest? Had word somehow reached the Estovers that their long-lost heirlooms had turned up at an auction in a small country town and had been sold to one of whose name they were as yet unaware? Candell & Inchpin, she knew, maintained the strictest professional etiquette and would reveal nothing of the private details of their clients—not even, it seemed, in response to a ducal enquiry. To whom should the frustrated nobility turn in matters of confidentiality but the police? Mr. Foxon was an experienced detective: he might reasonably be expected to learn more, enquiring in person, than even a duke or duchess over (one assumed) the telephone, or by letter. Superintendent Brinton had sent Mr. Foxon to Brettenden to—Miss Seeton gasped and turned pale at the realisation—to detect *herself*!

With her eyes suddenly bright, she fumbled at the catch of her handbag, reaching for the Candells catalogue. There was a snatch; a cry; and a clatter, as the forgotten umbrella slipped from her grasp to the ground.

"Whoops!" He'd been right—it'd got to her at last, poor old girl. Too upset to know what she was doing. "Let me, MissEss—no, don't worry." Though a fat lot of use it was, saying that . . .

Watched by a now blushing Miss Seeton, Foxon bolted down the steps in pursuit of the wayward brolly: which, bouncing on its ferrule, had begun a swift somersault descent to the street instead of rolling to a bumpy halt at the brink, arrested by the handle—

Arrested. Miss Seeton quailed at the very idea. Surely not. Lady Colveden had assured her—

But then she was only the wife of a magistrate, not the magistrate himself—

But she had bought it in good faith, even if the circumstances had been—

"Mr. Foxon!" Miss Seeton's voice quivered as the

young detective, grinning in triumph, came loping up the steps to present her with his trophy. "It really was—thank you so much—an accident. Do please believe me"—her tone was almost pleading—"when I tell you I had absolutely no intention—as you will see, if you will only look at this"—she handed him, in belated exchange, the catalogue—"which is not marked, as I understand people do when they intend . . . and in any case, we were looking for a barometer. And perhaps a fireside chair as well. For his birthday, or a late Christmas present. Surely if you explain to Mr. Brinton—ask him to tell them—that is, surely one cannot be—be prosecuted, over what was a genuine mistake?"

Foxon, slow-witted from sleeplessness and baffled by the intensity of this remarkable plea, gazed wildly about him for inspiration. His gaze fell upon the umbrella he had so recently retrieved, which its owner now clutched in a trembling hand. Jumpy as a kitten: and no wonder, in the circs. Well, pushed for time he might be, but cheering her up with a quick joke wouldn't hurt.

"I suppose," he offered, "we could always do you for Litter, Miss Seeton—I mean we could've, if I hadn't picked it up—but it's far more likely to be Lost Property, and we don't charge for that. Which means you're in the clear." He took pity on her perplexed expression. "So why don't you just *clear* off home?"

He didn't wait for her to smile: any fool could see she was too upset for that. He hurried on, "You'll feel a hell of a lot better when you're back in Plummergen—and never mind Old Brimstone, I'll tell him all about it." *And* bend his ear—as far as a humble plainclothes sprog would dare bend anything belonging to a super—about putting pressure on old ladies who weren't up to it any longer, and deserved a bit of consideration after all they'd done for the force over the years. "I'm sorry I can't offer you a lift myself, but you can imagine I'm still a bit tied up, with sorting out the leftovers of you-know-what in there." And he jerked his head with a wink towards the auction house door.

"But never mind that," he reiterated hastily as she turned pale again. *Fool* was the word, all right! Opening his big mouth and plonking both his great flat feet inside, reminding her of what he'd just been telling her she'd no need to think about any more—overworked or not, he ought to kick himself.

He didn't, though: too dangerous, on top of these rain-slippy steps. He biffed himself reproachfully over the head with the absent-minded paper cylinder he'd made by rolling up the catalogue . . .

The catalogue. He unrolled it. Why had she supposed Old Brimmers'd want to see—he peered at the date—last week's sale listing? He frowned. Last week. Wasn't that when the super'd sneaked off to buy an apology for his wife, and had come back late with nothing to show for his pains but a brooding silence for the rest of the afternoon? Did . . . something, but he couldn't imagine what, happen there? Might this catalogue hold some clue to the death of Terry Mimms; to the burglary that had preceded it?

"Come on, Miss Seeton, don't be a tease." He lowered his voice and held out the catalogue with a conspiratorial gesture. "I promise I won't let on," he whispered. "But if you could just give me a hint, then I'll tell the super, and no bones broken. And I bet you'd rather I kept your name out of it, wouldn't you?"

"Oh, Mr. Foxon!" Miss Seeton was immeasurably cheered by this kindly offer. "Oh, if only you could, I would be so grateful—unless, of course, it happens that by doing so you will yourself get into trouble. I should feel—"

"Trouble?" And just when she'd been starting to relax. Keep her happy: pile it on thick. "Trouble? Not me. I'll be the super's blue-eyed boy, honest." Miss Seeton was somewhat puzzled by his air of certainty, but as he caught her wondering look he smiled, nodded, put a finger to his lips, and winked.

Miss Seeton, allowing herself to be reassured, smiled back at him, accepted the catalogue, and turned quickly to the relevant page.

"It's this one," she said, pointing. "The carved oak chest. The written description, of course, doesn't include the words on the inside of the lid, or the contents, because it was locked." She regarded him wistfully. "If you are quite, quite sure, Mr. Foxon, that Mr. Brinton—that nobody—will wish to speak to me . . ."

Dumbly Foxon nodded. Miss Seeton ventured a smile.

"I had, you know, planned to go along to the library after coming here. It was Lady Colveden's suggestion," she added as he looked surprised. "Neither of us felt it appropriate to ask the dear vicar for his assistance."

Foxon blinked. Was she turning in desperation to the church? Were the years of strain making her hanker after the peace and quiet of a convent? Sister Emily of—despite himself, he grinned—the Sketchpad, perhaps?

Miss Seeton smiled back, though her voice at first was grave. "A dreadful cold, you know, like poor Martha, though she is almost better, thank goodness—but in the vicar's case they have a tendency to go to his chest. There can be little fear of pneumonia—Miss Treeves takes excellent care of her brother, and should there be the least anxiety she would, I know, ask Dr. Knight to call—but the last thing anyone who is at all under the weather wants is a—an intellectual problem, no matter how intriguing. Whether or not it turned to bronchitis. With being locked, you see, for so long, and the inside naturally not visible from outside." Foxon had stopped smiling some moments before. Miss Seeton, drifting away on a tide of historical intelligence, continued to smile vaguely at him.

"Much longer, of course, since the break from Rome, even if they did, I believe, continue to use it for some years afterwards—William Tyndale, you will recall, was during

Henry's lifetime—though Mary's subsequent return to Catholicism was of comparatively short duration. King James the Second, as far as I remember, didn't impose his religion upon his subjects at all—but it is certainly not used in Anglican services today, although he is sure to have a certain basic knowledge. Unless they are extremely high. Even if he didn't, as Lady Colveden said, have a temperature. We thought the library would be the best place to find a dictionary, you see."

No, he damned well didn't: not unless she was saying that *he* needed a dictionary. The way he was feeling right now—his tired brain turned to cotton wool, his ears obviously out of focus—he wouldn't argue with her. From where he stood, for the last ten minutes or so MissEss had been talking gibberish: she'd made even less sense than usual, which for her was quite an achievement. The one thing he'd got out of it—he thought—was that *she* thought the Mimms murder was something to do with some wooden chest sold by Candell & Inchpin in last week's auction . . .

He thought. He was willing to admit he could be wrong: who was he to interpret MissEss once she got going? With him being only a humble detective constable . . .

He'd play it clever. He'd remember his rank, and keep his place, and hold his tongue about whatever-it-was . . .

He'd leave everything for Superintendent Brinton to sort out.

CHAPTER 19

Miss Seeton was the last to alight from the bus. Of the many Plummergen ladies who had taken advantage of the modest break in the weather to indulge in a trip to Brettenden, she was the only one not to hurry, laden with bags and bundles as they all were, straight from the bus stop into the post office. The most territorially-minded shopper could not claim that local emporia provided for every possible want, a sentiment with which the proprietors of these emporia never argued. Instead, they cheered (in silence) the invariable incursion, once the returning bus had disgorged its passengers, into their emporia of said passengers, each ostensibly bent upon acquiring such items as had, once examined by the light of a Brettenden day, failed to meet the exacting standards of a Plummergen eye. That such incursions rendered the exchange of gossip gleaned during the Brettenden trip much easier—and cheaper—than a telephone call from home was, of course, mere coincidence.

But it was raining again: not hard, yet enough to make Miss Seeton's thoughts—which had never, in any case, been directed towards gossip—turn to slippers, and tea, and fireside toast, thickly buttered. She adjusted her handbag—

so much more awkward than before, with the Latin dictionary and her other library books—and smiled to herself as she opened her umbrella. The fire, she knew, would not be as she had left it. Despite all her protests that she was quite as capable as Martha of arranging coals, kindling, and crumpled paper in their correct order in the sitting room grate, Mrs. Bloomer, domestic paragon, remained convinced that she was not. Miss Emily (Martha was wont, with some eloquence, to insist) needed Taking Care Of. Miss Emily couldn't cook as well as Martha (Miss Seeton acknowledged the truth of this: few could); Miss Emily didn't have the same knack with a duster or a mop; Miss Emily—

"Miss Emily. Miss Emily!"

Miss Seeton—her inner vision focused on brass-handled forks and strawberry jam, her outer vision limited by the spread of her umbrella, her ears filled with the patter of raindrops and the splash of her puddle-skipping feet—did not, at first, hear the breathless call from the female form hurrying towards her up The Street.

"Miss Emily!!"

Miss Seeton became suddenly aware that Martha Bloomer—in a plastic rain hood, a lurid mackintosh, and gumboots she could only, from their size, have borrowed from Stan—was blocking her path. "Oh, Miss Emily—I'm glad I've caught you. The bus got in a bit earlier than I expected . . ."

Martha paused to inhale. Yoga might do wonders for her employer, but for herself she got enough exercise in the normal way, thank you, running around clearing up after folk who couldn't, never mind what they said, clear up nearly so well as others. Just because they could tie themselves in knots on the floor as the fancy took them, and she couldn't, didn't mean she couldn't run up The Street from her cottage to the bus stop, if the weather was fine—which it wasn't—and if she didn't have the remains of a cold . . .

"Martha?" Miss Seeton peered through the rain and the

uncurtained light from nearby windows at the panting paragon of domesticity on the pavement before her. "Why, Martha, is anything wrong?"

Martha emitted one final wheeze, shook herself, and nodded. "There's no way to make it easy, dear—but we've had burglars, of all things! Well, one, anyhow," she amended as Miss Seeton gave a little cry of alarm. "Tough-looking little beggar he was, too—not as that's got anything to do with what you're asking, of course, but yes, there's something wrong, because if breaking and entering's not wrong, then I don't know what is, dear. And you won't tell me otherwise, Miss Seeton!"

"Why, I wouldn't dream of it." Miss Seeton truly had no idea of how her perennial attempts to see the best in everyone often drove more pessimistic persons to distraction. "Burglars? This is shocking news, and I'm so sorry. I hope they didn't take too much, or"—she sighed—"do too much damage. And anyone would agree that they—or, as you said, he—had done wrong . . . But you're naturally upset, Martha dear. And what does Stan have to say?"

"Nothing repeatable," replied Martha, almost forgetting her troubles to grin, then sobering quickly to explain in full. "I'm sorry, Miss Emily, I didn't make myself clear as it was your cottage he broke into, not ours. What've we got that's worth pinching? But you, with all them lovely things left you by Mrs. Bannet, not to mention— Now, dear," she said as Miss Seeton uttered another little cry, "there's no need to take on, because aren't I telling you I stopped him in his tracks before he did hardly more than poke his ugly head through the door?"

"Oh. I'm so sorry—are you?" Miss Seeton decided surprise must have made her miss that part; but she had no time to enquire further as Martha, having broken the bad news, gathered up her employer and began to escort her homewards down The Street, huddling under the shared umbrella partly for shelter, and partly for reassurance as she continued:

"On my hands and knees, I was, when it happened, doing the hearth. A shocking mess it's got into, these last few days, and you know how those red tiles can come up lovely if only you give them a *proper* rub. And there was this new polish I'd seen in the shop I thought I'd give a try. Only I was late getting started, because that Tibs was in the front garden. I had to chase her out before Stan saw her—*you* know, Miss Emily."

Miss Seeton nodded: she did. Everyone did. Tibs, the tabby from the police house, was the most infamous feline for miles. Rumour had it she was afraid of no creature smaller than an elephant, and would eat, fight, or forcibly mate with any creature smaller than a tiger. When Tibs was on the prowl, Plummergen dogs skulked in their kennels, and superstitious villagers made signs against the evil eye, for she was popularly suspected of shape-changing at the full moon. Villagers who were not superstitious were rather more energetic with their sign language as they ejected the Cyprian marauder from shrubberies, flower beds, and vegetable patches. Martha wasn't superstitious, she insisted—not really—but then she didn't want her hands scratched . . .

"So I got rid of her in the end with the broom. Digging great holes to bury her mice as bad as a dog, or worse—and having to fill them in again before Stan found out—so when the bell goes, I get all tangled up in my apron strings as came undone where I knelt on them by accident, not properly fastened on account of that wretched cat and being in such a rush. And by the time I get myself sorted out and to the door, he's gone—though I must say he give it a good, long ring." Martha paused: for emphasis, Miss Seeton supposed, or perhaps the aftermath of her cold. It did not occur to her that her loyal henchwoman, accustomed as she was to detailed and tortuous narratives, didn't generally deliver them while trotting in the dark through the rain.

Mrs. Bloomer recovered herself and plunged on with her story. "Must be important, I thought, so whoever it was is bound to call again, or phone, or pop a note through the door. I didn't bother looking outside because I wanted to get back to the hearth to have it done and the fire laid proper''—even now, Martha couldn't resist that little dig— ''before you came back, and so I was on my hands and knees, dear, like I said, when I thought I heard a noise outside, round the back. Only with the rain, and the weather, and that cat, I wasn't going to get up again in a hurry, and of course that'll be when he must've looked through the window and thought the place was empty. And there was this funny sort of scratching, and a rattle, and suddenly there he was, bold as brass, opening the door of the sitting room and me on my hands and knees in front of the fire.''

The enormity of what had happened was taking a long time to sink in. Miss Seeton responded on automatic pilot with a faint ''Good gracious, Martha, you must have had a shock.''

''Not half as much of a shock as him.'' Martha—who, as the pace of her narrative increased, had perforce slowed the pace of her walking to save her breath—now quickened her steps again as the climax (and, coincidentally, the cottage) came in sight. ''I yelled at him what did he think he was doing, and he jumped back pretty smartish, I can tell you.'' Martha clutched Miss Seeton's arm in the agitation of reliving her exploits. ''I grabbed the poker and was up from my knees in a second,'' she said proudly. ''Chased him right out of the house and down the path—but then,'' she said with a sigh, ''I lost him. Had his car parked just outside the bakery, jumped in, and was off up The Street without switching on his lights—I never even got his number. I'm sorry, dear, I really am, but with the sun down by then, and The Street not lit, I just couldn't, though I did my best.''

''You did more than enough,'' said Miss Seeton, her voice unsteady—and not from the speed of her walking. ''Oh, Martha, suppose you had been hurt? I would have

felt so very much to blame, for no amount of—of sentimental attachment to one's belongings," said Miss Seeton
firmly, "can equal the kindness of one's friends. I would
always have had my memories, Martha dear, no matter
what he had taken, and—"

"Now, don't you fret, he didn't take nothing." Martha's
clutch tightened as she shook her employer's arm. Drops
of rain splattered from the umbrella to the ground about
their feet. "I could see that much, for all he turned tail and
ran—not unless it was small enough to fit in his pockets,
which I've had a quick look and I can't say I noticed anything's gone. Mind you, Ned Potter says you'd best check
round for yourself, so's to know—"

"Constable Potter?" Miss Seeton halted in her tracks,
disturbed more by this final intelligence than she'd seemed
to be by all that had gone before. "Oh, dear. Martha, I'm
sure—indeed, I know—that you acted from the very best
of motives, and I am most grateful—but when the police
are always so busy with important matters, and as you say
he stole nothing—"

"Nothing *I* could tell, dear. But two heads are better than
one. And me and Stan, we were very fond of old Mrs.
Bannet," returned Martha mysteriously.

Miss Seeton's eyes pricked with sudden tears. "I know,
Martha dear. So was I." She sighed. "If one views this—
this escapade in the light of a—of an affront to her memory—exaggerated though this may sound when, on
reflection, I cannot help but think of it as a—as a prank,
which went wrong: a case of mistaken identity, perhaps,
and although rather *foolish,* not, I feel sure, malicious . . . but if Mr. Potter believes it to be necessary, then
naturally I will do as he suggests. He is, after all, more
expert in these matters than myself."

He was also (though unknown to Miss Seeton) a young
man with a healthy sense of self-preservation. During the
first foray into the Plummergen affairs of Miss Emily Dorothea Seeton, her adopted community had become in-

volved in drugs-related murder and attempted murder, a vicious drowning, various car crashes, gassing, shooting, abduction (of Miss Seeton, by a youth with ginger hair), and embezzlement (of client funds, by a solicitor with a booming voice). After the little art teacher's second, equally irregular irruption into local life, Superintendent Brinton had, in desperation, drawn up his Standing Orders. With these, PC Potter—on pain of dismemberment, demotion, and (the ultimate deterrent) Traffic Duty—had strict instructions that he must at all times comply. If anything— *anything*—untoward relating, however remotely, to Miss Seeton, should occur at any time within a five-mile radius of her person—or, in her absence, her cottage—such occurrence must be reported at once and without fail to Potter's Ashford superior: even if (a rider Old Brimstone had added in a spirit of desperate self-sacrifice) it occurred in the middle of the night, or on the superintendent's day off.

PC Potter was not only blessed with a strong sense of self-preservation: he was blessed with a happy marriage to wife Mabel, and with daughter Amelia as happily settled at the village school. He was, in short, contented with things as they were: he had no wish for change. Neither had he any wish to put ideas into the head of Superintendent Brinton, whether about his competence (and consequent fitness for promotion) or lack of it (with subsequent risk of demotion to traffic wardenhood). For the past seven years, PC Potter had walked a narrow tightrope in his dealings with Ashford headquarters, and knew to a nicety which untoward occurrences he should report to his apoplectic superior, and which might safely be ignored.

"Burglars," groaned Brinton, over a snatched cup of tea in his paper-piled office. "Why did it have to happen now? Come to that, why tell us at all? Doesn't the idiot realise we've enough on our plate with two murders to solve, and no idea where the hell either case is going, to start chasing burglars?" He drew a deep breath, gulped a mouthful of tea, and glared at Foxon as if that young man were personally to blame for his Plummergen colleague's behaviour. He sighed. "Sometimes, laddie, I wish Miss Seeton had stayed in Hampstead and given the lads on Parliament Hill something to take their minds off cruising homos, or people walking mad dogs, or idiots flying kites too close to the air lanes—and if I didn't know Potter better, I'd think he was trying to take the Michael. Especially as the blighter got away without a sausage, by all accounts."

Foxon closed the file on the Quendon killing, hesitated, and pushed it aside without a word. This uncharacteristic taciturnity went, for once, unremarked by Brinton, who was so full of his own misfortunes he failed to notice his generally ebullient junior's current low score on the irritant scale.

Foxon was too busy pondering a moral dilemma to play his usual part as the super's mentally stimulating sidekick. As he drew the Mimms update towards him, he hesitated again. Hadn't he promised? But then MissEss couldn't—could she?—expect him to keep quiet when they'd started trying to steal the vital evidence of her sketchbook from under the very noses of the force. He'd done his best to keep his word—suggested to Brinton it could be worth checking on who'd sold what, and who'd bought it, in the records the Candell burglar had made such a mess with, as if he'd been looking for something and had chucked the lot on the ground when he couldn't find it . . . He'd asked if Brinton didn't think, sealed or not, the sooner the auctioneers got their files in order, the better; and Brinton had said he couldn't agree more, but the whole affair seemed to have sent the one woman who understood the system into hysterics, and until she was in a mood to get back to work, there wasn't much they could do, so they'd have to rely on good old-fashioned detection the way they always did.

"Miss S. was in a funny mood this afternoon, all right." Leave it to fate: if Brinton took S for Stanebury, that was Foxon's mind made up, he'd hold his tongue, and suggest some other course of action once he'd thought of it. But if the old man took it he'd been referring to Miss Seeton . . .

"Funny mood." Brinton repeated the words in a hollow tone. "Funny mood?" He started, set down his mug—some of the tea splashed over the top—on his blotter, sat up, and glared across the room. "Foxon! I ought to bust you back to uniform, you—you—insubordinate—insubordinate . . ." Struggling for a suitable epithet, he turned an interesting shade of purple. Foxon jumped from his seat in alarm.

Brinton gave up the struggle as the young man drew near. "You've been sneaking off to Plummergen without telling me," he roared, "when you were damned well meant to be checking statements at Candells—and you've been fobbing me off with some tom-fool excuse about getting them typed up properly! You—you've known all along about this blasted burglary, you—you—"

"Steady on, sir. I can explain—please, sir, put that paperweight down—I *am* waiting for the typists, and—hey!" Foxon sounded genuinely aggrieved as the missile missed his head by half an inch, crashed against the far wall, and fell with a horrid thump to the ground.

There followed a thoughtful pause, during which Brinton sat breathing hard, and Foxon dropped heavily on his superior's visitors' chair for his own spell of laboured respiration. "Come off it, sir," ventured the young man at last, as the face behind the desk slowly regained its normal ruddy hue. "That was a bit much, if you don't mind me saying so. I mean, you might have killed me, if I hadn't got such quick reflexes."

Brinton grunted. "My aim's better than that, laddie. If I want to hit you, I hit you. When I think of all the peppermints I've wasted on you over the years . . ."

The truth of this claim could not be denied, and Foxon acknowledged it with a faint grin. When Brinton did no more than groan and roll his eyes, it seemed worth pressing on with the explanation that had been so vigorously curtailed slightly earlier in the proceedings.

"Honest, sir, I haven't been to Plummergen in weeks, not since Christmas. Miss Seeton'll tell you the same, because the first thing she did was wish me a Happy New Year when I met her—by accident, sir—this afternoon, in Brettenden. Right outside Candell and Inchpin . . ." Foxon regarded his superior with an expert and calculating eye. That mention of peppermints had reminded Brinton of the presence in his desk of an unopened packet: the clench of his jaw had relaxed, and he was groping happily for the handle of the top drawer on the right.

He'd risk it. "Well, coming down the front steps, sir, actually." Brinton popped two mints in his mouth but said nothing. "She'd just finished inside, sir—as far as she could, I mean." An accusing note entered Foxon's voice as, in Brinton's continued silence, he continued to speak. "She was a bit bothered, sir, that she hadn't managed to—to get anything useful, if you know what I mean." Brinton's raised eyebrows and vicious crunch suggested that this knowledge was denied him, and Foxon had better elucidate quickly.

"I know she often needs a bit of—of coaxing, sir, to hand it over, but when she seemed so—so upset," said Foxon, still accusing, "I didn't sort of think it was exactly my place, sir. Not when you were the one that'd asked her, and I was sure she'd bring it along in the end, the way she always does . . ."

Brinton closed his eyes, crunched once more, gulped, and swallowed noisily. He opened his eyes in a bleak, desperate glare. "Are you trying to tell me, Foxon, that Miss Seeton has been—has been Drawing again?"

"Of course, sir. As you—oh." Light, at last, dawned. "As you don't," Foxon said, "know. Er—do you, sir?"

"I do now." Brinton buried his face in his hands. "Oh, I do—and I wish I didn't. Damn and blast you, Foxon. Why the rip-roaring hell did you have to tell me about it?"

CHAPTER 20

"But—sir, I thought you knew. Miss Seeton was talking as if you did . . ." Then Foxon frowned. "At least, I—I think she was."

Brinton lifted his head, his eyes rolling again. "You think. *Think* means something else, laddie, and right now you damned well don't! *Nobody* does, where Miss Seeton's concerned. It's all guesswork and waiting for inspiration and translating what the wretched woman sees into something even more obscure . . . No," he said as Foxon opened his mouth to protest, "you're right. I'm being unfair." He shot a quick sideways look at his subordinate. "I think." He even managed a grin. "She's helped us in the past, and no reason why she shouldn't again. I suppose." He sighed. "But you know *I* can't cope with her, Foxon. She makes me nervous. She's more the Oracle's pigeon than mine, for all she lives in my manor. For some crazy reason, he seems to understand better than most what makes her tick. Which probably," he said with a wry twist to his mouth, "says something about the man's subconscious I'd rather not know. And if you tell him I said so, I'll have your guts for garters."

"As if I would, sir. But . . . talking of Mr. Delphick, if we—you—can't make any sense of MissEss's doodle, couldn't we ask him, once she's brought it in?"

"We don't know that she will." Brinton groaned. "Come to that, we don't even know if she *has*—done any doodling, I mean, because you're not really sure *what* she said. Are you? Well, then. But if you *are* sure she said I sent her off sketching the scene of the crime at Candells, all I can say is, I didn't. The Yard promised her years back—well, I don't recall the exact words, but you don't send Miss Seeton into every blessed case that turns up, not unless you've got nerves of steel, you don't, no matter how desperate you are—and we aren't that desperate yet. The Mimms business was only a day or so ago, dammit. Let's give good old foot slogging a proper chance before we bring in the Battling Brolly—if," he added heavily, "we do. If it's worth the effort. From what you say, strikes me the poor old girl's cracked at last and started imagining things—"

"Oh!" This final suggestion had jogged Foxon's memory. "Oh . . ." He became subdued as Brinton fastened him with a full-power glare. "Sir, I'm sorry. I think I might have got it a bit wrong. She mentioned you—and sketches—and of course I thought . . . but then she fished out a Candells catalogue and was going on about—about barometers, and chairs, and a wooden box they sold last week. And—and I think—some sort of mistake—"

"Mistake?" Brinton slapped his hand so hard on the blotter that his forgotten mug of tea leaped up and almost tipped over with the force of its tidal wave. "You *think*? Like hell you do! It's you that's made the mistake, my lad. Candell auctions—wooden boxes—why, the blasted woman's changed her mind about keeping the perishing thing, that's all . . ." And he delivered, in sulphurous tones, a far more detailed account of the previous week's occurrence than his lacerated nerves, at the time, had allowed.

To this account Foxon gave his full and undivided attention. He listened gravely, saying nothing as Brinton wound up with a scathing condemnation of half-baked plainclothes fools who didn't know their whatsit from their epithet; and only offered his apologia once the superintendent had come to a final, exasperated halt.

"Yes, sir, of course. And I'm sorry, I know I am. But— if you'll pardon the liberty, sir—just supposing—you know what MissEss is like—the way she has these funny sort of . . . connections with things even before she knows there's anything to connect—and now this burglar, sir— not the Candell one," he said hastily, "the one who broke into her cottage, I mean." Foxon leaned forward and fixed his gaze on the empurpling visage of his superior. "Suppose they *are* the same person, after all? Suppose he was trying to find out who bought that box last week, and where they live—and he wants to get it back?"

Brinton opened his mouth, shut it, shrugged, then bowed his head in a gesture of defeat. His wife still brooding, Miss Seeton starting up again: no peace at home or abroad. How much more could a man be expected to take? He moaned softly. Foxon said nothing.

Brinton ground his teeth. He sighed.

He sat up and reached for the telephone. "Switchboard? Scotland Yard, quick as you can. Quicker, if possible." He turned to his relieved subordinate and jerked his thumb at the desk on the other side of the room. "Hop along, laddie, and get listening on that extension. It was your blasted idea to bring the Oracle into this, so— Hello? That the Yard? Chief Superintendent Delphick, please."

Foxon, hopping as his chief commanded, didn't catch the Yard operator's reply, but could guess its import from the expletive that broke from Brinton as the tinny voice in the telephone earpiece fell silent.

"Out? Where? No, never mind, if you can't reach him anyway—and no, nobody else will do, unless it's that tame giant of his—no, I thought not. Where Delphick goes, young Ranger's never far behind. Damn. Well, can you ask

him to ring Superintendent Brinton as soon as he gets in?
B for burglar, r for ruffian, i for—for innocent—Brinton,
yes. Ashford. He knows the number.''

He rang off and addressed Foxon with an air of resignation as that young man, frowning, dropped his receiver
back on its cradle. ''We're on our own, then. For the time
being . . . but is Miss Seeton? If you're right, then who's
there to stop chummie having another crack at the crib,
occupant at home or not?''

''Potter said the Bloomers would keep an eye on her,''
Foxon reminded him. ''Not that they can stand guard day
in and day out, even if Miss Seeton'd let them—which
knowing her she wouldn't, sir, would she? Wouldn't want
to keep 'em away from their normal routine. She never
seems to think anyone's got it in for her especially—and
perhaps,'' said Foxon, trying to convince himself, ''they
haven't, after all. Houses are always being burgled, and
Sweetbriars is a nice-looking place—anyone'd suppose
someone with money lives there, someone with something
worth pinching. Maybe it's all been just a—a coincidence,
sir . . .''

He did not really believe this.

Neither did Superintendent Brinton.

It was not until late that night—it was almost the next
morning—that Delphick and Bob, assisted by a team of
well-built, hand-picked colleagues, made their latest
delivery of underworld citizenry to the cells of Scotland
Yard. Even as the last key turned in the last lock, the first
solicitor arrived, arguing with passionate eloquence that his
client—if none of the others—was innocent of all charges,
and should therefore be allowed bail, at the least. Of course,
it was his recommendation that these charges should be
dismissed; the evidence on which the police had acted had
been fabricated by his client's—he coughed—business ri-
vals, with intent to mislead: as it had. Witness the current—
he coughed again—misunderstanding. Allow his client his

liberty forthwith, and out of the goodness of his heart no
counter-charge of False Imprisonment would be made . . .

No sooner had this ingenious gentleman been sent, far
from rejoicing, on his way than another appeared, gifted
with similar powers of rhetoric. What remained of the night
was long, hard, and extremely tiring.

It was almost at daybreak that Delphick, rubbing his
eyes, looked with sudden dismay upon the drawn faces of
his subordinates, and issued the stern instruction that everyone, without exception, should go home at once to bed.

"Without exception, Bob." Even Sergeant Ranger's
mighty form seemed somehow diminished in the grey light
of the winter morn as they all trooped outside for a welcome breath of air. "This includes you."

"And you, sir." Bob wouldn't have spoken so freely if
the others could hear him, but their yawns and stamping
feet masked his courteous impudence. "We've done a good
night's work, sir—you most of all—but we're none of us
getting any younger. Rickling's a—a devious blighter. You
need to be on top form to deal with him . . ."

He yawned again. Delphick managed a bleak smile.
"Your fear that in my senile exhaustion I might not be
equal to the challenge of Public Enemy Number Two and
his advisors is—is misplaced, Sergeant Ranger . . ." Yawns
were infectious. "Or perhaps, in the current circumstances,
not."

"Perhaps not, sir." Bob chuckled. "I'd say he'd see it
as another challenge, to call him Number Two when he's
doing his damnedest to be Number One. And when you—
we—finally catch up with Cutler . . ."

"If we do." Delphick frowned and quickly amended this
remark. "When. Dammit, Bob, you're right, I'm losing my
mind. I've never yet given in to despondency, and I've no
good cause to be starting now—blame lack of sleep, if you
will. Off home with the lot of you," he commanded, raising
his voice so that all could hear. "I don't want to hear the
clatter of boots along the sacred corridors until the

afternoon shift, and that's an order. Thank you for your help—and goodbye.''

Whereupon, under Bob's watchful eye, the Oracle waved less affluent colleagues towards tube and bus, led the main body of the company to the car park, and himself headed thankfully home.

Had he only gone back to his office before signing off, he would have discovered Brinton's message: but he did not. And, in the flurry of changing shifts, and the excitement of the multiple arrests, the officer to whom the Ashford superintendent had entrusted that message found no chance to chase up its receipt, or lack of it. For the rest of the morning, and the early part of the afternoon, a scribbled sheet of paper in the middle of Delphick's blotter must wait for the Oracle's return . . .

But it had been a long, hard, tiring night. As Bob had pointed out, nobody was getting any younger. Police detectives need their sleep as well as anyone else, if they wish to function at maximum efficiency . . .

Miss Seeton didn't exactly feel that she was functioning at maximum efficiency, but was delighted at just how far from the minimum she felt herself to be. It must, she decided as she completed her final pose of her morning routine, be due to her yoga. Seven years of dedicated practice must surely count for something; the book had promised mental and— she hesitated—spiritual refreshment as well as physical relief from stiffness: she knew she had achieved the latter— her knees, in particular—and she supposed that, over the seven years, she had probably acquired something of the former, as well. Normally, a sound sleeper, she had stayed up far later than usual, poring over her various library books and puzzling over the Latin dictionary. In the end she had gone to bed, and had woken once or twice (which she seldom did) from dreaming, a state she almost never experienced, though she understood that one dreamed every time one slept, and only recalled such dreams when the sleep was troubled.

Not (she told herself as she prepared breakfast) that she was in the least troubled by recent events. Martha and Stan's fears that the prowler—or prankster, which seemed far more probable—would return were (she felt) needless, though it was kind of them—such dear friends—to be so concerned on her behalf. Stan had insisted on her leaving all her downstairs lights on during the night; with some difficulty she had refused his generous offer to sleep on the sitting room sofa with a mattock by his side; and she had discouraged him (she supposed: unknown to Miss Seeton, this discouragement had been in vain) from patrolling up and down her section of The Street throughout the hours of darkness. When one considered that it had obviously been a mistake—the man, after all, had taken nothing—and when there were far more pleasant matters to think about . . .

Happily buttering her breakfast toast, sipping her tea, Miss Seeton thought about them. Her mental checklist, first compiled with the enthusiastic help of Lady Colveden, had been much revised since, and now looked, she thought, rather promising. One could not, of course, telephone quite so soon: museums, she supposed, were like offices and banks, which generally opened at nine, or half past. Which would give her time to read once or twice more through her notes, and to make certain that her attempted translation of the carving round the inside of the lid was indeed—she'd taken the greatest possible care, but with foreign languages (especially when they were dead—and when one's linguistic ability was limited to begin with) one could never be too careful . . . that the translation was as accurate as she could, in the circumstances—she'd had to guess at the missing letters, and she wasn't sure all her guesses were correct—as accurate as she could make it.

Miss Seeton checked the number three times in the directory before she would allow herself to dial. She glanced at the clock: twenty-eight minutes to ten. That extra half-hour had been a most valuable lesson in self-control: one had no wish to overstate one's case. With a deliberately understated gesture, she dialled.

"Brettenden Museum," announced the receiver.

"Good morning." Miss Seeton cleared her throat. "Could I—that is, would it be convenient for me to speak to Dr. Braxted, please?"

"Putting you through." A click, a rattle, and a rhythmic hum, the ringing tone of an unanswered extension.

"*Good* morning," carolled the well-remembered voice. "Euphemia Braxted here!"

Miss Seeton had to smile. "Understated" was hardly the word for Brettenden's noted archaeological expert. Miss Seeton had a sudden vision of Euphemia's introductory declaration being accompanied, as were so many of her remarks, by that characteristic, expansive, outward flinging of her arms which so often resulted in those nearest her having to leap out of the way. With a smile for her folly, Miss Seeton nevertheless found herself holding the telephone two or three inches from her ear as she replied.

"Dr. Braxted, good morning. My name is Seeton—I don't know whether you remember me, but—"

"Seeton?" A blink of uncertainty, if that. "Plummergen—the Roman temple! Am I right?"

Miss Seeton, blushing, confirmed that she was.

"Siberius Gelidus Brumalix." The sheer relish of each syllable was indescribable. "What a man—what a memorial. The Temple of Glacia—the marvellous mosaic! Those wonderful pieces of silver plate! Best find we've had in years, and all thanks to you, Miss Seeton. Don't say," she exclaimed with a surge of still greater enthusiasm, "you've gone and blown up another oak and found some more remains. That would be simply too good to be true. Er—have you?"

She sounded so hopeful that Miss Seeton made haste to dispel any notion that she might have duplicated her recent unwitting disturbance of a World War Two hand grenade, in so doing causing the destruction of a centuries-old tree and revealing, beneath its roots, Romano-British artefacts of the very highest quality. "It is, however, a—a coincidence," she went on, "that you should mention *oak*, because . . ."

Miss Seeton launched into her tale. Euphemia Braxted, Doctor of Philosophy, listened quite as hard as any medical doctor, making the right sounds of encouragement when it seemed her patient might be flagging, taking notes of the more salient points as they arose.

"A Latin inscription?" This cry far out-decibelled the good doctor's earlier delight on hearing of the papers and parchment, the coronet, and the robes with their ermine trim. Artefacts, Euphemia had then reminded Miss Seeton, could always be faked: and—as she'd already pointed out—the Georgian era was more than a millennium after her time, historically speaking. If Miss Seeton wanted an expert—

Miss Seeton agreed that her accidental purchase and its assorted contents could certainly be fakes. She herself had no way of telling. The library books, undoubtedly interesting, had provided no reliable evidence in either direction. It had seemed advisable that, before she set out on a hunt for acknowledged heraldry and genealogical and documentary experts—most probably to be found in London, which would mean a journey she was not, in such unpleasant weather, especially keen to take unless it should really prove worth everyone's while. She was reluctant to disturb too many distinguished scholars—begging Dr. Braxted's pardon, of course, since she hoped she did not imply that Dr. Braxted was . . . was undistinguished: she remembered how cleverly she had translated the inscription around the edge of the silver salver; she had been foolish to imagine that with the help of a dictionary she, too, could translate accurately from Latin into English, and should have realised sooner—

"A Latin inscription? On your blessed box?"

All Miss Seeton's painstaking parentheses collapsed at this point. She hadn't expected Euphemia to say anything just yet, with her elaborate explanation still unfinished: she was so startled that the only reply she could frame comprised the three simple words: "Inside the lid."

"Inside the lid, eh?" The rustle of windmilling arms echoed down the line. "*Inside* the lid. Round the edge, or across the middle?"

"Round the edge—right round it. And—and not proper words, I think, from the dictionary." Miss Seeton decided this didn't sound quite right. "I mean, not *real* words— full words. Not all of them, that is—except the names. Which are, of course. Proper. Abbreviated, I mean. Many of the others—indeed, most."

"Aha!" Euphemia Braxted could construe not only Latin, but also Ancient Greek, Abyssinian, and Egyptian Hieroglyphics. Miss Seeton's conversation, on the whole, didn't present her with any great difficulty. "Now this begins to sound more hopeful—oops!" There came a clatter down the line, as if in her mounting excitement she had dropped the receiver. Politely Miss Seeton waited for the genteel cursing to subside and the conversation to resume.

"Yes, well—sorry about that." Euphemia's words were half gasp, half giggle. It was clear that her emotions had been deeply stirred. "An inscription round the *inside*? Now, isn't that splendid!" She didn't ask: she stated, obviously expecting Miss Seeton to share her appreciation of this splendour. When, from the silence, it became apparent that Miss Seeton's understanding was limited, she relented.

"As I said, you'll remember, it's not that hard to fudge a set of likely-looking papers, if you know what you're doing—*and* fudge 'em well enough to fool most people, including me." She chuckled. "Wouldn't fool my sister, mind you. Eugenia's one of the queen bees up in the BM's Muniments Registry. My twin," she added, as Miss Seeton was suitably impressed at this convenient connection to the renowned expertise of the British Museum. "Lord only knows, though, what our parents were thinking of. A double helping of Miss E. Braxted, and all our private correspondence in a muddle—but there you are, nothing to be done about it." She chuckled. "Saved a fortune with Cash's, of course."

When Euphemia had finished enjoying the joke she had doubtless made before, Miss Seeton communicated her own discreet amusement for the ingenuity of the elder Braxteds in halving expenditure on machine-stitched name-tapes, as supplied by the celebrated school outfitters. But amusement was quickly muted, at either end of the line: there were more important matters to discuss.

"Besides, it was less of a problem," Euphemia continued, "when we grew up, because we went into different fields—Genie's not as keen on the mud-and-muscle side of history as I am, Miss Seeton. But when it comes to fake documents, believe me, she's your man. We could do a good deal worse than consult her . . ."

It was evident that Dr. Braxted had already embraced Miss Seeton's cause—the cause of the Estover dukedom—as her own. ". . . but not just yet. I'd like to have a proper look at the evidence before I send you off on what might be a wild goose chase, although I agree with you that to take so much trouble on the inside . . . Hang on a tick while I turn to a fresh page . . . Right. There are at least three different styles of pronunciation. Chances are yours and mine won't be the same—so give it to me letter by letter, and I'll see what I can do. Fire away, Miss Seeton!"

CHAPTER 21

The county bus ran only one day a week, Crabbe's supplementary service on two. This was none of them. Miss Seeton hesitated to ask for the lift she knew Lady Colveden would willingly offer, whether it was convenient or not: there was always so much to do, on a farm . . .

Miss Seeton chided herself silently as she dialled the number of Crabbe's Garage. Wasn't honesty the best policy? Very well, then. Lady Colveden—and Nigel—had been kind; more than kind. But . . . but it had been—and she blushed—her discovery, in the beginning, not theirs. Her mistake: just as it was her responsibility, now, to see that whatever Dr. Braxted had found out should be imparted at the earliest possible moment to the appropriate authorities . . . whoever they might be. The Colvedens, as members of the aristocracy—Sir George, in particular, as a Justice of the Peace—might well know—and would be consulted, of course, for the benefit of their advice; but . . . but perhaps, for a little while, she might have the—she blushed again—the romance, and the fun, of the Estover Secret as all her own—

"Crabbe's," said a sudden voice in her ear; and Miss

Seeton, waking, blushed for a third time.

From what even she had to acknowledge might be the workings of her subconscious, Miss Seeton found herself asking to be set down outside Brettenden's library, not its museum. In answer to the solicitations of taxi driver Jack Crabbe, she promised to telephone if, once her business in Brettenden was complete, she could find nobody to bring her home; no, she had no idea how long she would be, so it really was not worth dear Mr. Crabbe's while to wait. In her eagerness for him to be gone, Miss Seeton almost dropped her handbag as she fumbled with the catch in the hunt for her purse and his fare. The ferrule of her umbrella caught in the open door of the cab; her arm jerked sideways, and the half-open bag emptied itself on the ground.

"Careful, now—here, let me." Gentleman Jack was out of his cab and gathering Miss Seeton's assorted impedimenta before she could do more than click her tongue and rebuke herself for her carelessness. "Dictionary, eh?" Mr. Crabbe picked it up with a grin. "Setting up in competition, Miss Seeton?" And he laughed richly. It was an open secret in Plummergen that, under the pseudonym "Coronet" (he always said he'd got a kinder heart than folk supposed), the great-grandson of the garage proprietor was a successful composer of cryptic crossword puzzles.

"Hey, now." Jack whistled. "Latin! My word, you'll be showing me a clean pair of heels and no mistake, Miss Seeton. Never one for dead languages, I wasn't. Reckon I'll be on the dole before— Hey! No," he said at her anguished exclamation, "I was only kidding. You go ahead, with my compliments, Miss Seeton, I'm not one to stand in anyone's way. Room for another good 'un any time, the editors allus tell me. Seems those as like 'em can't get enough. Not as if they stick to just one and won't dare look at the rest—no more than if a chap as likes Dickens thinks it a disloyalty, dipping into Thackeray once in a while, or Wilkie Collins.''

He handed over the last of his passenger's belongings—a bulging envelope in stout brown manila—and clapped her kindly on the shoulder. ''You need any help, Miss Seeton—get stuck with the grid, or short of the top right-hand corner—you give me a ring, see?''

And he embarrassed Miss Seeton even more by refusing the offered fare, on the grounds that he'd been no more than doing a favour for a fellow professional; and drove off with a merry tootle of the horn which made her feel more guilty than she remembered feeling since she didn't know when.

Or rather, she did. Since the auction. The auction at which she'd bought the wooden chest . . .

The chest which was the reason she'd come to Brettenden in the first place . . .

To reconcile her conscience, Miss Seeton returned to the library the Latin lexicon she'd intended to keep until she'd seen Dr. Braxted, and blushed as she agreed with the counter assistant that it had indeed been most helpful. Then, with her heart beating a little faster than usual, she headed out of the library into the High Street, and trotted off in the direction of the museum.

Euphemia had said it was impossible to miss her office. She was, in fact, right, though her visitor was given no chance to test the theory. Dr. Braxted was waiting for Miss Seeton in the entrance hall, her eyes lighting up as the heavy swing door was pushed open and the little figure in the tweed coat and remarkable hat peeped inside.

''Miss Seeton!'' Euphemia came leaping from the bench on which she had alternately sat, twiddling her thumbs, and leaned, gossiping with the uniformed guide. ''My friend, at last,'' she explained, in a whispered aside. ''I'll take her right along with me—we'll have coffee in my room, Miss Seeton, and I'll show you my treasures!''

Two turnings off a straight corridor, and they were there. "Told you so," said Euphemia, opening the door and ushering Miss Seeton into a room that was probably larger than it seemed, so cluttered was it on every side with books and cardboard boxes, with balls of string and pottery shards and—balanced one upon the other—a dustpan, a brush, and a wind-up tape measure in a circular leather case. "I simply couldn't wait, not once I'd got the final drop on it—by the way, do sit down." She gesticulated expansively towards what might have been—beneath its high-piled obscurity of learned journals (bound and unbound), and bundles of clipped newspapers—a chair.

"I didn't want anyone to know what we were up to," went on Euphemia, oblivious to the confusion of her guest as she darted around the desk to snatch up a notepad, covered in black spider tracks. "Told 'em," she said, "you were interested in . . ." But Miss Seeton was never to know. "Now, you just sit down and we'll talk!"

Euphemia perched herself on the one clear corner of an otherwise cluttered desk in what must, Miss Seeton supposed, be her habitual spot. So intent was she on the substance of her spider tracks that she had no thought to spare for Miss Seeton: who took one more look at the hypothetical chair, knew she would never dare to touch the teetering heap thereon—knew likewise she would never dare to disobey Euphemia—and sank, after a moment's pause, to the floor. She knew she would find it difficult, in her skirt, to achieve the Lotus Pose without some unseemly revelation of her person; but the lower half, as it were, of her favourite Cow Face Posture—*Gomukkhasana*—must be unexceptionable. She duly rucked her skirt up just above the knees to prevent bagging; knelt; spread her back-bent feet far enough apart and no farther; and lowered her rear end neatly between them, at the same time with her hands turning out her heels, to point her toes forwards. When one normally assumed this posture in one's underwear, it was surprising how inflexible one's shoes, when worn, could be.

Euphemia didn't so much ignore these contortions as fail to notice them in the first place. "Listen," she commanded; and prepared to read aloud from her notes.

"First I'll give you *my* translation: see how it compares with yours. *This work was made in the Year of Our Lord 1525 at the expense of Adelard Hedgebote, son of Adelard, son of Florence*—in this case male, but of course it can be used for females, too—*Florence, son of Adelard, son of Bennet, husband of Adeline, daughter and heiress of Adelard Turbary, on whose souls may God have mercy.* Interesting," she added as Miss Seeton sighed with quiet pleasure at the near-accuracy of her own translation. "*Propicietur* is a post-Augustan usage—Augustan in the Roman sense, not Queen Anne—but it's interesting in other ways, too. Seems your Benedicta came from pretty remarkable stock, Miss Seeton. *Daughter and heiress* seems to run in the family, don't you think? Adeline Turbary way back in the fourteen hundreds, I should guess—and then Duke Bennet in the Regency period."

She lowered the notepad and regarded Miss Seeton with a glittering eye that entirely overlooked the fact that the object of regard was resting several feet below her on the floor. "Sounds to me as if you could have hit the jackpot again, old girl: mosaics one minute, dukedoms the next—and now let's see that parchment of yours!"

Meekly Miss Seeton handed up the brown manila envelope. Euphemia opened it. She studied the contents in silence for a while. She frowned.

"I told you I was no expert," she said at last. "Mind you, even without seeing this, from the inscription I'd have risked a small flutter you and Lady Colveden were absolutely right—but you need to be sure, with a title at stake. And that's what I've tried to do."

She leaned forward from the desk at a precarious angle and whispered in thrilling tones, "I had a word with Genie, not half an hour ago. Hope that's okay with you," she said as Miss Seeton looked somewhat startled, "but we don't want this hanging around for some outside blighter to pick up and have all the fun with. Do we?"

Miss Seeton, blushing at this echo of her own emotions, relieved that they seemed to be shared by an eminent scientist and were therefore perhaps not as unreasonable as she'd feared, agreed with a gasp that they didn't. And she didn't. Mind, she meant. Not at all—apart, of course, from the fear that she might be wasting Dr. Braxted's time, and that of—of her sister . . .

"Dr. Braxted," said Dr. Braxted with a twinkle. "Genie's a Ph.D., too. And she looks exactly like me. You'll feel quite at home with her."

Miss Seeton blinked. Euphemia glanced at her watch. "Now then, if you step on it you'll make the next fast train to London. Genie's expecting you. I told her I'd ring," she said above Miss Seeton's audible squeak of surprise, "once you were on your way. I'm no mediaevalist, of course, but I've picked up a little from Genie over the years: I'll take some instant snaps of the parchment while you powder your nose—no time for coffee, I'm afraid—then I can give her what I can over the phone before you get there with the real thing. Should give her a head start. From what she's heard of the story, she's just as keen as we are to find out what exactly it is we've got. Now then!"

Flinging out her arms for balance, she hopped down from the desk and headed for the door before Miss Seeton had even begun to unfold herself. "Come on," she enjoined with her hand on the knob; and whisked out of the room with Miss Seeton, trying to catch her breath, pattering anxiously down the corridor behind her.

*   *   *

In London, it was raining again. The queues at the
Charing Cross taxi rank were as long as Miss Seeton
had ever seen them, and she thought her chances of
hailing a cab outside the station very poor; but she was
reluctant to entrust herself and her precious burden to either bus or tube. It took ten minutes patrolling the
Strand before her quick eye and waving umbrella between them brought one of London's philosophers to a
hissing halt beside her.

"Where to, luv?"

Miss Seeton asked to be taken to the British Museum,
and settled herself damply, mourning the cockscomb that
drooped over her brow, on the smooth leather seat. Perhaps
it was inevitable that the subject on which her driver chose
to philosophise all the way to Bloomsbury should be the
weather.

There was a distinct sense of déjà vu as Miss Seeton
arrived at her destination to be saluted by a vigorous lady
in sprightly tweeds.

"Miss Seeton!" It wasn't a question: umbrellas might,
on such a day, be more than fashion accessories, but only
a complete disregard for fashion could justify such a hat.
"Eugenia Braxted. My word," she said, shaking hands,
"do with warming up, couldn't you? Come along to my
hidey-hole, and we'll have coffee."

Dr. Braxted didn't wait for coffee before, like her sister,
she had whipped out a notebook. "Phemie wouldn't make
an archivist, but she knows enough to be a pretty useful
long-range assistant. As soon as she'd given me the first
few words . . ." She cleared her throat. "Let's see if she
was right, shall we?"

Divining her meaning, Miss Seeton reached into her
bag and produced the brown manila envelope. Eugenia's
hand was steady as she took it from her and raised the
flap.

"Ah," she breathed, taking out the soft, creamy-grey
folds of parchment. "Feels genuine . . . and," she said,

opening it, "looks genuine. So far . . ." Gently she opened the box on its crimson ribbon. "And so does this. My goodness me. The Royal Seal . . . Edward the Second. Ties in with the rest very nicely. Very nicely indeed . . ."

She didn't remove the seal from its box, but studied it carefully. "Edward enthroned recto, on horseback verso—that's the usual style, and I imagine it's no different in this case—front and back," she translated as she looked up and caught Miss Seeton's eye. "Sorry. My sister may have told you I'm a bit of an enthusiast about my work—and this is such a splendid example . . ."

"Then," Miss Seeton could hardly bring herself to ask, "the document is—is genuine?"

"Looks very much like it." Eugenia beamed at her. "One of Edward's Letters Patent—from the Latin, *patere,* to lie open." She pronounced the word with three syllables. "Letters Patent are public, that's to say government, documents, issued through the office of the Lord Chancellor, and sealed with the Great Seal of England." She launched into what was evidently a set speech, to be delivered to all comers before her ears should be lacerated by a mispronunciation. "Pat, not pate. Patent leather is quite another matter—but you know this, of course," she said as she recalled that her visitor was no careless student, but a responsible adult, willing to be informed. "Letters Patent: official documents, open"—she spread the parchment on her desk—"to the public, and conferring an exclusive right or privilege, such as the right to exploit an invention to financial advantage. Think of the chaps who thought up safety pins, or ballpoint pens. Or the ownership and inheritance of land. Or . . . the right to a title of nobility, Miss Seeton."

Miss Seeton, holding her breath, nodded.

"Pretty rare, you know." Eugenia beamed again. She had her notebook in one hand as she smoothed the parchment with the other. "Wonderful, this stuff. Use the whole thickness of the skin, that's vellum; split it into layers, and it's parchment. Pickle it in salt, stretch it nice and thin, dry it and bleach it in the sun, and it'll last a hundred lifetimes. Even the writing. Know what they used for ink?"

Miss Seeton shook her head.

"Oak apples boiled in sulphuric acid. Etches its way into the surface, so it doesn't matter if it flakes off, we can always read the traces by ultraviolet. Not that Phemie needed to, of course." She coughed. "Shall we see how she did? *Edwardus Dei gracia rex Anglie dominus Hibernie et Dux Aquitannie omnibus ad quos presentes littere pervenerint salutem.* 'Edward, by the grace of God, King of England, Lord of Ireland and Duke of Aquitaine, to all those into whose presence these letters might come, greeting.' Wonderful!'' She flung out her arms, dropped her notebook, and addressed herself gleefully to the original. "*Sciatis quod de gracia nostra speciali concessimus et licentiam dedimus pro nobis et heredibus nostris.* He wants it known he graciously makes this special promise on behalf of himself and his heirs . . . *sibi et successoribus suis aut masculi aut mulieres pariter imperpetuum*—to the subject of this letter and *his* heirs in perpetuity. His heirs whether male—or female . . .''

Miss Seeton found that she was still holding her breath. She let it out now in a long sigh. Eugenia took no notice; she went on with her translation, muttering to herself and, when audible, sounding pleased. "Heirs male or female, on equal terms . . . crown—no, coronet—and the same robes to be worn by both male and female in identical fashion— ha! Never heard of that before: peers and peeresses always dress differently. Touch of the Piers Gaveston here, I fancy . . .'' She chuckled.

Miss Seeton, whose historical reading had not left her ignorant of the sexual preference of Edward II, nodded; but Eugenia did not see.

"Eldest son to eldest son, and failing sons the eldest daughter . . . equal rights and honours of inheritance . . ." She looked up. She smiled. "And the inheritance he's talking about, Miss Seeton, is the duchy of Estover!"

Miss Seeton smiled back a little nervously. "Then this is—is real?"

"As far as I can tell at this stage. I'll need to study this more closely and consult a few colleagues—swear 'em to secrecy, and so on—before I can give you a definite opinion; but I think you could really be on to something here. You've checked in Debrett, Phemie tells me."

"Only the current volume in our local library."

"No Estovers?"

"Not as far as I could see, but—"

"Not exactly reliable," said Eugenia. "Most of what's in the peerage books is supplied by the peerage themselves, one way or another. If they want to keep something quiet, fudge a few dates, it's not too hard. Who puts notices in the papers? Births, marriages, deaths? The family," she stated before Miss Seeton could reply. "Where do Burke and Debrett find most of their information? The papers. Who do they ask to check it before they publish it? The family." She glanced at Miss Seeton and smiled. "See what I mean?"

Miss Seeton saw. "An injudicious marriage," she suggested, "would, in the circumstances you describe, be only too easy to ignore."

"Ignore in the first generation; rumour in the second; forget completely by the third. What was the date on your Benedicta's note? After a couple of hundred years . . ."

"Who," enquired Miss Seeton, "would know now?"

Eugenia shrugged. "Royal College of Heralds? The Lord Chancellor? Far as I remember, anyone who wants to claim a title has to prove his or her identity and descent from the last known incumbent, if that's the word. Chancellor's happy, then they go to the House of Lords for a Writ of Summons. The Lords issue the writ, and that creates the title again, as it were—needs an Act of Parliament to revoke it. That's why it's so dashed difficult for the nobs to disinherit their sons. They can do the black sheep out of the money, all right, but the title's another matter altogether. And if the property's entailed . . .''

She favoured Miss Seeton with a searching look. "I'll give you all the help I can, of course, but I'm a mediaevalist. It's not really my period. Strikes me, Miss Seeton, you're in for a pretty interesting few weeks!''

CHAPTER 22

The Ashford police were proceeding about their business as they usually did, at a steady, careful, painstaking pace leavened by the occasional spurt of inspiration. Having two murders to investigate alongside the day-to-day enquiries into such crimes as burglary, assault, and motoring offences might be expected to cramp the investigative style to some extent: but Brinton, as ever, coped. By detailing junior officers to carry out routine legwork, by instructing that each and every resultant report should be duplicated and, in duplicate but digest form, should be sent to him, the superintendent tried to remain abreast of all the most important forensic discoveries while concentrating on that which he saw as his main job: solving the deaths of Terry Mimms and—despite the lapse of time, still no nearer a solution—of Professor Eldred Quendon.

When the telephone alarm was raised by Plummergen's PC Potter, it was Foxon who took the call. Brinton, buried in files, had barked one swift command to his subordinate, then submerged himself in paperwork again . . .

Until Foxon's voice brought him, with a jerk, right out of the reported past into the present.

"The—the body of a woman?'' Brinton looked up.
Foxon gulped. "In—in Sweetbriars?''

The train left Brettenden station, and so did Miss Seeton.
She was the only passenger to alight, emerging into the
gloom of the winter afternoon half hoping, half dreading
there would be a taxi at the forecourt rank. Everyone for
miles knew old and asthmatic Mr. Baxter's even older and
more asthmatic car; with luck—except that this seemed a
slightly ungenerous, not to say malicious, wish—Mr. Baxter might have, as he so often did, broken down, which
would leave her free to telephone for Jack Crabbe without
feeling selfish.

Miss Seeton's luck was in, as was Jack. He promised to
be with her inside ten minutes, and after he'd said goodbye,
Miss Seeton promised herself that, since he'd been so kind
about that morning's trip to Brettenden, she would insist
on doubling his fare for the return journey. Or else, she
thought, suppressing a yawn, she would make sure she gave
him a lavish tip . . .

She yawned again. It had been such a tiring, though at
the same time stimulating, day: which was, no doubt, the
reason she felt so tired. So many new ideas to absorb, and
Dr. Braxted—both of them—so . . . so enthusiastic. While
one always enjoyed watching an expert at work, somehow
one did not expect to be—to be swept up and carried away
with the sheer force of such expertise. But it had been,
without question, worthwhile. So interesting; so romantic.
Miss Seeton smiled for the romance of it all, and settled
herself in a happy daydream to await Jack's arrival.

Though a small, elderly, tweeded spinster would appear
at first sight to be no match for a strapping young man,
Miss Seeton—whose principles were firm, to say the
least—on this occasion prevailed. At the end of the journey,
Jack accepted his gratuity with a good grace, averring that
to justify such generosity he would personally escort her
up the short paved path to her front door, and would help

hold her handbag steady while she hunted for her keys.

The manoeuvre was smoothly executed. Jack made some joking reference to the way they worked together, and Miss Seeton blushed; but her hand was on the knob, and her weary thoughts were more inclined to slippers and tea than to crossword puzzles.

She pushed open the door. "Why, how strange. I would have supposed . . . coming in from the cold—not," she added hurriedly, "that I would for one minute wish to imply that the heating in your car was unsatisfactory, Mr. Crabbe. It was, indeed, most comfortable—which must, of course, be why." Miss Seeton smiled and nodded. "The contrast . . . yet even on such a chilly evening one would expect . . ."

"Boiler could've gone wrong," said Jack, his professional association with petrol inspiring the suggestion. "Flow can get pretty sluggish, this cold weather, especially if you're near the bottom of the tank, stirring up the sludge. Or you might have an airlock somewhere in the pipes. I'll take a look for you, shall I?"

Miss Seeton quickly weighed up the relative merits of allowing Jack, who was already on the premises, to supplant Stan, who wasn't. She would have to rely on the good sense of Martha to soothe her husband's feelings, should they be hurt if he ever learned that someone else had been carrying out what he saw as his especial and official duties at the home of his employer. To disturb him in—Miss Seeton stole a quick glance at the hall clock, just visible through the open doorway—in the middle of supper . . . "That would," she said, "be most kind of you, Mr. Crabbe, if you can spare the time. And should it prove simply a matter of bleeding them, I have a key by each radiator, and there will be no further need to trouble you. Dear Stan has shown me more than once what to do."

"Find out first, shall we?" Jack stepped aside to allow his hostess to precede him, and saw her shiver at a sudden gust of cold air.

Cold air which—he instantly recognised, if Miss Seeton did not—was coming rather too fast from indoors, for a house whose central heating had broken down.

Miss Seeton had always considered Jack Crabbe to be as polite as anyone in Plummergen. He must, she supposed, have a good reason for pushing past her in such a way and running down the hall. Puzzled, she hurried after him, and arrived at the kitchen door in time to hear a muffled curse.

"Burglars," groaned Jack, gazing at the broken window and its shattered fragments, scattered all over the floor. "No, Miss Seeton, you'd best keep out o' this. Don't want you treading splinters into your shoes and all over the house after, do we? You pop back to the phone and call Ned Potter, if you will."

"Oh, dear." Miss Seeton's dismay was tinged with some degree of guilt: twice in two days, and herself not here to stop the foolish prankster and send him, once and for all, about his proper business. Whatever would Martha say? "I'm sure," she said bravely, "that this is no more than a—than a mistake, Mr. Crabbe. A practical joke, carried this time beyond what ought really to be acceptable, and when I discover who is responsible you may be confident that I will—I will have something to say to them," she concluded, in her best schoolmistressy tones. "I hardly like to bother Mr. Potter at this hour, when he and his family . . . Oh. Oh!"

Family. Pedigree. Documents. The robes; the coronet! "Excuse me, please." And Miss Seeton was pushing in her turn, squeezing back past him into the hall, hurrying to the sitting room, opening the door . . .

On the threshold, she stopped.

Dead.

As dead, it seemed, as the figure on the sitting room floor . . .

"The—the body of a woman? In Sweetbriars?" Brinton snatched up his handset and clamped it to his ear. "You're not—'' Foxon gulped again. ''You're not saying it's—it's Miss Seeton, are you?''

''No,'' said the well-known—and injured—accents of PC Potter. ''If you'd just given me time, instead of jumping down my throat like—''

''Potter!'' roared Brinton.

Foxon removed the extension receiver from his ear and shook his ringing head. In Plummergen, Potter did likewise. Brinton modified his tone. Slightly.

''Potter, stop making statements in official jargon, damn you, and give us the facts in honest-to-goodness English. What the hell d'you mean, there are women's bodies dotted about all over Miss Seeton's house?''

''One woman, sir. In the sitting room.'' Potter cleared his throat. ''Looks as if she was hit over the head with the poker—Miss Seeton's very fond of toast,'' he added in partial explanation. ''Hit by person or persons—''

''Potter! I warned you . . .''

''Sorry, sir.'' Potter cleared his throat again. ''Anyway, sir, it's not as if the corpse is unknown. Miss Seeton has made the provisional identification as—''

Foxon erupted into a bout of spluttered coughing which made Brinton curse him with unaccustomed fluency. Potter said nothing until the pair had fallen silent. If Headquarters chose to take the matter lightly, well, that was their affair. Not, of course, that they did: it was just their way, making daft jokes, of coming to terms with the news of a third murder on their patch when the other two were, so far as he knew, no closer to being solved than they'd been at the start.

''A provisional identification,'' he repeated, after only a few moments, ''as Miss Myra Stanebury, who—''

''*Who?''* burst simultaneously from Brinton and Foxon.

''Who,'' said the much-provoked PC Potter, ''is—I mean was—the senior clerk at Candell and Inchpin, sir.'' He paused. From the Ashford end of the telephone came a seething silence. ''For which reason,'' concluded PC Potter of Plummergen, "I thought you'd want me to let you know even sooner'n usual. Sir. Considering."

Miss Seeton, after so many eventful years, was no stranger to police activity, though she generally, and happily, contrived to dismiss all or any suggestion that such activity was—could possibly be—anything to do with her.

Even she, however, was unable to dismiss the connection between the death of Miss Myra Stanebury, in the Sweetbriars sitting room, and herself. She had, indeed, been as shaken by the discovery as anyone had ever seen her.

Jack Crabbe, hearing her horrified cry, had rushed from the kitchen, taken one quick look over her shoulder, and swept her away back down the hall to the telephone, where he took it upon himself to ring in quick succession PC Potter and the Bloomers. Stan arrived with a spade in one hand and—for some reason he couldn't explain—the remains of his hot meat pie and two veg. on a plate in the other. Martha was at his side with knotted apron strings and the pepper-pot, prepared to join battle with whatever foe might still lurk on the premises of her dear Miss Emily.

Miss Emily was pale but composed to the eyes of all but those who knew her best, which meant the Bloomers. Stan took one look, plonked the pie-plate on the hall stand, shouldered his spade, and trudged outside on patrol. Martha scolded at ring marks on her polish, scooped up plate and employer together, and bore off both in triumph to the daffodil-bright cottage across The Street. When Brinton and the rest of the Ashford team arrived, they found PC Potter on guard indoors, while Stan and Jack were stationed at each of the two entrances, side door and front gate, to the scene of the latest crime.

Photographers, fingerprinters, and the rest were left to carry on under the supervision—to his proud delight—of Police Constable Potter; Brinton, with Foxon for note-taking and moral support, went to talk to Miss Seeton.

"I'm so sorry, Superintendent, I really couldn't say."

Miss Seeton, bravely swallowing the strong, sweet tea that had been forcibly prescribed by Martha for shock—one could not hurt her feelings, although surely, after so long, one's preference for weak, unsugared tea was recognised—was doing her best to be helpful, and feeling very guilty because she wasn't. Or couldn't. And when one was, albeit in a very minor capacity, by way of being a colleague, employed by the police as an IdentiKit artist on account of one's—admittedly small—talent for sketching, which necessarily involved using one's eyes—and one hadn't . . .

"What she can have been doing at my house, I mean. One would hardly imagine why a complete stranger . . . except, of course, that she wasn't. Not complete." Miss Seeton blushed for her forgetfulness, and felt more guilty than ever. "Because of having met her yesterday, at the auction house. Mr. Foxon may remember—but apart from that, definitely a stranger. Just long enough to recognise her face . . ."

"Yes," said Brinton quickly as her voice quavered. He glared at Foxon. "He does. Don't you, laddie?"

"Certainly do, Miss Seeton. Not that I actually saw the pair of you chatting"—Brinton glared at him again—"but I remember very well seeing *you*. Coming down the steps with your umbrella and showing me the catalogue from last week's sale." It was about the only certain memory he had of their encounter. The rest, as he'd already reported to Brinton, had been much too confused to register with any hope of usefully retrieving it.

Miss Seeton smiled. "Yes, indeed. My chest—that is," she said as despite himself Brinton's eyes darted to her meagre bosom and then, in apologetic embarrassment, to her face, "I suppose I should rather say the Estovers'. Or the Pottipoles'—it's always so confusing when one deals with the British aristocracy—as you yourself no doubt find, Superintendent. Chief Constables," said Miss Seeton, with vague memories of knights and earls in official dress at school speech days, "and so on. And even when it *is* the

same, the spelling need not be. Carrington and Carington—
one sometimes wonders how they know which they mean,
except that if one is born to it, of course, there is probably
no problem.''

''Very probably,'' said Brinton as she seemed to expect
some reply, and nobody else was willing to oblige. ''Er—
not,'' he added, in case the negative made more sense.
''But please go on,'' he prompted before he could be asked
to enlarge on this. ''You were at Candells yesterday,
and . . .''

''And I asked her about the provenance. And she said
she didn't know. And she couldn't find out, because her
files were in something of a muddle . . .'' Miss Seeton
would have blushed, fearing it tactless to recall how the
blame for this muddle had been apportioned by Myra to
Brinton's men, when recollection became sudden realisation. Turning pale, she sat up. ''Oh. Oh, dear. She must
have managed to sort them out and found my name and
address, and was kind enough to call in person to let me
know, and—and . . .''

''Yes, very kind,'' interposed Brinton before she could
become still more distressed. Both he and Foxon privately
wondered why whatever information Miss Stanebury had
wished to impart could not—knowing Miss Seeton's name
and address—have been passed on by telephone. It wasn't
as if MissEss was ex-directory, much though they and their
colleagues might wish, on occasion, that she was.

''Very kind,'' Brinton said again absently: his mind was
working furiously. Granted, it was only six miles from
Brettenden, but the bus wasn't running. She must have
made a bit of an effort to get here. Why come all this way
on a cold, wet January day just to speak to Miss Seeton?
Was the provenance (for whatever—though, taking into account yesterday's unsuccessful burglary at Sweetbriars,
he'd hazard a fair guess) so earth-shattering it could only
be revealed in a face-to-face meeting? If that's what she'd

meant to tell her, of course. Whispered, no doubt, for greater secrecy.

Guessing was all very well: knowing was better. "The provenance of what, Miss Seeton?"

Miss Seeton blinked; but a gentlewoman tries never to express surprise. The superintendent, naturally, had a lot on his mind and couldn't be expected—any more than could Mr. Foxon—to remember every conversational detail, no matter how recent that conversation might be. "My chest, Mr. Brinton. The carved wooden box I—I bought last week. At the auction." She paused. Would it be tactless to . . . ?

Tact was unnecessary—at least on Miss Seeton's part. "Oh, God, I knew it." Brinton rolled his eyes expressively in the direction of Mrs. Bloomer. "We'll be wanting a good long talk with you later, Martha, but for now—Miss Seeton, this box. Locked, wasn't it? And none of 'em knew what was inside. I remember they made a big mystery of it to push up the bids, but nobody was biting . . ." And he'd bet someone had realised, too late, that they should have bitten harder . . . "Then you go asking questions about where it came from, but you couldn't learn anything, because of the files being in a mess after the burglary."

Miss Seeton opened her mouth to explain that it had all been a mistake: a practical joke. Martha, a loyal audience at the interview—she'd like to see anyone, police or not, try turning her out of her own front parlour when Miss Emily needed her—stirred on her chair, but had no time to speak before Brinton was pressing on with his train of thought. Two burglaries in as many days: that box in both places, and Miss Seeton, of all people, another link. No need to upset her more by telling her of Terry Mimms's murder—a murder he was becoming more and more certain (for all young Chrissie's insistence they'd gone to Candells by sheer chance) could have been a case of thieves falling out . . .

Falling out . . . over what? "What happened, Miss Seeton, to make you go asking these questions? You seemed quite happy with the thing at the time you bought it.''

''I . . .'' Miss Seeton faltered. ''I should say *we* managed to unlock the box.'' Her continued pleasure at this achievement should not, she reminded herself with a blush, moderate in any way the accuracy of her statement. ''Undo it, I mean, between us. That is, dear Nigel and his mother tried first with knitting needles, though without much success. It was Mr. Eggleden who so cleverly knocked out—the spindle—which is nothing to do with wool,'' she added in the further interests of accuracy. ''But in the hinges, at the back. So that one could tip it back, to the front.''

It needed neither Brinton's muffled groan nor Foxon's wince to persuade Miss Seeton that her desire for accuracy had resulted in something closer to confusion: which was, one couldn't help but feel, embarrassing. ''And—and so he opened it,'' she concluded with another blush . . .

And she thought it safer, in the interests of accuracy, to say no more.

Brinton's imagination had long since begun to run riot. Thieves, as he knew, could fall out over the most trivial things: but a locked chest—a treasure chest?—was hardly trivial. Jewels and gold, rare porcelain and glass, works of art—trust MissEss and her brolly to find 'em if anyone could . . . If she had. She'd buttoned her lip pretty damn quickly once she'd said her final piece. ''So then what was inside, Miss Seeton, once you'd got it open?''

Accuracy. One must remember in what order the things had been taken out: it might be important. ''Papers,'' said Miss Seeton, frowning. ''Handbills and engravings—a few letters—a journal—props and costumes . . . a robe, and a tiara—no, a coronet . . . and—''

Brinton passed the reference to clothes. Silk, satin, and lace couldn't compare with—his eyes gleamed—the richness of ornaments and precious stones. ''A coronet?'' Miss Seeton, thrown off balance by the interruption, nodded. He waited for her to go on. She didn't. ''That's all?'' It

couldn't be. The fuss the damned things had caused, he'd
have expected the Crown Jewels, at least. "Nothing
of . . . particular value, I suppose?"

Miss Seeton hesitated: accuracy. "Oh, dear. That is, I
understand they are of little financial value in themselves,
although the *content* . . . They date back to Georgian times,
you see."

It was clear from Brinton's expression that he didn't.
Miss Seeton tried again. "Most of them, that is, though the
Letter Patent is from the fourteenth century." She began
warming to her theme. "Edward the Second, on parchment,
and beautifully written. But everything else—the marriage
certificate, the diary and personal correspondence, the theatre handbills and engravings—they're stippled, you know,
and in quite remarkable condition, in the cir—"

She broke off, blushing. Her artist's enthusiasm had got
in the way of accuracy. "The robes were a complete set,
if that is the correct term. The Colvedens, I expect, would
know. They also are in surprisingly good condition, if a
little faded, after so long. Like the cap of—of maintenance,
with the coronet. For—for a duke. The Duke of Estover.
Or," she continued as accuracy yet again overcame her,
"the Duchess."

Brinton looked at Foxon. Foxon shrugged. Did Brimmers
think he spent his spare time reading the society pages? If
he did, he was wrong.

"Duke of Estover? There's no such person, dear," said
Martha Bloomer very gently. The two policemen jumped:
she hadn't spoken—for Martha, this was rare—for so long
that they had almost forgotten she was there. "It's the
shock, I dare say," she said aside, as Miss Seeton looked
as startled by this interruption as the two detectives. "I
know you've your job to do, but couldn't you ask the rest
another day? Give the poor soul time to finish her tea in
peace, for a start—dukes, indeed!"

"Indeed yes, Martha." Miss Seeton's correction was not
only courteous, but slightly guilty in tone. Martha, so dear

a friend of such long standing, might justifiably feel hurt that the first exciting revelations (if true) of the old wooden chest had been shared with others (some, virtual strangers) before her cold-riddled self. But there had been—Miss Seeton sighed—that selfish wish to play one's part as a—as an historical sleuth. The challenge, the mystery of the search . . . "The romance," murmured Miss Seeton, and sighed again.

Brinton, Foxon, and Martha Bloomer exchanged speaking glances. The shock must really have upset Miss Seeton if she was suddenly confessing to a fondness for hearts-and-flowers fiction. As far as any of them knew—and Martha, domestic paragon, must know better than the others—she read little but biographies, history, and nature books: birds, and gardening—wildflowers, too—and, since the admiral had presented her with a pot of his famous honey, bees and other insects. Mrs. Bloomer's reading taste, apart from her cooking and sewing journals, ran more to magazines and papers of the lighter kind, with gossip columns and society photographs. "There isn't no Duke of Estover, Miss Emily, dear," she said as gently as before . . .

And her next glance in Brinton's direction carried a clear warning about pushing people further than he ought.

CHAPTER 23

Martha might have known Miss Seeton longer: Brinton
wasn't so sure she knew her better. In some ways, at least.
"Er—what makes you so sure there is, Miss Seeton?" he
enquired. "These . . . documents you found?"

"Dr. Braxted seems to think so." Miss Seeton ventured
a peep at Martha, then recalled that she was supposed to
be making an official statement. Accuracy. "Both of
them."

Damn. Maybe she did: Martha, that was. Know the old
girl better. One minute she says the box is full of papers,
the next, just two: and that shifty look of hers—no, not
shifty, just sort of lopsided, somehow. She'd gone over the
edge at last.

In which case they weren't going to get much out of her
until, as Martha had said, she'd had a decent rest. They'd
be busy across at the cottage for a few hours yet, so . . .

"D'you think you could put Miss Seeton up in your
spare room? You'll sleep sounder," he explained as Miss
Seeton began to protest that she had no wish to cause anyone any inconvenience, "if you haven't got bluebottles in
boots buzzing about downstairs all night keeping you

awake. We should be done by tomorrow, I hope. Until then . . .''

''Course I can,'' said Martha as Miss Seeton attempted another protest, then remembered that the police, quite rightly, would expect her to do as she was told, and fell silent. ''I'd have asked her myself, if you hadn't first. Me and Stan wouldn't want to think of you alone over there anyway, dear, so let's have no argument. You'll be swamped in one of my nighties, of course, but Mr. Brinton won't mind if I slip across to fetch a few things, will you?''

''My toothbrush,'' said Miss Seeton faintly, as Brinton ran a quick mental check. ''My slippers—dressing gown . . .''

The forensic crowd should know by now whether chummie—either of them—had gone on the prowl upstairs. ''Should be all right,'' he said at last. ''Foxon will have to escort you there and back,'' he told Martha, ''but don't worry, Miss Seeton, he'll keep his back turned in the bedroom like a proper little gent.''

Miss Seeton smiled, though with an effort, and her eyes could not meet his. They fell instead to her hands, clasped on her lap. Brinton's gaze followed hers. Her fingers were white: white with the effort of keeping still? The superintendent stiffened.

''Toothbrush, slippers, dressing gown—and sketchbook,'' he said slowly; and saw Miss Seeton's clasped hands give a convulsive jerk. ''Yes. Now, the way I see it, Chief Superintendent Delphick's going to want to know what's been happening to his favourite art consultant, Miss Seeton—but the Oracle's a busy man. Can't always get down here as often as he'd like, so what *I'd* like is to let him take a look at this famous wooden box of yours. If Martha brings your gear—pencils and so on—can you have something ready by the morning?''

''I will certainly do my best,'' said Miss Seeton, and her hands unclasped, to stretch and writhe as if trying to fix an invisible seal to that promise. Brinton nodded, satisfied in more ways than one.

Martha jumped to her feet, eager to speed these visitors on their way.

"Stan's in the kitchen, dear. While I'm out, will you slip along and tell him to put the kettle on? You'll be wanting a hot water bottle. *And* something hot inside of you, tea isn't enough even with biscuits—not that you had any— and you'll share it with us," she said as Miss Seeton tried to say she wasn't hungry. "Seeing as we never finished ours, what with one thing and another, and reheating never tastes the same—which reminds me, Mr. Brinton, if we've time, I'll get the torch to light us over. We might spot Stan's knife and fork he dropped on the way. Rings on Miss Seeton's hall table's something I'm sorry for but can always be polished out, only once you've lost part of a set you can never make it up again, can you?"

"Oh, Martha, I am so very—"

"Never you mind my nonsense, dear." Martha was quick to break into what had obviously been intended as an apology. "It's not your fault, and you aren't to go thinking for one minute it is. It's that burglar's to blame, blessed cheek, come back a second time to help himself and bringing half Brettenden with him. Once Stan and I've got you settled, I'm going to have a good long talk to the superintendent, and he'll sort everything out. Won't you, Mr. Brinton?"

"I'll do my best." He could hardly say less: he wished he could say more. Maybe, tomorrow, he'd be able to.

Martha, the torch, and the detective escort set off for Sweetbriars. They left Miss Seeton to oversee the boiling of the Bloomer kettle while she pondered her latest challenge, that of sketching the Estover chest from memory, for Brinton was unhappy about allowing her home again until all traces of recent events should be removed.

He was made unhappier still when Foxon, having watched Martha hurry homewards with Miss Seeton's gear, decided to share his own misgivings.

"Sir—about this murder. I've been thinking."

Brinton grunted. Foxon took this as an invitation to continue. "Well, sir, she's—she was, I mean, smallish and—and faded, sort of middle-aged to look at, especially in a hurry, I imagine. Spinstery," said Foxon as the superintendent suppressed a groan. "Of course, we don't know yet whether the two of them came here together, or not—but suppose they didn't. Suppose he didn't bring her, but got here after, and broke in the same way he did yesterday, when Martha scared him off—and he finds this spinstery type in what he's got to know is a spinster's cottage, sir . . ."

"You needn't say any more," said Brinton, suppressing a shudder. "That blasted auction—this blasted box!" He ran a pensive finger over the carved surface and sneezed as it came away dusted with white powder. "Never mind scorch marks on the mahogany and half a canteen of her second-best cutlery littered up and down the road—Martha Bloomer's going to have a fit when she sees this lot."

"Martha's got brains enough to know about fingerprints." Foxon produced a neatly folded handkerchief from his pocket and shook it out. "Here, sir. It's a spare," he added as Brinton's ruddy face expressed surprise.

"Thought it didn't match." Brinton accepted the plain white square with a nod of acknowledgement for his subordinate's always sprightly, sometimes startling sense of fashion. "So your theory," he said as he rubbed his hands, "is that chummie somehow missed out at the auction and decided he'd better pop along to rectify matters once he'd got the name and address from the Candell files?"

"Yes, sir. Subject to modification, of course—and if I'm right," he said nobly, "then I must've been wrong before. He probably isn't one of the sale-room people after all."

"How d'you reckon that?"

Foxon took a deep breath. "Well, sir, we don't know yet what Myra was doing here, but she was doing it in working hours. Either she helped herself to time off—phoned in sick, said she'd got the plumbers or something—or she was given it. If she was given it, if it was official, then she either meant to fudge what she'd been supposed to do— which in a place the size of Brettenden would be too easy to check afterwards—or . . .''

''Or,'' supplied Brinton, ''she did it. Yes, I'm with you so far. Did it, with their blessing, and got murdered for her pains. But . . .''

''But, sir, if they'd known enough to send her—if it was important enough to kill for—why send her? Sanctity of human life and all that, but she was only a clerk. You'd think it'd be one of the high-ups they'd send to explain to MissEss they'd made this horrendous mistake with selling the box, and asking for it back. They wouldn't know she's the sort to let it go without a fuss once she'd realised she'd no real right to it. They'd bring out the big guns, to make it sound more impressive. To make sure.''

''To make sure they got it back,'' muttered Brinton. ''And you're saying they didn't, so they can't have known she was coming? It's a theory. But suppose she simply took a day's holiday and didn't bother saying why?''

Foxon's face fell.

''And suppose,'' continued Brinton, gleefully usurping his subordinate's customary role of Devil's Advocate, ''they *did* know she was coming? Suppose they were willing to let her try getting the box back from Miss Seeton with a touch of woman-to-woman sympathy? It'd explain how she got here when the buses aren't running. They'll have dropped her off with her instructions; arranged to pick her up again, with the box, once she'd let them know she'd got it. In this place, strangers tend to stick out like a whole casualty ward of sore thumbs. And strange cars—Foxon, stop smirking.''

''Sorry, sir. But—not outside pubs, they don't. Stick out, I mean. Has anyone checked over the road at the George yet? Or she could have come by taxi—or hitched a lift—"

"Or come on a bicycle," agreed Brinton glumly. "More legwork—but we can't do everything at once, dammit, not with the manpower we've got. Not even in a case of murder—though I think," he added, "we'll chance a spot of doubling up from the Mimms enquiry."

"And if they *did* mean to collect her and the box later, sir—why didn't they?"

The superintendent brightened. "Maybe they did, saw what had happened, and got the hell out of here before anyone saw *them*." Then he gloomed once more. "Endless possibilities, Foxon, that's what we've got. Questions to ask, statements to take, statements to check and check again . . . and about all we know is that it's something to do with this box. Probably."

"I'll bet Miss Seeton's wishing she'd never gone to that auction, sir."

Brinton sighed. "I wish *I* hadn't. I wouldn't feel so bad about not having sorted out the whole damfool mistake as soon as she made it, instead of letting her talk me into thinking everything was fine and sending her off on her merry way into the usual chaos—oh, I wish the Oracle was here! How he does it, I don't know, but he can cope with her, and I just can't. Why did the chummies in Town have to try a takeover bid now, of all times?"

"You've asked her to Draw, sir. You might get something from that."

"Pigs might fly. I won't. She's Delphick's pigeon, laddie, and no point in trying to beat him at his own game. If I hadn't done an Oracle and given her that blasted brolly for Christmas, none of this would have happened—but it has." He gave the treasure chest an ill-tempered thump with his fist. "It has, and we're stuck with it, whatever it is—and according to Miss Seeton, we need a historian to tell us. Documents! Dukes! Dr. Braxted!" He paused. He frowned. "Hmm. Foxon, perhaps we should be talking to the fair Euphemia."

"Tomorrow might be better, sir. By the time we've finished here, not to mention all the checking on the Candells crowd . . ."

Brinton tore at his hair. "Checking! Oh, I know you're right, laddie. It's routine that solves cases, ninety-nine times out of a hundred. Flashes of inspiration come in handy when you get them—but they're the hundredth. And when you *do* get them, it takes an Oracle to translate them." He fastened Foxon with a penetrating gaze. "Once I've got my hands on whatever sketch Miss Seeton comes up with tomorrow, you'll be on the first train to London. I wish I could spare a fast car, but . . ."

"Manpower," said Foxon. "And money." He'd heard the superintendent hold forth on these topics more than once in the past. "The first train, sir—so long as he knows I'm coming. He's never answered your original SOS, has he?"

"That," said Brinton, "was no SOS, laddie, that was just a—a hint. This," he said, striding out to the telephone in the hall, "is an SOS." And, with Foxon hovering at his elbow, he picked up the receiver and began to dial.

The greater part of Brinton's team had already returned to the Ashford station, where, for the second time within a week, the forensic department was subjected to even more overtime. Brinton, Foxon, and a small but dedicated crew remained in Plummergen, Brinton and his ebullient junior to investigate Miss Seeton's house while the rest, armed with powerful torches, checked her gardens (front and back) and the immediate area up and down the unlighted Street.

The absence of street lamps was less of a hindrance to this checking than might have been expected. Before the police had prowled more than a few yards beyond the Sweetbriars boundaries, curtains were a-twitch in every window that overlooked that part of the village's only road, as well as in those of optimists farther to the north who had been alerted by telephone that Summat Was Up. Oblongs of spilled electric light gave the smooth asphalt a curiously striped appearance: black, brilliant, black, brilliant, black. Only in that stretch where The Street narrowed to cross the bridge, a lane running between cottage fences on one side and Miss Seeton's high brick wall on the other, was the search performed by official torchlight alone. Martha Bloomer's tongue could not only wag, but it could also—as her neighbours well knew—excoriate, in a good cause. And what better cause could there be for the Bloomers than the welfare of Miss Emily Dorothea Seeton?

Despite the relative darkness at the southern end of The Street, the search was methodical, though slow. It was little more than half an hour after it had begun that the cry went up from PC Potter, down by the concrete pillbox beside the canal. A favourite place for courting couples and the occasional shelter-seeking tramp, this symbol of England's most desperate hour still stood, squat and square and grey, within daylight view of the canal bridge, the top of the church tower—and the bottom of Miss Seeton's back garden.

''A bicycle, sir,'' said PC Potter, breathing hard from the exertion of his sprint up the gentle slope of the lane. ''Dark green, I think, and a ladies'—and it's not local, or I'd know it, even in the dark. There'd be no mistaking that great wicker basket on the front, or the splash-guard at the back all over flowers, sir. Horrible pink it looks to me, though we can't be sure till day, of course.''

''Well done, Potter.'' Brinton, at the telephone, was already dialling. ''I'll have 'em ask the Brettenden beat bloke whether Miss Stanebury rode a bike, and get a full description—but I've a feeling it won't be necess— That you, Mutford?'' he said as there came a click on the other end of the line, and the lugubrious tones of the desk sergeant identified Ashford Police Station. ''Brinton here.''

He issued his instructions, stressing—as he suppressed a yawn—that they should be carried out promptly, but not instantly. First thing in the morning, he said, would do. Yes, he was quite sure he didn't need to know any sooner than that. It was late; he doubted he'd be able to make too much sense of the information even if they rang back within minutes, most of all because he wasn't going to be here then, with luck. He was going to be on his way home for a few hours' much-needed kip: and he'd see Mutford to-morrow—or rather (with another yawn) later today.

The disapproval of Desk Sergeant Mutford radiated at him down the wire. Mutford was one of the staunchest members of the Holdfast Brethren, a sect celebrated for holding fast to the letter of the strictest law, whether tem-poral or spiritual, and for obeying any (legitimate) order far above and beyond the call of ordinary duty. It was a police officer's duty to solve crime: any slowness in such solving was, to the mind of the Holdfast Brethren, an offence against duty, and not to be encouraged. If the superinten-dent (volunteered the self-appointed saviour of Brinton's soul) liked, Sergeant Mutford would obtain a camp bed for his office—

The superintendent did *not* like. Through gritted teeth, he thanked his sergeant, pointed out that sleeping overnight at the station would require his sharing a room with Foxon, who snored, and repeated that he would see the man to-morrow morning, and not before.

"I suppose," remarked Foxon to nobody in particular as Brinton banged down the receiver, "I don't *mind* being slandered, so long as it's all in the course of—ahem—duty." He sighed. "But honestly, sir, couldn't you find a better excuse than saying I snored?"

"Not at this hour of the night." Brinton stretched and shook himself, blinking. "Doesn't he realise most folk need to sleep if they've got to think?" He pondered the immi-nent round of face-to-face interviews with assorted Can-dells, Inchpins, and friends and relations of Myra. He'd need to be right there on the ball and more, with the Mimms cross-referencing he'd have to do at the same time . . . "You can't help wondering sometimes if Mutford's really human."

"Slander again," murmured Foxon with a grin.

"Not," said Brinton, returning the grin with a ferocious grimace of his own, "if it's true. *I* wonder, even if you don't, so shut up. Potter, we'll detour past your pillbox on the way home: and we'll be back tomorrow morning at a civilised hour for a chat with Miss Seeton, heaven help us. I won't ask you to keep an eye on her for what's left of the night, because if the Bloomers can't look after her, nobody can." Potter took this in the spirit it was intended and nodded cheerfully. Like the superintendent, he enjoyed his eight hours when he could get them. "And don't," continued Brinton, "let her wander off after breakfast by herself, if Stan and Martha decide they have to go work."

"Shouldn't think they will, sir. Not both of 'em leave her at once, I mean."

"Nor should I, but," he said in the voice of experience, "where Miss Seeton's concerned, you can't be too careful. No popping off to the middle of nowhere watching birds, or picking wildflowers—well, not in January, but you know what I mean. She's to stay over there with or without the Bloomers until we've had a proper talk, and taken her statement . . ."

Her statement which would in turn be taken, through the good offices of Foxon and of British Railways, to London: to Scotland Yard: to Chief Superintendent Delphick.

CHAPTER 24

Conscious that Brinton was relying on her, Miss Seeton had done her best to remember what she could of the events leading up to—and her impressions of—her first, and only, meeting with Myra Stanebury, as she now knew the dead woman to be. Except, of course, that when she had met her at the auction house, she wasn't. And now she was. In her sitting room. Miss Seeton sighed, even as she recalled Brinton's hope that everything would be back to normal by the morning. Or at least, had been. It was a cruel, and wicked, return for such great kindness in taking time from her work merely to reassure . . .

Miss Seeton frowned. Or maybe not. Since poor Miss Stanebury had died before having revealed what she knew of the provenance of the treasure ch—

No. *The carved wooden box.* She must never, ever again allow herself to think of her purchase in any other way. It was her fault, hers alone, that harm had come to poor Miss Stanebury. Entirely through her romantic—she blushed—folly, an inflated idea of the value of the box and its contents must somehow have become general knowledge, must have tempted some callous thief to break in and—

Miss Seeton gave one little gasp, then firmly shut her mind against all thought of what had happened next. She had been asked to sketch a likeness of the chest—*the box*—to show Mr. Delphick, who was busy in London and could not spare the time to come down to Kent. She would have offered to take it up to him herself, but Mr. Brinton had not seemed to think this a good idea; and, since he had said he wanted to send Mr. Foxon first thing in the morning and would not let her back in the house until later, she would have to sketch it from memory. Yet memory, she feared, might prove, after—after what had happened . . . might prove less reliable than Mr. Brinton evidently supposed . . .

She explained all this, and more, to Brinton when he and Foxon arrived at Martha's door on the dot of nine next day. "I am so sorry, Superintendent." Her hands moved restlessly on the closed cover of her sketchbook, and her eyes wore an anxious, guilty air. "So very sorry—but somehow I cannot, in all honesty, feel that my drawings are likely to prove particularly helpful. The details of the carving—apart, that is, from the Latin, where letters and words are easier to recall . . . but I hope you won't think it a—an impertinence for me to say that I—I believe Mr. Foxon could, in these distressing circumstances, use his time rather more profitably than in taking my foolish doodles up to London."

"He couldn't use it less," Brinton told her, slandering his subordinate with the very best of motives. Everyone who'd ever had dealings with MissEss and her Drawings knew that she more often than not had to be coaxed into handing them over. "He might just as well waste it annoying the Oracle instead of me, for once, then I could get some good honest coppering done in peace and quiet. You'll be doing me a favour, Miss Seeton—both of us, in fact. If I can only get him out of my hair for a few hours, I'll be far less likely to want to chuck things at him once he's back under my feet again."

Miss Seeton turned a startled face to where Foxon stood

at Brinton's shoulder. The younger man was a strangely reassuring sight as he winked and nodded as if agreeing with every word the superintendent said. Which, if Mr. Brinton had been serious about—about throwing things at him, could well be true. Except, of course . . . She had always accepted that her sense of humour was possibly not as—as robust as that of others; and Mr. Brinton, she had remarked before, had a certain tart sense of fun to which his colleagues must be far more accustomed than she. Even if she, too, ought perhaps to consider herself a colleague, since she was, after all, paid a retainer for her artistic services—

"Oh!" The faint cry signalled a sudden realisation of her failure, so far, to justify that retainer. Recalled to duty, Miss Seeton blushed, smiled her polite acknowledgement of Mr. Brinton's little joke, and handed him the sketchbook without further demur.

As the train rattled out of Ashford station, Foxon found himself a comfortable seat in a No Smoking compartment, opened his newspaper, and under cover of *The Daily Negative* studied Miss Seeton's first sketch.

Well, it was a box. He supposed. But she'd shown it so piled round with such an assortment of junk he wouldn't care to swear to it. A barometer, a set of golf clubs, a wrought-iron bedstead; a set of arrows with matching bow; a spur-heeled chicken with a malevolent glint in its eye; binoculars, very small, in a case; a violin, likewise small, but perfectly drawn to the last detail.

Detail. That's what he ought to be looking for. What had MissEss taken most trouble to draw?

To Draw, he meant. Because if Old Brimmers was right, that was what she'd done with this lot . . .

Lot. Foxon chortled for a few moments. She'd drawn the auction, where all this had started: he'd bet a fiver these were some of the lots she'd seen that day with Lady Colveden and, later on, the super. Not that Brimstone had said he recognised any of 'em, when MissEss handed over the book: a quick thank-you and goodbye Foxon, that'd been the size of it. Probably rather not know the worst until he had to . . . Until the Oracle had given him the translation. Foxon wished him joy of translating this lot.

He chortled again and turned the page. Another box, or the same one, more visible: carved, bound with iron bands, and with a sprig of—he thought back to Christmas—mistletoe, of all things, poking out of one of the padlocks. Next to the box, a couple of books, encyclopaedia-sized, and on them a heap of what looked like papers, closely written. Foxon realised that he was squinting in an attempt to read the words. Detail. Papers?

"Paper violins." It sounded even more daft when he said it out loud. Just as well nobody else had got in when the train stopped at Headcorn; they'd've thought he was crazy. Which he probably was, trying to do the Oracle's job for him when even the super gave up without a fight . . .

He turned to the third sketch. Evidently Miss Seeton had been unhappy with her previous attempts, for here was the carved wooden box again, this time with its lid open and a necklace of what might be diamonds spilling over the side from among a wealth of treasure: gold coins, crowns, sparkling stones. On the edge of the open lid perched the glint-eyed chicken, with the violin case in its beak and a piece of that close-written paper in one upraised claw. Against one side of the chest, the set of golf clubs leaned; around the other side, pooling in front under the necklace, a mass of dark material, trimmed with ermine, sprawled.

Foxon muttered something and turned the page.

Miss Seeton's fourth effort showed an altogether smaller box. It was plain, not carved, open as before but with a display of knives and forks in neat rows, rather than a jumble of jewels. Beside it stood a male figure in mediaeval dress—flat, feathered cap, tunic and hose, and over all a long, fur-trimmed robe, reaching almost to the ground. In one hand, he held another sheet of paper; in the other was a violin, full-sized, and about his neck hung, not a necklace, but a heavy, ornate chain of office.

"The Lord Chief Justice?" Foxon shrugged. "The Lord High Executioner?"

There was no box (of whatever size) on the fifth page. A sheet of paper, beautifully written in what it was easy to see was a foreign language, and with what looked like an official seal at the bottom, was held in the wicked beak of that same malevolent chicken, perching one-footed on the bridge of the violin while its free claw clasped a briar pipe, from which woolly white circles puffed slowly upwards. "Smoke signals," said Foxon. And wondered.

Miss Seeton had obviously made a desperate effort for her sixth, and final, sketch. With nothing cluttered about it to block the view, there was the iron-bound wooden chest. Its lid was open, and there were carved letters around the inside rim; but in place of jewels and gold, the chest held bundles of knives and forks, and spoons with curlicued handles and deep, rounded bowls.

"And that," said Foxon, "is the lot."

He didn't chortle this time.

It was auction day at Candell & Inchpin, one of their regular Fine Art and Furniture sales for which an advertisement had appeared for the past three weeks in numerous trade and public papers. Had it not, the senior Candell repeatedly insisted, they would have closed the establishment for the day, as a mark of respect. A loyal employee of such very long standing as Myra Stanebury . . .

"Don't worry, sir, I quite understand. And I'm sure she would, too," soothed Brinton, as Mr. Candell wrung his plump hands together in a frenzy of mingled guilt and embarrassment. "I should think you'd find it almost impossible to turn folk away when they could be coming from the other end of the country, for all you know. If Miss Stanebury was as devoted to the interests of the firm as you suggest—"

"She was! Oh, she was. From school, you know, she'd been with us full-time. Even before then, she worked here at weekends, and during the holidays. She was"—Mr. Candell closed his eyes, evoking a vision of dedication beyond the call of duty—"a veritable legend about the place, Superintendent. If she took a holiday, I'm sure I can't remember when. We paid her double for those weeks," he added hastily, in case Brinton should suspect him of exploitation. "And she was *never* ill." Brinton's look expressed surprise, but he had no time to comment before the eulogy resumed. "Always the first to arrive in the morning, the last to leave at night. She knew the business inside out— and I simply don't know what," he said, wringing his hands again, then plunging his right into his trouser pocket, "we're going to do without her."

As he paused at last to blow his nose, Brinton managed a few words before Mr. Candell, oblivious to anything but his loss and the requisite tribute, broke in on him. "Never ill? Didn't it strike you—?"

"*Never.*" He leaned forward to wag an arch finger under the superintendent's nose. "Now, this is in confidence, Mr. Brinton. You may consider my remarks somewhat lacking in taste—mean-spirited, even, but in a case of—of—" As so many did, he baulked at that six-letter word for death. "In such a shocking case, Superintendent, it would be . . . ridiculous not to give you the fullest facts."

"Which are?" enquired Brinton as Mr. Candell's red silk handkerchief was once more applied to his nose.

"Which are that poor Myra—Miss Stanebury—has— had—the most ghastly mother you can imagine, Mr. Brinton. Calls herself an invalid—ha! Lazybones would be a more suitable term." Mr. Candell crushed the scarlet silk into irritated invisibility in the palm of his plump hand. "The tyranny of the possessive mother, Mr. Brinton, that's what it is—was. And poor Myra too devoted—devotion was in her nature, the dear thing—to realise how she was being exploited. Mama," he said, grimacing awfully, "must have attendance danced upon her at every free moment of the day. Her digestion was so delicate, her nerves were so frail, that she had to have the best of everything, in case she might suffer a relapse." Mr. Candell didn't quite say *Faugh!*, but his distaste for the ailments, real or imagined, of Myra Stanebury's mother needed no such gloss to be fully understood.

"She had no social life, Mr. Brinton—Myra, that is, not her dear mama. Mama believed that social intercourse of the most exclusive nature, among equally refined and delicate souls, could only serve to ease her weary path through life. And what mama wanted, she had."

"In Brettenden?" Brinton could hardly believe his ears.

"In Brettenden. Mrs. Stanebury contrived—heaven knows how—to achieve for her sickroom the reputation of a *salon* in the most fashionable sense of the word." Once more, Mr. Candell grimaced. "Whether or not such reputation was justified, I am in no position to judge. Mama was careful to hold court only while Myra was out of the house, and always dismissed her guests just minutes before her daughter was due home—a home which was, by all accounts, luxurious in the extreme. The salon itself, I gather, is a marvel, the very picture of an eighteenth-century literary meeting-place—and all paid for by poor Myra! Of course, we only charged her cost price plus ten, you know, when she bought from Candell stock."

He sniffed. "Mama, you see, dared not fritter away her precious widow's pension on such frivolities as chandeliers and French windows to the conservatory—with a grapevine," he added grimly—"and miniature peach trees— poor Myra! One day, mama maintained, her daughter would marry, leaving her alone and destitute. Against which day—a day she took the greatest care Myra had no chance to see—the pension must, of course, be hoarded. There was never any suggestion that Myra might wish to save her wages on her own account—and, poor girl, as far as I know she didn't."

Mr. Candell shook his head. "She'd been brainwashed, Mr. Brinton—brainwashed almost from birth. Her papa succumbed to a heart attack after no more than a year or two of wedded bliss—and that," he concluded, "is the reason, I suspect, for her willingness to spend so much time here at work." He waved an airy hand to emphasise his suspicions. "Oh, it was subconscious, I've no doubt, but she must have realised that the longer she was out of the house, the less opportunity mama had to play her nasty little games. And"—he hushed his tone to become still more confidential—"I also suspect that of recent years the worm had begun to turn—that some of those double holiday wages went into a separate account: I do hope they did. I believe poor Myra was not only escaping, in daylight hours at least, from her dreadful parent: I believe she could actually have been planning her escape! When she had saved enough money, I suspect that Myra Stanebury was going to slip her leash completely, and be off . . .

"But we would always have cherished the hope that she might one day come back to keep our books in order and our files straight. Now"—he sighed, from the heart—"that hope is gone. And what we're going to do without her, I simply do not know!"

"If she was so indispensable," said Brinton, seizing his chance, "I'd have thought you'd be surprised when she never showed up yesterday for work. Didn't—?"

"Oh, but she did." Mr. Candell was so keen to set Brinton straight that for the second time he interrupted him in mid-question. "She arrived in the morning at her usual hour—such devotion! She tried so bravely to work through as she always did, and it was only after lunch that she admitted she didn't feel quite the thing. A migraine—and who could blame her? She took such a pride in her work, she had invented a filing system unique to our requirements, and when the burglar made that terrible mess, not to mention the shock—that poor young man . . ."

He rapidly shook the crumples out of his anguished

handkerchief, and blew his nose again. Nothing, it seemed, would persuade him to speak the full enormity of what had happened to Terry Mimms: and—Brinton silently echoed Mr. Candell's own words—who could blame him? "One thing after another," he observed. "For instance—"

"It most certainly is!" Mr. Candell sat up, looking positively affronted. "It seems that Brettenden is suffering a veritable crime wave, Superintendent! If it weren't enough that our premises should be burgled, and our employees"—he took a deep breath—"attacked—and what she was doing in Plummergen, of all places, I'm sure I couldn't say"—Brinton heaved a sigh of relief that one of his unasked questions had been answered—"but after last week's dreadful affair at the museum, I might almost begin to believe there was a—a jinx on Candell and Inchpin. Only consider how—"

"Museum?" This time it was Brinton's turn to interrupt. "Jinx? What affair? Oh, yes," he said before Mr. Candell—looking amazed that this knowledge could have been denied a superintendent of police—should enlighten him. "I remember the report—they had a break-in a few days ago—but I don't know that I'd call it a burglary, because—"

"A matter of days," said Mr. Candell, his voice deep with meaning, "after the curator had attended our Household Sale! And the items he acquired at that sale were vandalised, Mr. Brinton—vandalised before there had been time for a proper cataloguing of the contents. How can we be sure that nothing was stolen?" He wagged another finger. "With our records in a muddle, we can't."

"We can't," agreed Brinton slowly. At the back of his mind, an idea was beginning to stir: but he needed time to think it through. "You're right, we can't . . ." And the look he directed towards Mr. Candell impelled the latter to respect, for once, another's silence, as the superintendent pondered those preliminary stirrings . . .

No. The coincidence was impossible.

Wasn't it?

He took a deep breath. "Was it—was it the same sale where you had an old wooden box—fancy carving, iron bands, jammed locks—bought by"—he gulped—"an old lady with a blue umbrella?"

As Mr. Candell was on the point of answering him, the telephone rang.

CHAPTER 25

Mr. Candell halted in mid-reply, glanced apologetically at
Brinton, and—as the other nodded—reached, with a frown,
for the telephone receiver. "I thought it was understood
that while— Oh. Yes. It's for you, Superintendent."

"Me? Thanks . . . Brinton."

"Sir, I'm at the Yard." The excitement in Foxon's voice
was evident despite the forty-mile distance. "With Mr. Delphick. He's had a look at MissEss's drawings, and—well,
sir," he said as a baritone commentary could be heard in
the background, "he *says* it's only a guess, with not knowing all the facts because I haven't had time to explain—
but it sounds pretty good to me—"

Brinton broke in with a quickfire burst of what-the-hell-
are-you-babbling-about noises. Foxon wasted no time in
apology before saying, "Peace Radwinter, sir. That's who's
suspect number one for our murders, according to the
Ora— Ahem! According to Mr. Delphick, sir. And I reckon
he could be right."

"Radwinter? Radwinter." Brinton frowned, too busy
concentrating on the elusive train of thought set in motion
by Foxon's words to spare his immediate thoughts for the

continued presence of the fascinated Mr. Candell. "Peace Radwinter . . ."

There was a click on the line. "According to Miss Seeton," came the modest amendment from Chief Superintendent Delphick. "There's no point in my going into details, Chris: time enough when Foxon makes his full report. We'll be bringing him back to you in a fast car as soon as possible." He paused; Brinton, still concentrating, said nothing. "But we—and Miss Seeton, it would seem—strongly recommend that you brook no delay in repairing to the house of one Neville Chamberlain Radwinter. Whose name, from Foxon's reaction when I first made this tentative suggestion, may be better known to you than it is to the Metropolitan Police. To whom, I might add, it is not entirely unfamiliar . . ."

The telephones at the London end of the connection waited in silence for some response from Superintendent Brinton in Brettenden. "Radwinter," he repeated at last. "Peace Radwinter . . . Got it!"

The discreetly mute and intensely curious Mr. Candell was not the only one to jump at the crack of hand on brow as Brinton's wayward memory lurched at last into action. "That blasted auction!" Mr. Candell uttered a squeak of protest. "He was there! I'd swear to it, Oracle. I only spotted him out of the corner of my eye, and what with MissEss and her brolly going into overdrive, I didn't pay too much attention, but if I had," he said as he clumped himself across the forehead again, "I might've started to wonder why he was doing his best to keep out of my way—him and his guilty conscience both. He must've seen me and got nervous about watching out for who bought what . . .

"But why?" After his first flush of enthusiasm for the unexpected lead, the superintendent subsided. "It doesn't make sense. He can be an ugly customer, yes, but only when he's panicked, and Peace has never been the sort of bloke to get the collywobbles *before* he's done the job—and he hadn't done a sausage at that stage. As far as we know,'' caution made him add. ''And where do your lot come into it? What's it to you if young Foxon comes back by train or—or push-bike? Why the red-carpet treatment and the fast car?''

''Fast cars,'' returned Delphick, ''may prove rather more apposite than you realise, Chris—but I'll explain later. I'm serious about urging you to visit Radwinter just as soon as you can—but not alone. Some backup could be essential, and certainly won't do any harm.''

''Backup? With the manpower I've got, I—''

''From what Foxon tells me,'' Delphick insisted, ''you have no other serious lines of enquiry. If Miss Seeton and I are wrong, you'll have wasted perhaps half an hour pulling a few men off other aspects of your various cases. If, however, we're right, you could be putting your hand on the collar of a triple murderer, as well as—''

''A triple murderer?'' Brinton gasped; Mr. Candell, still avidly drinking in the sensational scene unfolding in his office, goggled. ''*Three* murders—you mean you reckon he's our lad for the Quendon killing, too?''

''Explanations in due course, Chris. We're leaving ten minutes ago, and so should you. Seriously,'' he added as Brinton made a faint attempt at a further demand for enlightenment. ''But before you and yours descend on friend Radwinter, might I also suggest that you alert the Brettenden fire brigade? And not just because of Miss Seeton,'' he said as Brinton uttered a curse which made Mr. Candell blink. ''From my own recently acquired knowledge of this case—of these cases—I feel it would do no harm to have the support of a tender or two as you approach the house. As soon as you can,'' he reiterated.

And rang off.

Brinton stared for three seconds at the buzzing receiver in his hand, then shook himself awake, sighed, and clicked the cradle up and down. ''How do I get an outside line?'' he demanded as Mr. Candell nerved himself to ask what might be going on.

"Er—there's no switchboard. If you—"

Brinton was already dialling. "Mutford? Brinton. Put me through to whoever's in charge of the chummies' address-book, will you? Fast."

Sergeant Mutford had not forgotten his superior's recent dereliction of duty in the matter of camp beds and catnaps.

"Might I ask from where you are speaking, sir?"

"Candell and Inchpin. Yes, they found me from the Yard, if that's what you're getting at—but don't let's waste any more time. I need that address yesterday, Mutford!"

"I regret, sir, any disrespect." The tone in which he said this did not convince. "But how can I be sure this is not an attempt by some fraudulent mimic to obtain highly confidential information under false pretences?"

"Dammit, Mutford—"

"Highly confidential information," repeated Mutford, with relish, "which it is my sworn and official duty to protect from all unauthorised persons, especially such as use the medium of the telephone rather than applying in person, when their identity might be checked by—"

"Mutford!" Brinton added something which induced his sergeant, gasping with indignation, to recognise his superior with no further delay. Twenty-three seconds after the telephone in the Ashford operations room had been picked up, Brinton was writing down the required intelligence with a pen Mr. Candell had been only too happy to lend him.

"Thank you, sir." Brinton gave him an old-fashioned look as, having issued quick instructions to a haughty Mutford and broken the connection, he began to dial again. "I'm sure I don't have to remind you of the need to be discreet. Do I." He was not asking, but telling.

Mr. Candell looked hurt that anyone, least of all an officer of the law, should feel he needed to be told. "In my business, Superintendent, discretion—"

"Fire station? Superintendent Brinton, Ashford police. Look, this may sound crazy, but we've had a tip-off there could be a spot of bother before long, out Les Marys way—

no, not that blasted nightclub,'' he said, referring to a previous occasion when the Half Seas Over had been burned down by a proprietor with financial problems. He gave the correct address. ''No, I can't tell you any more than that.'' *Because I haven't the foggiest myself,* he added silently. *The only people who can see through this particular fog are the Oracle and—heaven help me—Miss Seeton* . . . ''But I'm heading that way now, and some of my blokes are meeting me there. It may be a false alarm, but in this case I don't believe we ought to take the risk.''

''A tip-off, you say.'' There was doubt in the voice at the other end of the line: calling out the Brettenden Fire Brigade was not to be lightly undertaken. As in many country districts, the market town relied heavily on a Retained service, where a large proportion of the crew members had other full-time jobs—mostly on the land, since all crews had not only to be able to reach the fire station within five minutes, but must also be in the peak of physical condition. It might not be as serious in sluggish January as in harvest-home July to summon a farm worker from the fields to attend a false alarm, but serious it undoubtedly was. ''Reliable, your source, is it?''

Superintendent Brinton hesitated for only an instant. He could almost swear he heard the Oracle egging him on by saying that perjury, in a good cause, was worth it. Well, he'd meet his friend—and Miss Seeton—halfway. ''Pretty reliable, yes. I'm bringing a couple of cars in from other enquiries as backup, and I wouldn't be doing that if I didn't feel I'd need 'em more likely than not.''

''One appliance, then,'' said the voice. ''One to start with—you can have another if the man on the ground thinks you need it. All right?''

''Thanks,'' said Brinton, wondering, now he'd burned his boats, whether the Police Benevolent Fund would run to the hefty fine he envisaged for having wasted everyone's time. If he had. Or would it count as a False Alarm, Good Intent?

Two telephone handsets clattered into their respective cradles in different parts of Brettenden as Brinton and the fire station operator went to Action Stations. Brinton said his farewells to Mr. Candell, promised to be back, and bolted from the sale-room to his waiting car. Foxon usually drove him, but the lad was in London—was, according to the Oracle, on his way back from London, in a Yard car full of Yard men, top speed down the motorway. It wasn't just that the younger man did all the fast driving that made his superior regret his absence: he had an uncomfortable feeling, nowhere near the back of his mind, that if he hadn't sent him off to Town with Miss Seeton's sketchbook in the first place, he could still be living the sort of peaceful, plodding life he hadn't had nearly enough of over the past seven years . . .

"What the—? Buckland!" Brinton took two steps backwards to gaze at the uniformed figure in his driver's seat. "What the hell are you playing at?"

"Chauffeuring, sir." PC Buckland leaned across to open the passenger door. "Sergeant Mutford radioed you might fancy a spot of company on the road, seeing as Foxon's up in Town and missing all the fun, for once. Les Marys, right?" he assumed as Brinton climbed in and fastened his seat belt.

"Right." And he could trust Mutford, he knew, to have passed on the address.

"Siren, sir? Lights?"

"Not unless you see a pillar of fiery cloud up ahead. Let's use a bit of discretion and get there without letting 'em know we're on our way—but don't take all day about it, either." To some, this might seem a tall order: but Buckland knew his job. He was, as Brinton was aware, one of Foxon's cronies: the detective constable had taught his uniformed pal quite a number of his favourite driving tricks. They'd chased each other up and down the police skid-pans more than once, and he himself had turned a tactful blind eye to the book some of the bloods in the station canteen had been running on which of the pair could do the most handbrake turns in a given time in a limited space. He'd been about to risk his money on Foxon when Desk Sergeant Mutford had got wind of the contest and, preaching hellfire and disapproval, had squashed the whole thing . . .

"Next turning but one on the left, sir."

Brinton jumped. His thoughts had been so busy with Foxon and Mutford and the Holdfast Brethren that he'd managed to forget all about Miss Seeton—about his reasons (whatever they were) for rushing off to Les Marys with a fire engine on full alert somewhere or other in the neighbourhood. Somewhere or—

"Fire appliance coming up fast behind." Buckland had checked in his mirror before signalling the turn.

Brinton didn't dare look round to confirm the statement. He closed his eyes, thankful that he didn't—as yet—have to close his ears against the ringing bells and flashing blue lights that would only attract public attention to his growing wretchedness.

"Down here, sir." Buckland slowed, changed gear, spun the wheel, and set off down the quiet side street. "Looks like another of our lot, coming the other way . . ."

Brinton kept his eyes closed. He slumped in his seat, cursing himself for being every kind of fool. Why the hell hadn't he insisted on waiting for the Oracle to arrive from London? Then the Yard could have gone halves in sharing the blame for whatever fiasco was about to—

"Hey!"

There was a jolt, a swerve, and the stench of burning rubber as Brinton was flung sideways. Juddering, the car came to a halt. His eyes flew open as the breath was driven from his body by the hot diagonal friction of the seat belt, by the jerk of his lowered head upflung by the forces of propulsion. He had not heard the squeal of the burning tyres—he did not hear the screech of mangled metal; Buckland's breathless gasp was as inaudible to Brinton as the startled braking, the horrified bell of the approaching fire appliance . . .

For every sound had been drowned out by the noise of the explosion.

CHAPTER 26

The shock had caused Buckland to steer into the side of the road: into a concrete lamppost which stood six inches from the edge of the footpath, next to a waste-bin. As the front tyres bounced up and over the kerb, the nearside wing and bonnet of the car crumpled against the concrete, and a carelessly aimed drinks can flew up from the gutter to clang with a burst of spider-web cracks across the laminated glass of the windscreen.

It was through the side windows that Brinton, and the hard-breathing Buckland, watched a plume of purple smoke and yellow-green flame erupt from a house halfway down the road. The oncoming police car vanished within seconds, blanketed from view by thick billows of aubergine and black, crested by a scurf of gun-metal grey shot through with speckles of sulphurous chartreuse.

"B-bloody hell." Buckland's hands shook as he fumbled at the clasp of his seat belt. An angry bruise branded his forehead where the rim of the steering wheel had caught it. "Are—are you all right, sir? We—we'd better see—if we can help, but . . ."

Brinton had to clear his throat twice before answering.

"I'm . . . all right, thanks." His neck, shoulders, and spine jangled from the crash; he shook his head; groaned; and the groan became a cough. "How—how about you?" He was struggling with his own buckle. "Just look at—hey!" His hands were suddenly still. He sniffed; he spluttered. "Petrol! Petrol—and I reckon it's us. Out of here—on the double, lad—blast this door, it's stuck—get *out,* Buckland. Stop fussing about me, damn you! Get out before this deathtrap blows us both to kingdom come!"

"Bugger that for a lark—sir." Buckland knew that his burly superior would find it no easy matter to scramble unaided out of the twisted passenger seat, over the gear lever and under the steering wheel to safety. He reached back in to grab as much of Brinton's bulk as he could, half pulling, half dragging him by sleeve and collar and—as there came a sudden rip—trouser waistband, towards the driver's door.

"I told you," gasped Brinton, kicking furiously as his foot jammed under the clutch pedal, "to get the hell out of this! If"—he kicked again; Buckland, sweating, tugged and heaved—"you're trying to be noble—"

"Not—me—sir." Buckland gritted his teeth. "Just—getting—in—a—spot—of—extra—weight—training—"

"Move over, son." The exhausted constable found himself suddenly plucked out of danger's way by a dark-blue-uniformed hand. Two other hands, attached to muscled arms attached in turn to a sturdy shape in fireman's costume, performed with practiced efficiency those miracles of contortion which should liberate Superintendent Brinton, with barely time to spare, from the wreckage of the car.

"The house," choked Brinton, staggering to the far side of the road, where Buckland, now white and trembling, waited. "My lads—the other car—"

"All under control." The fireman, having run an expert eye over the Ashford men, was eager to be off. "You'll do, so long as you keep away from that tin can of yours until we've checked it out. There's another tender or two on the way, so you've no need for heroics—you're done in. The pair of you," he added over his shoulder, hurrying to join his colleagues as the fire engine made its steady advance through the eddies of smoke and flame. "Don't let your boss start trying to win medals, will you?"

Buckland could only grin weakly. From being white, he had turned green; it wasn't easy to tell whether he was supporting Brinton, or Brinton was supporting him. Various well-intentioned occupants of nearby houses tried to urge the pair indoors for sugared tea and comfortable sit-downs until the ambulance should come. Neither man had any mind to accept these kindly, but misguided, invitations: Brinton, bruised and stiff, agonised over the fate of his men trapped in that hazy purple embrace, while Buckland felt sick, and saw throbbing lights before his eyes that had little to do with the warning beacons on the fire appliance—

Appliances, plural. Bells ringing, lights strobing, two more engines raced to the scene, with an ambulance close behind them, and a panda car bringing up the rear. Brinton, bestirring himself, hailed these reinforcements, and tried his best to issue intelligent instructions even as he and Buckland were swept into the protective custody of the one-hundred-per-cent-fit professionals. Short of bopping the entire medical team on their several noses, the superintendent had to accept that he was destined to play no further part in these proceedings. As a second ambulance, and a fourth police vehicle, appeared around the corner of the street, he sank thankfully into the rough red welcome of woollen blankets, leaned back against the cool metal wall, and closed his eyes upon the reassuring sight of Buckland, on a stretcher, being tended by a fatherly man whose white coat had three buttons missing.

His last thought, as the ambulance rumbled away in the direction of the hospital, was that when the Oracle and Foxon finally arrived from Town, they'd have a hell of a lot of explaining to do.

*　　*　　*

"Explanations?" Delphick's smile was faintly mocking. "As any explanation must inevitably involve Miss Seeton, Chris, are you sure your nerves are equal to the strain?"

Superintendent Brinton skewered Foxon (whose chortle had been just a little too loud) to his chair with one blistering glare. "I'm sure. Strain, shock—so what's the difference? I'll live. They said so." Despite protests, he had discharged himself from hospital the instant he'd heard that Buckland was in no danger, and was now—battered, weary, but triumphant—holding court in his office. "I wouldn't care to guarantee your chances of survival, though, if you don't tell me what the hell's been going on. And what," he added, "I'm supposed to put on the charge sheet, for heaven's sake."

"Sergeant Ranger, the evidence, if you please." Delphick smiled again. "And I don't, just yet, mean the sketchbook," he added for Brinton's benefit. "Foxon still has custody of that particular item—thanks, Bob." From his sergeant's huge hand he gently took a charred sheet of paper, which he passed to the superintendent without a word, watching with interest as Brinton narrowed his eyes, trying to make out the spidery scrawl.

"Need a magnifying glass for—oh. 'The production of—of ionised species of naturally nuclear'—no, 'naturally nonpolar compounds.' " He blinked. He drew a deep breath. He tried again. "Can't make out this bit, either . . . ah. 'Its standard octane rating of zero would be altered dramatically if . . .' If what? The chap could've used a few hours with a copybook . . . uh-huh '. . . series of experiments with high voltage elec-electricity'—no, 'electrolysis has been designed. If the status'—no, 'the static charge from a van der Graaf gen . . .' " He looked up. "That's the lot. Might as well be talking Russian, for all the sense it makes to me. Do you seriously mean to say it's for the sake of this"—he brandished the paper—"this dammed jargon that three people died?"

"Indirectly, yes." Delphick reached into his breast

pocket for a folded envelope, on the back of which he had made a few notes. "I took the liberty, while you were *hors de combat,* of phoning the Yard and speaking to one or two of our explosives experts. They confirmed the rumour that reached me only this morning, but which had reached certain members of the criminal fraternity some weeks ago— that, according to this, the self-styled Professor Eldred Quendon was working on a method for turning seawater into what we may, for convenience, call petrol."

"Quendon? Seawater—into petrol? You're joking."

"I'm not. Nor, from what the experts tell me, was Quendon, necessarily. May I?" He gestured for the paper, and Brinton passed it over with a grimace. "Unlike you, Chris, I was not suffering, even in the mildest sense, from delayed shock when I first saw this." He raised a warning hand as Brinton opened his mouth to protest. "In the very mildest sense," he said firmly. "As you yourself agreed, you'll live—but it's bound to have addled your thinking processes to some extent."

With a grunt, the superintendent acknowledged the truth of this, then grimaced and said he doubted he'd be any less addled if he looked at the thing for a week. He was a good, honest, straightforward copper who liked his cases good and straightforward, too. Which wasn't how he'd describe secret damned petrol formulas, not by a long chalk it wasn't.

Delphick did his best not to sound smug. He almost succeeded. "I was able to make out a few words more than you—a very few, but significant, I gather." He tapped the note-scribbled envelope, then readdressed himself to the charred paper. "Ahem. 'The best fuel economy credible with existing engines for domestic vehicles, which can be remedied by'—and here, Chris, we meet—'the production of ionised species of naturally nonpolar compounds.' And, again," he said as Brinton could only blink at him, " 'generation of the species . . .' " He stopped. Even the Oracle must boggle at the pronunciation of $C_7H_{16}^{++}$. After the briefest of pauses, he smiled. "The species—ahem—blank is what would, in theory, 'dramatically alter the standard octane rating of zero.' Don't ask," he entreated, as Brinton prepared to demand enlightenment, "what it means. I may be able to decipher it, in part, but beyond that I have to confess to being utterly perplexed."

Delphick contrived, by his manner, to suggest that such utter perplexity was a rare experience indeed for the Oracle of Scotland Yard: as Brinton had silently to admit that it was. "You'll hazard a guess, though," he said aloud.

"Hazard implies risk." Delphick's self-satisfaction was evident. "I risk little, I believe, by basing my submission on the conjectural ability of the Yard boffins—who, admittedly, can't be completely sure of their facts without seeing the exact formula, the remainder of which appears to have been lost in the explosion. Whether they'll be able to make any use of this, to my eyes inadequate, remnant is, however, neither here nor there: you—we—have evidence enough, I submit, to charge Radwinter, when he is fully recovered, for the murders of Quendon, of Terry Mimms, and of Myra Stanebury. And with the burglary at Sweetbriars, even if we can't really do him for the attempted murder of Miss Seeton," he added. "In this aspiration he was not, I suspect, unique—but we'll come to that later," he added as Brinton groaned. "And I doubt we should hold him personally to blame for the decease of Artie Chishall, even if—"

"Who?" The Oracle was going too fast for a man suffering from shock. "Chishall? Never heard of him."

"An informer, given to turning his coat at an alarming rate for which he was notorious among the fraternity. At a critical point in his latest double-cross, his . . . carelessness rendered him liable to the extreme penalty—though in London, not Kent. Radwinter has the parochial instincts of his kind. He may well have been inspired by Cutler to kill three other people, but realistically we shouldn't blame—"

"Cutler?" This was altogether too much. "Who the hell

is—? No, wait,'' he said as Delphick prepared to explain.
"That bloke who choppered his way out of Pentonwood,
right?'' The ferocity of his look subdued explanation to a
silent nod. "You mean,'' Brinton said, "he's been holed
up in my manor all this time?'' Delphick nodded again.
"While you've been chasing about Town looking for the
blighter?'' Another nod. Brinton gritted his teeth. "So
when I yelled for help, you—you damned well needed it
as much as I did?''

"The perfect professional partnership,'' Delphick said
cheerfully, gesturing to Foxon. "Assisted, of course, by
Miss Seeton and her invaluable doodles—thank you,
Foxon.'' He rested the sketchbook on his knee and tapped
the closed cover with his forefinger. "It's all in here, Chris,
though I appreciate you're in no fit state yet for the full
rigmarole: I'll be letting you have a written report once I'm
back at the Yard, by which time your concussion, or whatever it is, should have lapsed. Or whatever it does.''

"I haven't—oh, what's the use?'' Brinton closed his
eyes. "Where that woman's concerned, I *feel* as if I've got
it even if I haven't, if concussion means your head goes
round in circles and you haven't a clue what's what. Which
is why,'' he reminded his colleague, "I asked for a trans-
lator in the first place. So go ahead and translate before *you*
become liable for the *extreme penalty*. It'd almost be worth
losing my pension for—but not quite. Just tell me what's
been going on, and why. And then we can all be happy
again.''

"Cheap, virtually limitless fuel," said Delphick, "must be the ultimate dream of the inventor. It would not be over-stating the case to say that such a fuel would have a rev-olutionary effect on world economy: lower manufacturing and transport costs of goods are only two of the most im-mediate effects that spring to mind. Not that the oil industry would regard such a fuel with approval, of course. Legends abound of people who have discovered a water-based power as, ah, powerful as petrol, who have been paid vast amounts of money to keep their mouths shut.

"Professor Quendon hoped to make millions from his discovery, whether by marketing it in the usual manner or . . . by taking the other way."

"Blackmail," said Brinton, scowling.

"Commercial opportunism," Delphick corrected him drily. "A not uncommon characteristic: and he wasn't, though I very much doubt that he was aware of this, the only opportunist in the case. He must naturally have sup-posed that the oil companies, should they learn of his work before the method had been perfected, would try to prevent its successful completion: but he had no reason to expect that Cutler would display his own—considerable—interest.'' He indicated the sketchbook, which Brinton had placed cautiously in the middle of his blotter. ''Miss Seeton gives us no firm idea of how Cutler came to learn of Quendon's work, though I suspect the secrecy with which he apparently surrounded himself would have stimulated some curiosity among his neighbours, not all of it legitimate. Once the gentleman in question is again in a fit state to be questioned, the exact method may become clear, though it hardly matters. His grape-vine, even in prison, was invariably efficient.''

''Efficient enough,'' grumbled Brinton, ''to organise his personal flying taxi to pick him up whenever he felt like it, for a start.''

''Whenever he felt like it?'' Delphick raised an eyebrow. ''I've no doubt he felt like a change of scene on many occasions, but he never took the chance. He's a scientist: he would have calculated the odds and decided that staying in gaol, at the known centre of his information network, was a safer bet than making the break and risking an even greater loss of freedom after his inevitable recapture and reduced parole. All along we kept asking ourselves why, so close to the end of his sentence, he would hazard everything as he did. The stakes had to be pretty high: and they were. Cutler wanted the formula for seawater petrol . . . which he had already failed to acquire by more orthodox means.''

Brinton sat up. ''The burglary! When they hit the poor bugger over the head and killed him—that was Cutler?''

''That was Radwinter. Cutler, remember, was still in prison: but there's little doubt he was the moving force behind the break-in, though for myself I have considerable doubts as to whether he would have ordered Quendon's death, at least not until he'd learned how close the research was to completion—whether he, with a few picked assistants, would have been able to bring it to fruition without the professor, and make the best use of its possibilities. You may recall that Cutler is a chemist of some ability, but with a specialised subject like this, it's far more probable he would have preferred trying to coerce the old man into joining his team . . . We'll ask him that, too, once he's out of hospital.''

Involuntary memories of disinfectant and floor polish tickled the inside of Brinton's nose, and he made a frantic dive into his trouser pocket. "It'll be—achoo!—some time," he observed grimly. "Achoo!"

"Bless you." Delphick, Foxon, and Bob spoke together: but Delphick was a chief superintendent. It was he who continued, in answer to Brinton's observation, "Indeed it will. Which is all to the good, as it may, I fear, be some time for us also, before we have a case anywhere near strong enough to bring before the courts. With Radwinter's house completely destroyed, and the laboratory equipment with it—but I digress," he said as Brinton raised an exasperated face from the depths of his handkerchief. "The basic facts for now: the details must wait for later."

Brinton grunted, finished blowing his nose, and returned his handkerchief to its proper place before folding his arms and leaning back in his chair. "The facts," he said, with as much command in his voice as a man suffering from shock may achieve. "Please!"

"Sorry. I'll try to keep it short. Briefly, what seems to have happened is that Cutler heard about the petrol substitute, wondered if it would be worth his while to follow up on his release, and arranged, through his second-in-command Wimbish, for Neville Radwinter—I beg his pardon, for Peace—with or without companions we don't yet know—to burgle Quendon's laboratory and report back on what they found. It wouldn't have been a quick job. Radwinter's no chemist; and before they'd learned anything remotely useful, they were disturbed by Quendon, whom they killed. This left Cutler worrying that the professor's goods, chattels, notes, and equipment might be acquired by people who either wouldn't understand their true worth, and

would destroy them—or who would, and whose exploitation of the process would be well advanced before he could
do anything about it.''

He paused. He caught Brinton's eye and received a nod
in return. ''So far,'' said Delphick, ''so good, then. Cutler
escaped with Wimbish's help from prison, and took refuge
chez Radwinter. Peace found out when Quendon's effects
were coming up for auction and escorted Cutler there to
examine the lots to be sure of buying the right packing case.
And while they were making sure . . .''

''In walked Miss Seeton.'' Brinton shuddered. ''And me.
I *saw* the little creep and didn't cotton on—I could kick
myself!''

''That's hardly the way to speak of a professional colleague, Chris.'' Delphick hid a smile. ''It was hardly Miss
Seeton's fault that her path crossed that of Cutler: call it
fate, if you must, but don't call it creepy. It was . . . one of
those things that seems to happen, when Miss Seeton and
her umbrella—any of her umbrellas—are around.''

Brinton shuddered again. Foxon sniggered and turned it
into a cough. Big Bob Ranger shifted on his chair.

Delphick ignored them all. ''Radwinter recognised you,
of course, even if Cutler didn't, and warned him to duck
out of sight. They didn't dare draw attention to themselves
by putting in their bid when they'd just seen Miss Seeton
signalling, as they thought, to you: they hung around long
enough to realise you weren't going to do anything right
away, then took the opportunity to head for safety when
you, ah, started to—to create a—a slight disturbance.''

''That bloody wooden box,'' moaned Brinton with his
eyes closed. ''That damned umbrella! I should have
known . . .''

''But you didn't know. Nor did they—that it was a simple mistake, a happenstance: a coincidence, nothing more.
It's a pity they didn't. Their consciences began to trouble
them: Miss Seeton ought to be silenced, for the common
good: she might at any time inconveniently remember what

and who she'd spotted to inspire her to signal as she did before she was—ahem—distracted." He ignored Brinton's muttered curse, though he smiled as he went on:

"But they had no idea who she was or where she lived. Nor did they know who had, in the end, bought the professor's equipment: hence, the burglary of Candell and Inchpin where Terry Mimms and his young woman were unlucky enough to get in Peace's way—and the ransacking of the files that so distressed Miss Stanebury."

Brinton opened his eyes. "Yes, what about her? Had *she* recognised the chummies, as well as Miss Seeton? As well as they thought Miss Seeton did, I mean, because she didn't, of course." He sat up. "Did she? Were they right? Not that she was signalling, I mean, but that she'd spotted there was something a bit odd about 'em?"

"According to Miss Seeton—with whom I've had time for only a brief telephone conversation—she noticed nothing untoward. Consciously noticed, that is, though her subconscious noticings are quite another matter, as we all know." Brinton muttered something that his friend chose to ignore. "It was her subconscious that produced those Drawings on your desk—and as for Miss Stanebury, my guess is that she, likewise, noticed nothing. She wasn't given to attending sales on the floor, I gather. Her filing system appears to have taken up most of her working day— and if you're about to ask me why she was killed, don't." He allowed a smile to quirk his lips. "Ask Foxon instead."

"I was right, sir," chirped the irrepressible one, as Brinton favoured him with a resigned but enquiring glare. "It *was* mistaken identity: he thought she was MissEss. The first time he broke into Sweetbriars he bumped into Martha, and he knew *she* wasn't—she's twenty years younger, for one thing—but the second time, I suppose he was worried he'd bungle it again, and he'd only ever got a quick look at her the day of the auction—so when he found her, that's Miss Stanebury, inside Miss Seeton's cottage he was sure that's who she was, and he—he killed her, sir. By mistake. Like I said. Sir.''

"So you did.'' Brinton glared at him again. "What you *didn't* say was what the Stanebury woman was doing there in the first place. I don't—I won't—believe she'd just dropped in out of the kindness of her heart to tell MissEss where that blasted box came from, not if you try till doomsday to make me believe it.''

"Then we won't,'' said Delphick as Foxon subsided. "We will rather explain that it is a—a second strand to the mystery: the subplot we should have suspected from the very beginning, given our knowledge of Miss Seeton. A second coincidence, yet related to the first in that the unfortunate Myra Stanebury's encounter with Miss Seeton only came about in the first place because of the wooden box, and Miss Seeton's earnest desire to know its provenance. Myra, you see, also suffered from an over-sensitive conscience. When Miss Seeton came asking her innocent questions, Miss Stanebury began to lose her nerve. It can't have helped, of course, that after speaking with her Miss Seeton went straight into a conversational huddle with Mr. Candell. Miss Stanebury, we must assume, had an attack of panic, and decided that she must be silenced. For,'' he repeated, with another quirk of his lips, "the common good.''

"Oh, God. Let me guess: she was running a brothel in the back room, doing fancy things with four-poster beds and antique rolling pins, and MissEss upset her—no?'' as Delphick, looking shocked, shook his head. "Go on, then. Tell me the worst.'' And the superintendent drew himself to his full height, breathed deeply, and gripped the edge of his desk in a frenzied grasp.

It seemed doubtful he could take much more. "Embezzlement,'' said Delphick simply. "There hasn't been time yet to check every detail, but Myra Stanebury had almost total control over the firm's books and files. It seems she persuaded one or two of the firm's partners—I'm almost sure they're innocent of anything except undue trust—to sign cheques out to legitimate clients, whereupon she altered the names of the payees to her own—she'd doctored the ink to make it easy to erase—and deposited the money in a bank account she kept secret even from her—ahem—rather forceful mother. When Miss Seeton started asking questions, she reacted as we've seen—and in due course suffered the same fate she had planned for someone else."

"Oh," said Brinton after a pause. "Is that all?"

"Near enough. It was Radwinter, of course, who at the instigation of Cutler broke into Brettenden Museum. He was after Quendon's notes, which were in the same lot as the Van der Graaf generator bought by the curator for educational display purposes: electrical currents and so forth. I'm told one stands on an isolation block with a hand on the globe, and when the circuit is complete, your hair stands on end as it discharges heaven knows how many volts from the mains. Very popular with children, they tell me, though not being a family man, I can't—ah, yes." Delphick eyed his friend thoughtfully.

He decided to take the chance. "Family. Yes. Wimbish, a gentleman with whom we in London have been long acquainted, is Peace Radwinter's cousin, Chris."

Brinton groaned. "I might have known! That blasted basement computer of yours'll have the whole damned family listed to the fifteenth generation, twice removed. Where's the old-fashioned coppering in just asking a machine?"

"Using its brains more profitably with the time saved from routine," returned Delphick, who had some sympathy with his hard-pressed colleague's complaint. "Which, indeed, we did, as soon as Miss Seeton had given us the vital clue. It was Peace Radwinter, the local, who first heard rumours of Quendon's work and passed them on to his big-shot cousin Wimbish as someone who would know how to make best use of the information; which was another reason for Radwinter's being the logical choice of refuge while

Wimbish waged all-out war in London on Cutler's behalf. Both men were doubtless promised great things, once Rickling's bid for power had been suppressed—a business rival,'' he quickly translated as Brinton quivered, and from the china mug of pencils near his blotter came a rattle of skeleton bones.

"Rickling, however, is my affair, not yours," Delphick continued smoothly. "You may rest easy on your laurels, Superintendent Brinton . . ." Then, as his friend seemed to relax and opened the top drawer of his desk, he decided to take a further chance. "Yours—and Miss Seeton's . . .''

Something in the way Foxon leaped sideways on his chair warned Delphick to duck—just in time—out of the flight-path of an infuriated high-velocity peppermint.

Bob Ranger wasn't so lucky.

CHAPTER 28

He had far better luck later. During the earlier telephone interrogation of Miss Seeton, Delphick had given due warning that a personal encounter—once the official business of the day had been completed—was probable; and Miss Seeton, in happy anticipation of a visit from her adopted nephew Bob Ranger and his kindly superior, had headed at once for the bakery on the opposite corner of The Street. From Mrs. Wyght she bought, among other delicacies, a thick slab of Bob's favourite gingerbread: it was sheer good manners now that compelled him to force down his third generous slice, with the pleasing prospect of others yet to come.

"And will you, Mr. Delphick, have another biscuit? Or a piece of Battenburg? A scone, perhaps? Or"—she twinkled at him across the table—"some of Martha's delicious fruit-cake?" Miss Seeton, always hospitable, that afternoon was even more so. She was in excellent spirits. A great weight had been lifted from her mind by the arrival of Chief Superintendent Delphick, and by his assurance that there was no need for her to feel in any way to blame for the unfortunate events of the past few days. The news that the prankster who had twice broken into her cottage was in hospital had, of course, come as something of a shock— but to know that her foolish pride in the romance of the Estover story had been completely innocent . . .

"A lemon-curd tart," she insisted, handing him the plate with a beaming smile. "Martha has been making up for lost time, you know, since recovering from her cold. And poor Mr. Treeves, according to his sister, is considerably improved, which is splendid news." The beam widened. "In fact, today has been a day for nothing but good news, hasn't it?"

Delphick mentally reviewed Buckland's concussion, Brinton's shock, the Intensive Care status of Cutler and his henchman, and the likely response of the insurance companies to the considerable damage done to the windows and roofs of the various properties either side of that demolished in the explosion—not to mention constabulary reactions at being one car short, and the likely views of Brettenden Town Council over its loss of the corresponding lamppost.

Then he saw Miss Seeton's smile . . . and substituted for his first list a second: an escaped prisoner found, a triple killer caught, a fraudster unmasked—too late, admittedly, for the law, but (according to the Candell accountant) just in time for the stolen funds to be recovered, for the tottering company to be placed once more on a sound financial footing.

"Nothing but good news," he agreed, helping himself (the gaiety of his hostess was infectious) to not one, but two of the dainty pastry rounds with their sharp, sweet, smoothly toothsome yellow filling, rich in stickiness and calories. "And nearly all," he added truthfully, "thanks to you and your sketches, Miss Seeton."

Miss Seeton blushed and murmured that she feared the chief superintendent was being too complimentary about her poor attempts at supplying him with that likeness of the box for which he, or rather Superintendent Brinton, had asked her. She had naturally done her best, but . . .

"But nothing, Miss Seeton. It was all there, after the very slightest mental adjustment had been made to what you had apparently drawn." Delphick picked up the sketchbook from its place at his side. "We will, of course, give you the usual receipt for this: Chris Brinton was adamant about that. I can't promise when your cheque will arrive, given the erratic behaviour of our basement computer, but rest assured that it will be a substantial one. We are more than grateful to you, you know."

Miss Seeton's modest denial of this knowledge was waved away by a third lemon tart as Delphick prepared to explain.

"It seemed, at first sight, that all you had done was draw the items you had seen at the auction: which, in a way, you had. But you drew only a selection. It was curious (and instructive) to note which of those selected you felt worthy of still more detailed observation—of emphasis, as it were. The golf clubs and the, ah, cutlery almost speak for themselves." He smiled. "But there was something of a puzzle in the violin, and the papers . . . and the man in the chain of office who Foxon was convinced must be the Lord High Executioner."

"Oh, no," protested Miss Seeton faintly.

"No," agreed Delphick. "The Lord Chancellor, perhaps?"

"Dr. Braxted," began Miss Seeton, "did say that—"

She broke off as she saw the Oracle shaking his head. Politely she waited for him to continue.

"A mediaeval costume, with associations of royalty and official responsibility: the Lord Chamberlain, I think, Miss Seeton. The repeated attention drawn to sheets of paper, that final sketch of the pipe of peace—ah, yes," he said as Miss Seeton uttered a little gasp of realisation.

Delphick smiled, rather sadly, as he nodded. "You and I, Miss Seeton, remember the Munich Crisis, and how Prime Minister Neville Chamberlain returned from Berlin waving his written promise from Hitler that there would be peace in our time.'' Miss Seeton shook her head—not in denial of his words, but in sorrow for the breaking of that paper promise, and for all the horror that followed. ''I doubt, however,'' Delphick hurried on, ''if you have even heard of one Charles Frederick Peace, and certainly I don't suggest that you remember him! He was a celebrated burglar of the Victorian era, as noted for his performance on the violin as he was for his steeplejack skills. Yes,'' he reiterated as Miss Seeton blinked. ''He carried his housebreaking tools in an old instrument case, was as agile as a cat, and so elastic in the facial muscles that he was a master of disguise. Charlie Peace was a thorn in the flesh of the Peelers for more than twenty years before he was caught and executed for killing two people.''

Miss Seeton sighed and shook her head again. Delphick said, ''Once the Cutler connection with what had been going on seemed likely, we fed his name, and those of his known associates, into the computer. Wimbish was already under some suspicion as Cutler's second-in-command: we fed in his name, asked for associates, and up came Neville Chamberlain Radwinter, alias—inevitably—Peace, resident of Brettenden. From that point,'' concluded the Oracle, a trifle smugly, ''it really wasn't difficult at all.''

Bob reached for another piece of gingerbread. ''So what happens next, Aunt Em? About the dukedom, I mean, not the rest. Is there some sort of—of blue blood authenticating service you could ask?''

''The Royal College of Heralds,'' supplied Delphick as Miss Seeton's burgeoning smile wavered and the old guilty expression crept back into her eyes. ''They'd be the ones, I fancy, and I've no doubt they could—if asked—draw up a family tree for the likely claimants . . . but it would take time, Bob. And money.'' He knew that Miss Seeton, innately honest, would never, in the cause of justice, grudge the cost; but he suspected strongly that she would regret losing the romance. For his part, he could see no good reason why she need suffer such a loss; and he set about calming her uneasy conscience with as much eloquence as he could muster.

"It's hardly a question of anyone's being in any particular hurry to claim the title, remember. I doubt if whoever it is has any idea at all that he or she might be the heir; almost probably it wasn't whoever put the box in the auction in the first place, since Miss Seeton has already explained that Candells have at last been able to supply her with the name, and she doesn't recognise it."

"Not yet," ventured Miss Seeton, casting a wistful eye in the direction of another heap of library books.

"Not yet," agreed Delphick. "But think how much more fun for . . . for everyone it would be, if Miss Seeton and the Braxteds and the Colvedens discovered the truth with no, as it were, official assistance. Think how they'll enjoy making a glorious present of their findings to—to whomever," he concluded. "I'm sure I would in their position."

He was much gratified to see the smile return, at full strength, to Miss Seeton's expressive countenance. "If," he added, "you were half the detective we believed you to be, Sergeant Ranger, you would have observed the large pile of theatrical biographies in library bindings beside Miss Seeton's chair; and you would have deduced that she is already well on her way to tracing the pedigree of the Pottipole family from the date of Benedicta's marriage."

Miss Seeton was nodding, seemingly much impressed by this display of Delphick's own deductive powers. "You would also," he went on, "have deduced that in London the good Dr. Braxted is working through the BM's— ahem—baronial archive in search of further clues, and that she'll be making regular reports of her progress as Miss Seeton, in turn, reports to her. Am I right, Miss Seeton?"

Miss Seeton's delighted blush confirmed the brilliance and accuracy of this chain of logic. Bob sat with the slice of gingerbread uneaten in his hand, muttering to himself for having missed the clue of the thespian tomes.

Miss Seeton smiled, rather ruefully, at her enormous young friend. "You aren't alone, I fear, in having to reproach yourself for a—a sad lack of observation. If I had only thought to examine these books before fetching them home, my first choice would have been those with the most comprehensive index—indeed, with any index at all. As it is, however . . ." She sighed. "Interesting though the subject matter might be in a general sense, it would have made it much easier to trace who is, or rather was, who. So many people in the theatre seem to marry others in the same profession, though they don't always change their names when they do. They can without, as well. Sometimes more than once. Bob Hope, of course, isn't so much a stage actor as a film star, but he was christened Leslie—and there's the chorus girl who called herself Dawn O'Day when her real name was Paris—which I would have thought charming in itself—and when she played Anne of Green Gables, she became Anne Shirley. I'm sure they must have done the same sort of thing in earlier times," said Miss Seeton, "which makes it all very confusing."

"But fun," said Delphick, "if I'm not mistaken. Yes?"

"Well . . . yes. Perhaps it *is* a little selfish—but, as you say, I'm not exactly . . . keeping it all to myself. Dear Nigel and his mother, and Dr. Braxted—and Dr. Braxted, too." She twinkled again. "Everyone agrees it's bound to be a slow and—and painstaking process, but if we could just find a suitable barometer, I would say that everything was really going very well indeed."

Bob choked on a mouthful of gingerbread; Delphick froze with his teacup halfway to his lips. Miss Seeton noticed nothing as she took a biscuit from the plate. "I had never been to an auction before, you know. I found it most enjoyable: and so very interesting—if a little sad, when one appreciates that many of the items for sale are the property of someone who has died. Were, that is, and all too often without family or friends. But the album, for instance, is a pleasant little keepsake. It reminds me of my schooldays, though Mrs. Benn's girls, being modern, had no time for such frivolities. And not too expensive,'' she added happily. "In Hampstead. I had considered, before the superintendent arrived, visiting the milliner as well, to find something to match: it is such an attractive shade of blue, and does deserve, I think, the extravagance of a new hat. Especially if''—the twinkle in her eyes was as bright as ever they had seen it—"I might one day have to pay a call on a duke. Or a duchess. And if her ladyship hasn't found one yet, I do hope she wouldn't feel it an imposition if I asked her to take me again . . .

"Do you think she would, Chief Superintendent?''

ABOUT THE AUTHOR

Hamilton Crane is the pseudonym of Sarah J(ill) Mason, who was born in England (Bishop's Stortford), went to university in Scotland (St. Andrews), and lived for a year in New Zealand (Rotorua) before returning to settle only twelve miles from where she started. She now lives about twenty miles outside London with a tame welding engineer and two (reasonably) tame Schipperke dogs.
Sold to Miss Seeton is Hamilton Crane's eleventh book in the series created by the late Heron Carvic. Under her real name, she has so far written four mysteries starring Detective Superintendent Trewley and Detective Sergeant Stone of the Allingham police force.